Harper Sloan is a *New York Times*, *USA Today* and *Wall Street Journal* bestselling author. Harper lives in Cumming, Georgia, just a few hours north of her hometown of Peachtree City. She (and her 3 daughters) enjoy ruling the house they dubbed 'Estrogen Ocean', much to her husband's chagrin. Harper has a borderline unhealthy obsession with books; you can almost ALWAYS find her with her eReader attached. She enjoys bad reality TV and cheesy romantic flicks. Her favourite kind of hero – the super alpha kind!

Harper started using writing as a way to unwind when the house went to sleep at night; and with a house full of crazy, it was the perfect way to just relax. It didn't take long before a head full of very demanding alphas would stop at nothing to have their story told.

Visit her at **AuthorHarperSloan.com**, on Facebook **/HarperSloanBooks** or on Twitter **@HarperSloan**.

Praise for Harper Sloan's sultry romances:

'Beautiful, mesmerizing . . . will charge its way into your heart and fill it with all the emotions available' Katy Evans, *New York Times* bestselling author

'Alpha heroes you'll want to kidnap and keep, heroines to root for, and sizzling love scenes with emotional punch' Carly Phillips, *New York Times* bestselling author

'If you're a fan of badass, protective Alphas with huge hearts, this is the series for you!' *Aestas Book Blog*

'This absolutely spectacular effort catapults Sloan to the top of her genre' *Publishers Weekly*

'So intense, so emotional, SO SEXY, so very well-written, funny, endearing characters you'll fall in love with . . . everything you want in a love story' *T and A After Dark*

'Absolutely perfect . . . . k, from susp . . . . ama to actio . . . . m in a nove . . . . .

By Harper Sloan

Coming Home Series
Lost Rider
Kiss My Boots
Cowboy Up

Cowboy Up

THE COMING HOME SERIES

HARPER SLOAN

HEADLINE
ETERNAL

The right of Harper Sloan to be identified as the Author of
the Work has been asserted by her in accordance with the
Copyright, Designs and Patents Act 1988.

Published by arrangement with Pocket Books,
A division of Simon & Schuster, Inc.

First published in Great Britain in 2017
by HEADLINE ETERNAL
An imprint of HEADLINE PUBLISHING GROUP

1

Cataloguing in Publication Data is available from the British Library

ISBN 978 1 4722 4777 3

Typeset in12.18/16.82 pt Adobe Garamond Pro by Jouve (UK), Milton Keynes

Printed and bound in Great Britain by CPI Group (UK) Ltd, Croydon, CR0 4YY

Headline's policy is to use papers that are natural, renewable and recyclable
products and made from wood grown in well-managed forests and other
controlled sources. The logging and manufacturing processes are expected
to conform to the environmental regulations of the country of origin.

HEADLINE PUBLISHING GROUP
An Hachette UK Company
Carmelite House
50 Victoria Embankment
London EC4Y 0DZ

www.headlineeternal.com
www.headline.co.uk
www.hachette.co.uk

To Lara Feldstein,
from book two to thirteen
Clay sends his love, darlin'.

Cowboy Up

1

CAROLINE

"Tin Man" by Miranda Lambert

— ★ —

The bright, speeding blaze of lightning shooting through and across the night sky illuminates the road ahead of me. The enormous boom of thunder that follows quickly on the heels of such a beautiful display makes me jump in my seat and grip the wheel tighter. Nothing but rain-soaked asphalt and darkness meet my gaze as I continue my drive. Normally, I would recognize the weather as an omen preluding my night's plans. A warning, perhaps, but one I won't be heeding. My mind is all over the place from my call earlier, and I just want to . . . escape, but, more importantly, I know I need a change.

"What am I doing?" I mumble into the emptiness around me.

No one answers. Of course no one does. I'm just talking to myself, like usual. Heavens me, if that's not a sign that I'm going insane, I don't know what is.

"That's what happens when you spend so much time closed off."

For the first time, the carefully constructed freedom that I've built for myself feels crippling. Or perhaps like it's caving in on me, the loneliness becoming too much. I've never been good at being alone, something I always knew, but I never realized how bad I was at it until now. I built my new life around just that, though, so like it or not, it's time to get over it. It could be worse, I remind myself. Shaking off the melancholy, I continue driving, knowing that when I reach my destination I'll be with people who care about me.

"Holy cow," I wheeze, gripping the wheel tighter when an even louder clap of thunder breaks the silence. I've always loved storms, but the sky's beautiful display is only amping up my already frazzled nerves, and I feel the unfortunately familiar burn of fear creeping up my spine before I can push it down.

I pull off the deserted back road and onto the shoulder, my headlights illuminating a sign announcing that I'm now leaving the town of Wire Creek. Beyond that is Pine Oak. It's a small town in northeast Texas, far enough from the big city for residents to be in their own little world. I grew up in Pine Oak, but after moving away just out of high school, I cut all ties and left some bad memories in my wake before returning to the area, opening up my dream bookstore, and calling Wire Creek my home.

I was close enough to feel the tug pulling me back toward Pine Oak every now and then, but far enough away that I wouldn't likely run into people who knew the old me.

My bookstore.

The Sequel.

It had been my second chance at happiness when I'd needed it the most—hence the name—and is something that I'm immensely proud of, even if being this close to Pine Oak brings back some bad memories I'd rather forget.

I have—or had, rather—a few friends in Pine Oak. It's not a stretch to think that they're still there—no one really ever leaves Pine Oak. I haven't seen or spoken to them in years though, so I think I've lost the right to call them friends. Actually, that right probably disappeared when I vanished without a word after graduation, and I'm not naive enough to think I'd be forgiven for that. But the stupid little hopeful cheerleader that pops into my mind every now and then likes to remind me that my girls from high school would welcome me back as though no time had passed, if I would just grow up and make my return to the area known. The fact that my mama's still there—not that it matters, since we don't speak anymore—is the driving force that has kept me at a distance, if I'm being honest. I don't need the memory of her to become a daily reality.

Not after everything that happened.

Never again.

"Get yourself together, Caroline. You're stronger than this," I mumble to the sign just outside my window.

I've *become* stronger than this. Logically, I know this, but still, old habits don't ever really die, do they?

I didn't survive the past twelve years to let fear keep me from living the life I've made. I promised myself that I'd take control of my life every day. It's time to stop making up reasons to stay closed off and not begin my new path of living. Impulsiveness might be something outside of my nature, but the only way I can think of to shake another call from *him* is to leap off the cliff of my comfort zone and *make* myself live.

I don't know why, after almost five years away, he started calling again. If it weren't for the memories long suppressed that hearing his voice brings back, I would thank him, though. It's because of that call that I was forced to really see my life, and what I saw, I didn't like.

Pushing *those* thoughts out of my mind, I turn the wheel to get back on the road and take the long way around Pine Oak's limits so I can get to the town on the other side—Law Bone. I could go home. I probably should, but I really don't want to be alone right now—something my mind knew immediately during that call, because I ran out into the storm the second I'd tossed my phone across the room. So I point my car to the one place I know without a shadow of a doubt will let me lose that feeling of being alone by finding safety in numbers but still remaining by myself at the same time.

- ★ -

Hazel's, the local honky-tonk, is just outside of Pine Oak—on the farthest opposite end of Wire Creek, inside Law Bone city limits. Okay, to call it a honky-tonk would be a stretch. It's a motorcycle bar that plays country music. It caters to a rough and rowdy crowd, but no one in there ever pays me a lick of mind. Of course, that's probably because one of my best friends is the owner, but even when he isn't there, I'm the last thing a man inside that place is looking for.

I'm shy by nature, an introverted book nerd who can handle fictional people a lot better than I can deal with real ones. I'm not a head turner. I never really gained the skills needed to make myself look anything but . . . well, plain. I tried. In high school, my best girlfriends always tried to teach me the ins and outs of being girly, but I was too interested in sticking my nose in a book and crushing on fictional cowboys to really retain any of it. I figured that, like in my books, the right man would love me for me and not for what the enhancements of makeup and fancy clothes could do.

I glance up at my reflection in the rearview as I pull into the lot and park, and fight off a cringe. I look sad, and that sadness makes me look much older than my nearly thirty years. My brown eyes don't shine with the mirth most women my age have dancing in theirs. Those are the carefree women who still believe they'll find a life partner to ride off into the sunset with. Just the thought makes me snort.

Where I always found my ordinary features and dull brown hair to be boring, I know the one thing I actually do have going for me is my figure. I've got the body of a dancer—thin and petite. It's my greatest attribute. I might not have all the curves most men seem to love, but I've been blessed with a body that requires minimum work to keep trim and firm.

There isn't anything about me that particularly screams, *Hey, look at me!* but I've been told men like my shape because it makes them feel like they were made to protect me—or so my good friend Luke always says.

"Speak of the devil," I mumble with a smile, seeing Luke standing under the awning outside of Hazel's front door, blowing a long stream of smoke from his mouth. The burning tip of his cigarette stands out in the darkness around him.

Luke Hazel, half of my best-friend duo, and twin brother to Lucy, is a dog, but at least he's an honest dog. Loyal to those he loves. Protective to the max. With his harmless flirting, he's also helped to give me back some of the confidence I lost over the years.

"Carrie," he drawls when I step out of my car and pull my cross-body purse over my head. I roll my eyes and cringe at the nickname he knows I hate.

"Lukie Dukie," I jest, tossing out the nickname that I know *he* hates, placing my hands on my hips and arching a brow at him.

Not even fazed, he kicks off the wall he'd been leaning against and walks my way. No, he struts. Because a simple walk wouldn't be good enough for this guy. He thinks he's God's gift to the females of the world. I laugh softly and fall into his arms for a hug when he reaches me.

"Not a good night to be here, sweetheart."

I push my hands against his abs and look up at him. "And what makes tonight different from all the other nights you say the same thing?"

"Rowdy, babe. Got some out-of-towners ridin' through lookin' for a good time. Not sure how they'll act when I pull the shotgun out if they try to get in your shorts."

I feel my nose twitch as I frown at him. "No one's gonna worry about me, Luke."

He shakes his head. "Not sure how many times I have to drill it in your head, babe, but every man in there is 'gonna worry about you.'"

"Don't be ridiculous, Luke. Even if you're right and I get some attention tonight, I've dealt with worse than some drunken bikers and you know it. And who says I wouldn't enjoy a little of their attention anyway?"

He frowns. "Yeah, Carrie, but that doesn't mean I want to put you through some bullshit just because I know you can handle it." His frown deepens, and I know the exact moment the rest of what I said registers. He doesn't call me on it, but he knows better than to ask if I'm ready for that kind of thing. "Told you, just like I tell Luce, this ain't a place to find a bedfellow."

I smile at the mention of Lucy. "You and I both know you're going to act like my babysitter the second I walk in there, so how about you stop acting like my big brother now and let me get a drink and forget about things for a while, hmm?"

His eyes narrow. "What you got to forget about, sweetheart?"

Too late, I realize my mistake. I haven't even talked to Lucy about the calls I've been getting, but with my emotions at the boiling point, my mind just slipped. Luke, the big macho protector that he's always been, isn't going to be happy without hearing what got me driving over to Hazel's on a Tuesday night either.

I sigh. "I promise, I'll fill you in later, but please, Luke, let me just forget about it all for a little while?"

He nods, but I can tell he isn't happy about giving in. One big, thickly muscled arm waves toward the door in a sweeping gesture for me to proceed. And even though he seems to be caving, I know a long talk will be coming. I just need to make sure I've had enough to drink so that I'm too intoxicated to deal with *that* chat tonight.

The heavy wall of smoke slams into me as we enter the bar. I always thought it was funny that Luke would go outside to have a cigarette when walking into Hazel's is probably the equivalent of smoking an entire pack of cigarettes in just one go. Most nonsmokers find the scent repugnant, but not me. I've always loved the smell of smoke—any kind of smoke—even if that is weird as hell.

An old Alan Jackson song booms through the air as we walk through the crowded bar. I feel the earlier tension slide off my body with each step and I know I made the right call in coming here. Luke grabs my arms, stopping me before I almost walk into a big, burly man, and pulls me to his side, securing me in place with an arm over my shoulders. I look up at him, smiling when I see his handsome face scowling down at me.

"What?" I mouth up at him, my smile growing.

He just shakes his head, continuing to guide me through the crowded room until we're at the very end of the U-shaped bar, closest to his office. He taps the shoulder of a man sitting down and, without a word, waves his hand in some sort of code that must say, *Get the hell up*, because the young cowboy doesn't even pause, sliding off the stool and disappearing into a darkened corner.

"You, sit." Luke pushes me toward the empty stool and crosses his arms with a glare at the men closest to the seat he demanded I take.

"You could say please, you know," I mumble under my breath, but I still follow his order.

"Could, but I won't."

"No surprise there, Lukie."

He bends down until his nose is touching mine. "Watch the 'Lukies' in here, *Carrie*."

"Whatever. How about a drink, Mr. Bartender?"

"Not joking, sweetheart. Don't want the men in here to think you're fair game."

"Look around, Luke. No one is worried about me." I don't know if that's actually true, but seeing as I've never been the type to turn a bar full of men's attention my way, I'm fairly confident in my assessment.

"Blind as a damn bat," he mutters loud enough for me to hear clearly over the noise, not backing away.

I open my mouth to give him a smart-ass retort but stop when I hear a deep, rumbling laugh to my side. I look over, not seeing much apart from the dark cowboy hat next to me. Its owner's face is concealed by shadows as he looks down at the golden-colored liquor in his glass. I can see a stubbled, very strong jaw though—the deliciously strong kind that's angled in such a way you could swear on a stack of Bibles on Sunday morning that someone carved it straight out of stone.

"Just please, stay here and out of trouble. You need to use the little girls' room, do it in my office. I can't run this place if I'm constantly worried about you."

"Got her, Luke," the stranger next to me mumbles loud enough to be heard over the music, still not looking up from his glass.

Luke flicks his gaze in my neighbor's direction, and even though there's no way he can see the man's face, he nods before pulling his attention away and back on me. "Be good, sweetheart."

He turns and stomps away.

"I'm always good!" I yell at his back, making the man next to me chuckle in such a low-pitched, manly way I almost feel like calling it a chuckle would be a sin. "What? I am," I defend.

"Sure you are, sugar." His deep, velvety smooth voice causes a wave of awareness to wash over me.

"Not that it matters, since I don't know you and all, but I'll have you know I'm the very definition of good. I wouldn't know how to be bad if it bit me in the butt."

He turns his head toward me. I'm unable to see his face, which is still hidden by the shadows, but I can feel his eyes on me. Their scrutiny is almost like a physical caress. "That so?" he rumbles after another few pounding heartbeats of silent study.

I nod mutely, wishing I had a drink to wash down the nervousness.

"How do you know Luke?" he continues.

"He and his sister are my best friends," I tell him without hesitation.

"Not your boyfriend?" he drawls.

"I— No. He's not my boyfriend," I answer, confused by his questioning.

"So what's a good girl like you doin' in a place like this?"

"Maybe I'm sick of being a good girl," I mumble, wishing I could see his eyes.

He continues to study me and I shift in my seat. Good

heavens, what kind of pull does this stranger have over me? I can't even look away, not that I want to, so I study him just as fiercely—even if I can't see his face, I can still see *him*. And what a mighty fine sight he is.

Dressed in the typical uniform of most cowboys around here, he's got his well-built frame in a navy-blue button-down shirt, tucked into jeans that I'm sure mold to his amazing-looking body perfectly when he's standing. Even in the dim light, I can see the dirty boots propped up on the step under the bar that keeps short legs like mine from dangling in the air. His hand wrapped around the tumbler is tanned, making me think he must work outside, but it's the long fingers that hold my focus as he uses them to slowly spin his glass against the bar top.

"Want to?"

Pulling my eyes from the strangely erotic sight of his hand, I look toward his shadowed face.

"Want to what?"

"Be bad, sugar."

Heat hot as fire washes over me with his words. Holy cow. My jaw works, but words elude me. I don't even know this man's name, let alone anything about him, and if my rusty knowledge of flirting is right, he just propositioned me. Why I find that as hot as I do, I'll never know, but before I even know what's happening, my brain finally figures out how to get the words past my shocked jaw.

"I think I do."

My eyes widen at the same time his hat dips, and then

he turns and holds up two fingers toward Luke farther down the bar. Call it male intuition, whatever kind of magic men have to know when another member of their brotherhood needs a drink, but Luke looks up the second the dark cowboy's fingers are in the air and nods. Not even a minute later, he's placing two glasses much like the one my mysterious companion just finished in front of us. Luke walks away without a word, clearly trusting this man if he's willing to let me drink with him *and* not give me a speech about drinking responsibly. When the chill of glass touches my knuckles, I look down.

"Somethin' tells me your mind might be ready to be bad, sugar, but your nerves aren't there yet. Goes down smooth, but sip it nonetheless."

My brain, still clearly under the dark cowboy's control, doesn't have a problem working now. My hand curls around the glass and I bring it to my lips, letting him control me without fighting it. He's not wrong—it goes down smooth as silk. At least, the first two sips do. Then I get a little confident and take a deep swallow, only to sputter my way through it.

"Sip," he calmly demands, leaning into me enough that I feel the heat of his body against my bare arms. "Want you feelin' calm when I show you how fun it is to be bad, not drunk."

"Who says I want to be bad with *you*?" I ask, taking a very small sip this time.

"Babe, you wanna be bad with me."

He's right, I do. "You seem confident." I look over the glass, trying to see through the shadows, but give up when I realize just how well he's cloaked.

He doesn't respond but instead takes a drink from his own glass.

"I don't even know you."

"Wouldn't make a difference if you did."

"You know, some people might actually think that you're actually just cocky and not confident."

"I'm old enough to go after what I want without playin' games. There ain't a thing cocky about that." *God*, his voice is pure sex.

"And what's that?"

"You'll find out," he promises darkly, playing the game despite his words.

"Cocky."

His deep laugh is low and gritty, almost as if it's a sound that normally doesn't come from him. For whatever reason, it makes me want to know everything I can about this man—this stranger.

We fall into a comfortable silence, but one that carries so much promise I can feel it building inside of me. Luke comes over to talk to me when he can, but it isn't often. My glass is never empty for long, but on Luke's fifth pass with the bottle of top-shelf whiskey, the dark cowboy places his hand over the top of my glass. I look over at him instead of Luke, to see him shaking his head.

"I got her, but how 'bout water and close out my tab?"

"You got it, Davis." Luke laughs, turning to grab me a bottle of water from the fridge behind him.

"Your name is Davis?" I ask the man next to me, weighing the sound of it.

He doesn't acknowledge me, waiting for Luke to come back with his credit card and his receipt to sign. He scribbles his signature and hands it back to Luke, dropping his feet to the wooden floor under us and stepping back. I follow his movements with my eyes, waiting to see what he'll do next, already anticipating the rush of disappointment when he leaves, knowing I'll likely never see him again. My jaw drops the second his hand comes out, palm up, in a gesture that clearly means he wants me to go with him. I look from his hand up to the darkness shadowing his face, wondering if I should actually be careless enough to go off with some stranger I don't know.

"You gonna give me shit about this?"

Confused, I look from that tanned hand with the long fingers back up at him, but I can tell by the tilt of his hat that he's speaking to someone behind me.

"Would it matter?" Luke laughs behind me and I turn to look at him.

"Not really. Only opinion that I care about is hers, but still askin'."

Luke shakes his head but still smiles. "Not her keeper, but I assure you if I had a problem with this shit I wouldn't

have sat her next to you *and* continued to refill her glass."
Luke looks down at me and gives me a wink. "Been a
while, darlin', make sure he wraps it up."

I gasp and feel heat blossoming on my cheeks as Luke
turns with a deep laugh and walks away. I'm going to kill
him.

Heat blankets my back a second later and two strong
hands clasp my hips. I feel him move until his breath is at
my ear. "Let's go be bad, hmm?"

Am I going to do this? Go off with some man I don't
know and sleep with him? Because I would be a fool to
think this is anything else. Earlier I promised myself I was
done living a ghost of a life and that I was going to find
a way to be wild and free. I've never slept with someone
I wasn't in a long-term relationship with. Oh, who am I
kidding, I've only slept with one man. To say I'm in over
my head here is an understatement. Lucy does it all the
time. Hell, she keeps telling me I need a good rebound
romp in the sheets. Screw it, I'll regret it if I don't at least
jump in the saddle again, letting this man go without
taking him for a ride.

I take a deep breath, lean back against the strong body
behind me, and nod. "Yeah. Let's go . . . be bad."

My back vibrates with his laughter, and I shiver in
his hold, my wide eyes meeting Luke's across the bar.
He gives me a wink and smiles his ruggedly handsome,
crooked smile, tipping his chin toward the door in
silent confirmation that he has no problem with the

stranger leading me away. Knowing that the dark cowboy has Luke's trust breaks the final restraint on my reservations. I turn, look up at my companion, and smile.

"Lead the way."

2
CAROLINE

"Bar at the End of the World" by Kenny Chesney

Deliciously reckless.

That's really the only way I can explain the feeling that's rushing through my body right now.

The darkness around us makes my other senses come to the forefront. The rasp of his five o'clock shadow against my sensitive skin as he kisses and licks his way down the column of my throat only makes my arousal spike to dangerous levels. Had we made it farther than even a foot into the motel room across from Hazel's, I would've turned on a light so I could finally see him, but now it's more fun to continue this ride with that unknown factor. He can be anyone I want him to be now. Or anyone I *don't* want him to be. For one night, I can take the pleasure my body hasn't had in years and live off the memories of it until I'm ready to give another man a chance. Hopefully I won't let another five years pass before that happens again.

I push my hands from his shoulders and palm his jaw as his stubble prickles against my fingers while my hands wander up to his hair. His hat falls to the floor with a thud and I know he's just as lost in me as I am in him, because he doesn't even make a move to pick it up. He lets out a deep grunt when I mold myself against his body, seeking some sort of friction. The next thing I know, my back is against the door and he's gripping my bottom. His mouth hits my jaw with a bite of his teeth, making a squeak of pleasure shoot up my throat, and his deep rumble of laughter reaches my ears as he presses me harder into the door with his hips. The heavy bulge of his erection against *that* spot makes me so desperate for him that I whimper in relief when his mouth *finally* closes over mine in a wet tangle of tongues.

I've never been kissed so thoroughly.

This is the kind of kiss that sets the bar for any that might follow.

The kind that shows you everything you've been missing and everything you never knew you wanted. I'm going to be comparing every kiss I ever have to my dark cowboy's, even though I know there's a good chance no one will ever compare. The sounds coming from my mouth, the ones being swallowed by his, are nothing short of needy. My hips move in tandem with the thrusts of his, and even though we're both fully clothed, I know it won't take much more of this for me to go off like the town's fireworks on the Fourth of July.

"Fuck, you taste just like apple pie," he whispers against my lips, breaking away with a gasp.

"Huh?"

"Goddamn, I love apple pie," he says before his mouth is back on mine, this time with a whole new kind of hunger deepening his kisses.

I'm held captive, enraptured. Then his hands move from my bottom to glide up my torso. He lifts his hard chest off mine and suddenly those delicious fingers are at my breasts. Even if I had big boobs his hands would dwarf them, I'm sure, but as it is he covers both with a firm grasp before adjusting his hold with a deft twist of the wrists. His mouth continues to feast on mine while his huge hands learn my body with slow movements. I tear my mouth from his with a breathy moan when he pushes my shirt up and slips his fingers into the cups of my bra to tweak my nipples.

"Oh, God," I moan when he does it again.

"I can't get enough of you," he rumbles.

"Please," I beg, not with the slightest clue as to what I'm begging for.

His hips dig even harder into mine as he leans back, supporting me against the door with that connection alone as he pulls my shirt off. The darkness makes me feel more confident than I normally would be, almost half naked with a man—no, a stranger.

"Yours too," I tell him as his fingers move to unclasp my bra. "I want to feel your skin on mine," I breathe, taking over the task so he'll hopefully give me what I want.

I fumble in my haste to feel more of this dangerous arousal he's creating in my body, but the second my bra is free and dangling toward the floor, his naked chest collides against mine, pushing me into the door with a force that sends the air rushing out of my lungs.

His mouth hits my collarbone at the same time his hands grasp my bottom, sliding me up the door until I feel the wet heat of his breath against my breast.

Then he stops.

"Wh-what are you doing?" I cry out, tugging him by his thick hair toward my aching breast. When he doesn't budge, I drop my head back with a thump hard enough to make my eyes water.

"Fuck, give me a second, darlin'," he rasps out, his heavy breath wafting against my flesh, causing my whole body to spark with another wave of need.

"Please, Davis," I whine.

He grunts, the sound of his name turning into a loud scream of pleasure when his mouth covers my nipple. Sucking deeply, he sends arousal shooting from every single nerve in my body. I've never in my life felt anything like it. One hand starts to caress and tease my other breast until I'm positive I'm going to come from this alone. My hips pump against his abs, and I wish I wasn't so short and that it was his crotch against mine, but with muscles like his, I'm thinking I still might be able to.

"More, need more."

He pops his mouth free, giving one more lick, then spins us and stomps away from the door. I'm so lost in him that when he drops me, I don't even think to panic. The hard mattress gives me enough of a bounce that when he follows on top of me we collide with dual grunts.

He's got me naked in a matter of seconds in a move so skillful I don't even realize I'm being undressed until a rush of cool air brushes against my wet core. I don't give myself a second to think about where he learned that; instead I push off the bed with my feet against the mattress and rut against his denim-covered erection. His groans mingle with mine, making me drunk with pleasure. The darkness around us, with not even the moon to cast some sort of light on us, only heightens the pleasure until I'm going out of my mind.

"I need you," I tell my dark cowboy.

"Fuck yes," he answers, but leaves me abruptly to stand.

I start to protest, until I hear his belt clang and the sound of his boots being toed off. "Light on or off, sweetness?" he rumbles.

"Off."

If he had an issue with my answer, he didn't verbalize it, instead he continues to undress.

"You taste like apple pie all over?" he oddly asks, when the sounds of him getting naked stop.

"What?"

"Never tasted anything better," he continues.

Lifting off the mattress with my elbows, I start to reach for him but stop the second he speaks again, and I know I'll spend the rest of my life swearing I saw the bright lights of heaven not even a moment later.

"Can't wait to find out if your pussy tastes as sweet as the rest of you."

Oh. My. "Heavens!" I scream when he grabs my hips and his mouth covers my sex. My eyes roll back in my head as I scream my throat raw, coming instantly with waves of intense pleasure that just keep getting more intense as his vibrating groans shoot against my core.

My toes curl, my fingers cramp as I fist the sheets, and I thrash my head from side to side with the roaring of my thundering heart matching the storm raging through my body.

He continues to drink from me. Sucking, nipping, licking, *devouring* me. The ragged sounds coming from me ring in my ears as I continue to come, begging him to never stop. All of this, without even knowing what the skillful man between my legs looks like, but knowing I will never forget him.

He gives me one long, slow lick from my clenching center to my oversensitive clit before releasing his hold on my hips and climbing up my body. Limply, I watch his shadow in the darkness move until something falls on my chest.

"You wanna be bad, sweetness, then let's be bad," he tells me against my mouth before kissing me. The taste of my arousal thick on his tongue makes me turn my head and deepen the kiss.

I could kiss this man for days and days.

He rolls us, my legs falling to straddle his hips as the hard length of his erection sits between my soaked lower lips. I start rocking my hips mindlessly, needing to be filled with him. He gives me free rein until his breathing is just as frantic as mine. Only then does he stall, his fingers digging into my thighs.

"Condom, get it on my cock and ride me until that sweet fucking pussy sucks me dry," he demands.

My hands shake as I search between our bodies for what he must've dropped on the mattress before rolling us. Finally finding it by my knee, I shift and grab his thickness gently. I give him a few pumps but stop when I realize just how big the man under me is. I look up and gasp, adding my other hand to better size him up. Holy shit, this will never fit inside of me.

"My cock will fit just fine inside of that sweet pussy."

"Shit," I hiss, giving him a squeeze with both hands. "You weren't supposed to hear that."

"Gathered that, sugar, but trust me when I say you're soaked and it'll fit just fine."

He's not wrong. I'm so wet I can feel the dampness

spreading across his thigh. I shift my hips, the friction making me pant loudly.

"Fuckin' hell. Get that shit on me so you can fuck me," he strains.

"What?" I sputter, freezing with both hands still fisting his huge erection. "You want me to . . ." I stop, unable to finish my thought.

"Say it, Carrie," he tells me, the nickname not bothering me as much coming from him. He must have heard Luke call me that and I don't correct him, using it as my own cloak. "Say you're going to fuck me. Tell me how you're going to ride my cock."

Oh my God, this man is going to be my undoing.

I squirm, but don't speak as the shyness I thought I'd lost comes roaring back. I start to drop him, but he must've realized I was losing my nerve. His hands shoot off my thighs and around each of my fists, closing around my hold roughly and pumping himself through our joined hold. A long and pained sound leaves him. He lifts up, one hand cupping my center, one long finger sinking into me and hooking inside my body as I scream.

"You feel this? Feel what your body wants? Or how fuckin' hard I am for you? I want you to use me, Carrie. I want you to ride me until I feel that wet pussy drippin' down my balls, and then I want to feel that sweetness of yours clamp down on me as you come. You'll keep ridin' me though, won't you, sweetness? You'll keep givin' me more because you want to know what bein' bad feels like.

And I'll give it to you just as soon as you give me what I want. Then I'm gonna flip you over until your ass is in the air and your ponytail is in my fist with my balls slapping against this soaked pussy until you come again. Fuck you so hard, darlin', you're gonna feel me for days. Then you're gonna get your sweet ass back against this mattress so I can put my knees at your sides and pump my cock until I come all over these fuckin' tits."

He slides his finger in and out of my body a few times, my core fluttering around him.

I'm ready to come again.

"Show me you wanna be bad," he says, his voice straining as his erection grows even harder between our hold.

I rip my hand away from his flesh and my mouth finds his as I search for the condom again. This time he's the one that finds it, but he pulls my hand from his neck and places the packet in my palm as I continue to roll my tongue against his. As I tear it open, my mouth leaves his and starts kissing every inch of his body while I fumble my way through putting a condom on. Then, thank the heavens above, I finish at the same time my mouth finds his nipple. I bite it, not even sure what's come over me, but I get a rush of power from the guttural noises spilling from him.

I scoot my knees until I feel him again between my legs, lifting up with my hands on his shoulders. "Put your cock inside of me," I pant against his mouth, shocked at the brazen words that left my own without thought.

"I thought you'd never ask, sugar," he grunts, one hand

leaving the breasts he'd been playing with to line himself up with my entrance. The second I feel his blunt tip, I let my body fall, taking every rock-hard inch of him at once.

The pleasure is blinding.

And I scream.

And scream.

And *scream*.

Every single time I go to lift myself off of him, I feel a strangled sound leave my mouth.

"Take it easy, darlin'. Fuckin' hell. Didn't think you would try to split yourself in two," he mumbles, kissing me sweetly while helping me rock my hips to get used to the size of him. It doesn't take long for those sweet kisses to turn desperate and my body to need more.

If he weren't such a large man, or maybe if I weren't such a small woman, I would have been able to ride him like he had wanted, but as it was, I couldn't even get myself halfway off his hardness before he realized I needed help. His hands clamp my hips and lift me all the way off before thrusting me down. We continue, both of us moving in a way that would make you think we'd been lovers for years. The sounds of my wetness fuel my desire as we swallow each other's moans.

"I'm going to . . ." I pant.

"Say it," he grunts when I stop speaking. "Tell me what you're gonna give me."

"I'm going to . . . God, Davis, I'm going to come!" I yell as I start to do just that.

He drops me, hard and heavy against him, and I start rocking my hips while my pleasure takes me to the brink of insanity. The whole time, he speaks soft words that I'm unable to understand through the force of my orgasm.

Then he proves he's a man of his word, because I come again on my hands and knees while he pulls my head back with a strong grip on my ponytail, his balls slapping against my hyper-sensitive flesh. Then and only then does he pull free of me, flip me onto my back, and climb up my body with his knees digging into the mattress next to my sides. I feel the tip of him touch my chest a few times as his furiously pumps himself; then the hot splash of his come hits my chest as he bellows out into the shadows around us. I hadn't even registered him removing the condom, so lost was I in delicious pleasure.

His body slackens when the last drop leaves him, giving me just enough of his weight but clearly not all of it since I can still breathe. I wiggle, the wetness on my breasts starting to roll toward my neck, and lift one hand up to swipe at it. I'm not sure what makes me lick my fingers clean, but when the salty taste of him bursts against my tongue, I moan loudly.

"Fuck." He hisses breathlessly. "Just came harder than I ever fuckin' have and I'm ready to take more from you. You too sore for my cock again?"

"Hmm?" I moan, still sucking the taste of him off my fingers.

"Doesn't matter, gonna fuck you again anyway."

And boy does he. By the time we finally fall asleep, he's taken me once in the shower and again in the bed before pulling me into his arms seconds before I pass out. The last thought that goes through my mind before drifting off is if this was how living wild and free feels, I am never going to stop.

Never.

3
CLAYTON

"Dirt on My Boots" by Jon Pardi

The overwhelming heat rushing through my body is enough to make me hate being a rancher during these hot-as-fuck summer months. The oppressing temperature assaults me the second I open my front door, the heat so stifling that it steals your breath straight from your damn lungs. The harder I work, the worse it gets, until I pray to whoever will listen for anything to filter some of these damn rays. Nothing changes the fact that shit needs to get done and I'm the one who needs to do it.

Trails of sweat drip down my back, slow tracks of fiery wetness that feel like they burn my skin on the way to my belted jeans. I drop the pitchfork I've been using to add straw to the horses' stalls and rip my shirt off, wiping my brow with it before placing my hat back on my soaked head as I toss the garment behind me and continue with my task.

Fucking Texas summers.

It feels like hell rises from the ground every day.

My days are all the same. I wake up, chug coffee, and work outside until well after the sun sets and the rest of the people in Pine Oak have set off for dinner with their families.

I'm alone, for all intents and purposes, and that feeling is even more pronounced on days when my brothers aren't around to distract me from my loneliness, which happens more frequently now that they're both married and living off the ranch.

But even if I wanted to find someone like Maverick and Quinn did, there's no place in my life for the responsibility of being the sole provider of someone else's happiness anymore. I'm at the tail end of my thirties, and it's too late for me to worry about finding someone I love.

No one can hurt me if I don't let them have the power to do it. Which means I'm better off alone.

"Fuckin' hell, old man, what's crawled up your ass and died?"

"Got shit to do, Mav," I tell my brother, not stopping in my shoveling.

"Looks like you need a break from that shit you gotta do, brother."

"Drew isn't here today. If I don't get this shit done, I'm

gonna be workin' all night. Tell me what you need so I can get this done."

"Leigh wants you to come to dinner tomorrow."

"Does she, now?"

"Says she doesn't see you enough, though I'm not sure why she fuckin' cares."

I bark out a laugh. "Jealous?"

"Fuck you," he retorts.

"Just saw her the other day when I stopped in at the PieHole. Why does she really want me to come to dinner?"

I hear my younger brother mumble something under his breath and smile despite the fact that I'm hot and exhausted, and my mind is in about a million other places. He continues to grumble—something he's always been mighty good at—as I finish placing the last few forkfuls of hay into the stall and turn to him. Even frustrated, I can see the contentment that his life now brings him written all over his face. I'm happy as fuck that he's got that. It hasn't been an easy road for him and his wife, Leighton, but they finally found their way back to each other. Took him almost dying, his rodeo career ending, and our father's death to do it, but it happened regardless, so if anyone deserves the full-to-bursting life he has with Leigh, it's my little brother.

"You didn't hear it from me, but she and Quinn want to corner you into comin' to their baby shower or some shit like that. Fuck if I know, Clay. I don't even want to be a part of it, but every time Leigh talks about the shower, her face does this thing that makes me want to give her anything in the damn world to keep it lookin' like that, so I'm here to make sure I keep gettin' those stars in her eyes and smiles on her lips. Even if it goes against everything to be beggin' my brother to come to a fuckin' baby shower."

I laugh, low and deep. "Admit you're just as over the fuckin' moon as she is and I'll be there." I don't need him to, but part of me loves to hear him talk about how thrilled he is that he's going to be a father. Even though I'm only three years older than him, I basically raised him and Quinn when our mama took off. I reckon this is as close to parental pride as I'll ever get, which is why I keep taking that pride whenever opportunities arrive.

He drops his brooding expression and gives me a smile that's usually only reserved for Leigh. "Shit, Clay. Can't even put it into words, but if that's what it means to feel like my heart is gonna explode daily, then yeah, I'm over the fuckin' moon. Scared outta my skull, too," he admits, his smile dimming a little.

"Why's that?"

"Did you know her mama had complications when she had Leigh? That's why they never had any more young'uns. She told me about how her mama almost died during childbirth and all I can think about is what I'll do if I lose Leigh."

No longer feeling the joy of his happiness, I prop the pitchfork against the stall, walk over to him, and clasp his shoulder in support. "Leighton's strong as hell and doctors are trained a lot better than they were thirty years ago, Mav. Don't let that ruin your excitement. She's gonna be just fine, and in the end you'll have a little piece of the two of you keepin' you up all night."

"I won't be able to move on if I lose her," he continues, completely ignoring my attempt at lightening the mood and I realize just how much this has been weighing on him.

"Maverick." I hiss through the thickness in my damn throat and pull my brother into my arms. His own come around me with bruising force.

"Can't talk to her about this shit, Clay. I don't want her worryin' about it when she should be focusin' on all the happy shit, but it's tearin' me apart just thinkin' about losing her."

"Fuck, brother."

Just like when we were younger and he was upset, he drops his forehead against my shoulder, and even though I'm no longer taller than him, he seems to shrink in my hold. It's then that I realize my baby brother—the badass ex–rodeo champion—is crumbling, his silent sobs only evident because of the choppy breaths coming from his lips.

"I could lose her."

"You won't."

"You don't know that," he bellows, ripping free from my arms and throwing his hands in the air. "Every day we get closer to the baby bein' born I feel like I'm losin' her. I can't turn it off."

Fucking hell.

I pull my phone out of my back pocket and move my thumb against the screen while he paces and mumbles in front of me, placing the device to my ear a second later.

"Hey," my sister sings through the phone.

"Tate around, darlin'?" Maverick stops in his tracks and looks over at me with a blank face. No hint of anger, the fear gripping him too deep for him to be mad that I'm bringing someone else into this and exposing his vulnerable fears to them.

"Yeah. Everything okay?"

"All's fine, Quinnie, just thought of somethin' I needed to ask him. Forgot the other day when I ran into him in town."

"Let me go grab him. We've been workin' on a junker he bought off Craigslist. Can you believe that? Only man in the world who would buy his wife a rust bucket as a gift."

"Sounds like the perfect gift if that wife is you," I tell her, forcing lightness into my tone while my eyes stay trained on Maverick.

"It is, isn't it." She sighs happily. "Here he is. Love you, big brother!"

"Love you back, darlin'."

I wait, hearing what sounds a helluva lot like them making out before he comes on the line.

"Hey. What's up, Clay?"

"Need you to come to the ranch, Tate. Keep that stupid smile on your face so Quinn doesn't think somethin' is wrong. Tell her I need help puttin' together a gift for the baby or some shit and come now. Got it?"

"Need me to bring any tools?" he plays along instantly.

"See you quick, Tate."

"Yeah, don't worry, I won't tell Quinn you're puttin' together a gift for her, man."

I hear Quinn make some girly as fuck noise as I disconnect the call and push the phone back into my pocket.

"You're gonna sit down and listen to what he has to say, Maverick. Then us three are gonna go inside and have some cold ones before you go home to your wife with a clear conscience. Got it?"

He grunts, doesn't speak but drops against the wall. He slides until his ass is on the ground and his head is hung low. The whole time my heart breaks knowing he's been carrying this load secretly until it became too much for him to keep buried. Work can wait for another day: right now, my brother needs me, and there's never been and never will be anything I won't do for the people I love.

I sit against the wall opposite him while we wait. Fifteen minutes later, Tate comes roaring down the driveway in the truck my sister restored for him almost a year ago. I'd sent him a text right after getting off the phone with him to let him know to find us in the old barn that we use for our personal horses. This one, while still nice, isn't top-of-the-line like the one we use to breed, and it lacks the air-conditioning system we put in the breeding stable a few years back. By the time Tate comes running in, I've finally gotten used to sitting in a puddle of my own sweat.

"Jesus Christ, Clay. Give me a fuckin' heart attack. What's going on?" he breathes, and I finally look away from Maverick. My sister's husband might not have been born and raised in Pine Oak, but all it took was one year back here and he shed every ounce of the city boy he'd become when he lived in Atlanta. Even if he still wears ball caps and not Stetsons, he looks like any other man that grew up here. 'Course, he would when Quinn's got his ass working on trucks, covered in dirt and grease.

"Maverick," I tell him, looking back at my little brother. He hasn't moved since I called Tate, who conveniently happens to be our town's lady doctor in addition being to our brother-in-law. If anyone knows the facts that can set Maverick's mind at ease, it's Tate. "Mav, want me to tell Tate or do you?"

He grunts, and I take that as him wanting me to fill Tate in, so I do. Each word that crosses my lips makes Tate look more and more sympathetic. His own wife, our sister, is due only a week after Leigh, so aside from Tate being one hell of a doctor, he can sympathize with Maverick on a level I couldn't begin to imagine.

"Jesus, man. That's some heavy shit."

"I'd die without her." Maverick finally looks up, his eyes pleading with the two of us.

"You wouldn't. Not because you'd move on, but because you'd have a reason to keep goin', but that's not gonna happen." Tate moves over to his side and starts spewing a bunch of medical knowledge that makes my ears bleed, but by the time he's done explaining to Maverick just how safe Leigh is, I finally see the tension leave my little brother's body. "Not only has medicine become more advanced, but we doctors are always thinkin' ten steps ahead, man. I promise you, Leighton and the baby are gonna be fine."

When the three of us are done talking, there isn't a sober one between us. Quinn came about an hour ago to pick up Tate, and Maverick just drove off with Leighton. Judging by him not being able to keep his hands off her when she showed up, I know I can go to bed tonight not worried about my baby brother.

The second their taillights disappear and the sounds of the night meet my ears, I feel the loneliness settle around me once again. Then I head back to the barn to finish the work I abandoned earlier this afternoon, but my mind is on my family and the apple pie I have waiting in the fridge, thanks to Leighton.

If I was a different man, maybe I'd do something about the deadweight of my solitude that's getting heavier and heavier to drag around. But I'm not, so I continue my work in silence before going to bed.

Alone.

4

CAROLINE

"I Could Use a Love Song" by Maren Morris

— ★ —

Dusting has become the bane of my existence. However, I do it with a smile because I love every second that I spend inside my bookstore. Even every second I spend outside of it, since my apartment is on top of The Sequel and the scent of books travels up the stairs and into my living space. There's no better smell on this earth than the pages of a book. Not one thing.

Well, maybe that of a certain dark cowboy . . .

I smile to myself. The memories of that night still hang with a delicious heaviness in my thoughts, even a month later. I always thought I wouldn't be able to detach the emotion from sex, but when I woke up alone the morning after that glorious night, all I could do was smile and take my well-used body home. I'd needed that night more than I thought. I needed to remember how to feel again without letting someone close. And it's been the memories from our night that have kept the loneliness I was drowning in at bay and a smile on my face. I think, in a way, my dark cowboy made it possible for me to not have any more lingering fear over the fact that my ex had started contacting me again.

"Thinkin' about that cowboy again?" Lucy sings with a smile, meeting me in the romance section toward the back of the store with her own duster.

"That obvious, huh?"

"Only on the days that end with *y*," she jokes.

"Yeah, yeah."

"You know, all you have to do is ask Luke. I bet he'd give you the stranger's name and you could enjoy another night of having your world rocked."

I laugh. "It was special, Luce, but I don't want to ruin what I got from him by tryin' to make it somethin' it isn't."

"And how do *you* know it couldn't be more?"

"How do you know it could?"

"Oooh, feisty."

The bell chimes, letting us know there's a customer, and Lucy takes off with a little skip, the smile still on her face. That girl is perpetually happy, and it doesn't take much to make her maniacally happy. She's been riding the same high as me for the past month, although she's been riding it for an entirely different reason. My best friend is just happy that I'm happy. For her, it's as simple as that. She's seen too many times when I wasn't close to that, been there for me since I met her at eighteen, and I know she'll be there for me until I die.

I hear her greet our newest customer and I continue dusting, moving through the romance books slowly as I study the spines. Romance is my favorite genre, the hopeless romantic in me still there despite everything my love life has been through, and I can't help it when my thoughts drift back to *him*. Our night together was the stuff fantasies are built from. There wasn't a single second of our coupling that gave me a hint to who he was. Even in the shower, we washed each other in darkness. He took me against the bathroom counter in darkness. We fumbled back to the bed in darkness. Even if a part of me wishes I knew who he was, I wasn't kidding when I told Lucy that I didn't want to cheapen the memory of our time together if he turns out to be less than the perfect man that I've created in my mind. It has nothing to do with what he might look like, but I'm afraid that if I were to find him and we had another chance at coming together, it'd never live up to the magic of that night.

So I'm almost completely content with never knowing. Almost.

"Did you move the pregnancy books?" Lucy asks, popping her head around the shelf I was working on tidying up.

"Oh, sorry. I forgot to tell you. They're toward the front now, over by the self-help books. I didn't think it was right to have them all the way in the back *and* on the bottom shelf. Makin' it a little easier for the mamas-to-be and all, keepin' them up front."

"Gotcha!" she says, smile in place and pep in her damn step.

I shake my head and smirk.

"Holy shit! Leigh, it *is* her!"

I feel my jaw drop and quickly turn with a squeak. No way. I haven't heard that voice or that name in years.

"Quinn!" I exclaim, placing my duster on the shelf and rushing forward to pull her into a hug about the same time I notice her round belly. "Oh my goodness, congratulations, Quinn!"

She pulls away, smiling and rubbing her swollen and very pregnant belly. "Thank you. I can't believe it's you. I thought I recognized your voice."

"Caroline?!" I hear behind Quinn, and then Leighton James is pulling me into her arms, hugging me just as tight as I am her.

"Holy crap! You too!" I laugh, looking from belly to belly, my laughter growing. "I shouldn't be surprised you two would be pregnant together. There wasn't a thing y'all did without the other growin' up! How close are your due dates?"

They both beam, then, simultaneously, exclaim, "A week!"

"Of course it is," I say, laughing even harder at the fact that the two childhood best friends, both born within the same week, are pregnant with their babies due a week apart. "It sure is good to see you two."

"Have you been livin' in Wire Creek long?" Quinn asks, still stroking her belly. "I thought I heard you were in Houston. Or was it Dallas?" She looks at Leigh in question before focusing back on me.

I shake my head. "Austin, actually. I lived there after college but moved to Wire Creek a few years ago."

"Never thought I'd see the day. You hightailed it outta here so quick I think you still had your cap and gown on from graduation." Leighton laughs.

She isn't wrong: I took it off on the road out of town and tossed it out the window. "What can I say? I was young and foolish."

"Who was it you were datin' back then?"

I know Quinn probably means the question as one of those toss-away ones old friends ask when they haven't seen each other in over ten years, but if she only knew how deep it slices me. I take a deep breath and school my features. It's in the past: no sense in bringing the details up to two girls whom I haven't seen in too long—two girls who were my closest friends years ago.

"John Lewis," I tell her, pretty damn proud of myself for keeping my voice even.

"God, Leigh, you remember John?" Quinn laughs. "You probably would've dated him too, had you not been all in love with Maverick back then. Hell, half the girls in school were in love with John, Mr. Quarterback himself."

"He did have quite the following, didn't he?" Leigh agrees, looking at me like she can read between the lines.

"So, who are the lucky men?" I ask, pointing to their bellies and changing the subject.

"You'll never guess who that one finally landed," Quinn jokes, pointing toward Leigh.

"No!" I squeak with excitement, catching on immediately. "Maverick?"

Leighton's whole face lights up at the mention of Quinn's older brother. Last I heard, he was on the rodeo circuit, making a big name for himself in the sport. "Finally wrangled me a cowboy." She giggles.

"I'm so happy for you," I tell her honestly.

"It wasn't an easy road, but I love my grump."

"You always did, honey," Quinn says with a smile.

"And what about you, Quinn?"

"You remember Tate Montgomery?"

"The boy who used to spend his summers at his grandparents'? Sure I do. You two were practically joined at the hip. What did you do, get married right after the dust settled around me leavin' town?" I laugh, but my smile slips when she doesn't join in.

"Nah, took us a while and a lot of distance to realize where we belong, but we finally did. We got married last year. Shortly after I found out about this little one."

She points to her stomach with a smile that doesn't quite reach her eyes.

I sense a story that isn't full of hearts and flowers and, knowing it's time to steer the conversation away from that, I nod.

"Well, what brings you two into my bookstore?"

They both laugh. "Why am I not shocked that you'd end up owning a bookstore. We never could get you to put down those Fabio books you loved so much back in high school."

I giggle with Quinn. "Hey, he was a stud."

"We're lookin' for those baby books for daddies. You know, the ones that tell them what to expect when a tiny little demandin' human comes from their wife and life as they know it is changed forever. Tate, love him to death, seems to think he's fine because he's a lady doctor, but no amount of pullin' babies from other women's vaginas can prepare a man for the birth of his own child. Don't even get me started on my brother. Man can ride the meanest of bulls without breakin' a sweat, but you talk about his baby comin' soon and he starts gettin' pale as a ghost."

"She isn't wrong. My husband is hidin' it well, but I can tell he's nervous."

We continue to laugh as I show them where to look, catching up with small talk as they thumb through the selection, pulling a few out to purchase.

"Hey, you should come to the baby shower in a few weeks. We're doin' the whole joint thing, since the whole town is basically shuttin' down. You'd think the president was comin' to town the way they're all carryin' on."

"I'd love to," I tell them, surprising myself with just how much I want to be there.

They give me the info and we exchange numbers, promising to catch up soon. Seeing Quinn and Leighton only drives home just how much I've missed having them in my life. My fears haven't just kept me from moving on romantically—they've also kept me from people who I know, with no doubts, would do nothing but enrich my life. Now that we've been brought back together, I can't imagine my life without them in it again.

"You should stop by the PieHole, too," Leighton says. "You remember my mama's pies?"

"Boy, do I ever. Best thing I've ever put in my mouth!"

"That's what she said!" Lucy calls out from somewhere in the back of the store.

We all dissolve into laughter, and by the time Quinn and Leigh leave, I have a date to stop by the PieHole after I close up tonight. The memory of Leigh's mama's pies is so strong I swear I can taste them.

- ★ -

Four hours later, having finally closed The Sequel up, Lucy and I head over to Pine Oak, the excitement of seeing my old friends again bubbling in my belly like butterflies the whole way.

Lucy and I make small talk during the thirty-minute

drive, but the second we hit Main Street and pass my mama's salon, I stop talking. The windows are dark, so I know she isn't there, but the thought of running into her at Leighton's bakery makes me feel like I'm going to puke.

"Thinkin' about your mama?" Lucy asks knowingly.

"That obvious?"

"I understand your history, honey, but don't you think your mama would be happy to see you and forget about that stuff that kept y'all apart?"

I shake my head. "I think those kinda hurts are unmendable. I was a kid when I left, Luce, but she was a grown adult who turned her back on me when I came back beggin' for her help. Sometimes the hurt inflicted by others is just too great to move on from."

She hums in agreement and we pull into the parking spot directly next to Leigh's place. Lucy turns off her car and turns to look at me. "I hear you, Caroline, I do, but you're still holdin' on to that hurt, so maybe a little closure would be a good thing. Just think about it. Now that you have a reason to come into Pine Oak more, it's not like you can avoid her forever."

"Probably not, but that's a bridge I'll cross when it's time."

She gives me a look of understanding before nodding. "I'm here no matter what. Luke and me. Family isn't just those you're connected to by blood, you know."

"I do, sister from another mister," I joke.

For it being six at night, things are still pretty crowded

inside Leigh's place. An older woman behind the counter calls out a greeting when we step in, causing every head to turn in our direction. My cheeks heat and my shoulders pull in under the crowd's scrutiny. Lucy just plasters on her pageant smile and walks confidently in front of me. What I wouldn't give to have just an ounce of her conviction. I've been disgustingly shy my whole life, something that will never change if it hasn't yet. I look down at the ground while following Lucy's booted feet farther into the room. She's used to me being like this, so even if she wasn't a ball of happiness, she would've taken the lead.

"Hey you!" Quinn calls, and I look up to see her waving us toward a big table in the back. The man next to her with his arm around her chair looks just like the Tate I remember. On her other side sits the unmistakable Maverick Davis. He isn't smiling like Quinn's husband, but he doesn't look like the grumpy teenager I remember either. And finally, my eyes land on Leigh, curled into his side, her hand on top of his resting against her belly.

"Hey y'all. I'm Lucy Hazel!"

"Any relation to Luke Hazel?" Maverick rumbles, looking away from his wife's belly and at my best friend.

"Only the best twin brother a girl could ever have."

"Good man," he responds, looking back down to resume his study, his big palm moving around Leigh's belly a little.

"The best," Lucy agrees. She looks over at Tate. "Hi! You're the lady doctor. Taking new patients? Hate my gyno." She thrusts her hand out. Only she would think that asking a man when she first meets him if he can take a look at her vagina is acceptable.

"Uh, yeah. Call the office?" he responds, a little unsure, but he takes her hand anyway.

"Will do!"

"You're a happy one!" Quinn giggles.

"Life's too short to be anything but."

"Pull up a seat. Jana can get y'all whatever you want."

Taking a deep breath, I smell a certain sugary confection that makes me smile, memories of a whole other kind of high making my cheeks heat. "Got any apple pie?"

"Does she have apple pie? It's only always here since Clay can't get enough of the gross stuff," Quinn hoots. "Just missed my big brother, too. He got a call about a problem with one of his pregnant horses, so he had to head back to the ranch."

"All he does is work," Leigh adds.

"He's running the ranch now," Quinn tells me, and I know exactly how much weight that comment holds. Something even half the size of the Davis ranch would be hard work.

"That's got to be something. Does his wife help?"

Quinn looks at Lucy like she has two heads. Her question wasn't one that merits that kind of reaction, so I look over to make sure my best friend isn't picking her nose or something, but she's just smiling like normal.

"Clay's allergic to relationships. I don't think he's been

in one in at least four years, maybe longer. He got a little serious once with a total bitch, but thankfully that didn't last. Since then, nothin'."

"Relationships aren't for everyone," I mumble, thinking about my own issues with them, though I can't imagine someone like Clay would still be single. He was the most beautiful man I had ever seen when I was coming around with Quinn and Leigh.

I look up and meet Maverick's eyes across the table. He's studying me with such an intensity, I blush and look down. He's always been intense, but when he focuses on you like that, you would swear he can read your every thought.

The rest of the night continues, and before I know it the room around us has cleared out and Jana Fox, the gray-haired woman I saw when I entered, who I've learned is the PieHole's manager, has long since said her good-byes. I ate two slices of the best apple pie I've ever had in my life, and enjoyed one of the best evenings I've had in years.

God, I missed being home. More than I realized. Now, being near these people again, I can feel that pull stronger than ever.

5

CAROLINE

"Speak to a Girl" by Tim McGraw & Faith Hill

"You stupid fuckin' bitch!"

I flinch, knowing what's coming before John grabs my biceps in a rough and painful grip.

He pulls me forward, my head snapping back. He's getting worse. The thought filters through my mind and I know, I know next time might be the time that he doesn't stop at just hitting me a little. It's been escalating over the years, but the past few he hasn't stopped at just the verbal abuse, manhandling me more and more roughly each time I do something that pissed him off until that doesn't even seem like enough for him. Even if it's just moving through our house, I never know what's going to set him off.

"I'm sorry, John!" I cry, holding my hands up in front of my face in case this is that time he doesn't stop.

"Fuckin' disgusting," he spits, giving me a shake before pushing me from him. I stumble but don't fall. "I asked for a Bud and you bring me this cheap off-brand shit. Go to the store and get my fuckin' Bud or you'll find out what it's like to be sorry."

I grab my keys and run to the car, my hands shaking the whole way. In the five years we've been in Austin, he's gotten worse and worse. Actually, the first couple years weren't bad. But when we turned twenty-one and he was able to get beer more often, things changed. The clerk at the twenty-four-hour mart doesn't even look at me while he rings up my purchase, handing me my change with a mumbled good night.

I spend the drive home thinking about just leaving. I could go. He's likely drunk off the very beer he turned his nose up at by now. There's nothing in the house I want. I long ago started carrying bigger purses so that all my important papers were always with me. My hands tighten on the wheel, the cross street that takes me back to our shack of a house just ahead. My foot pushes down on the accelerator at the same time that I decide to leave.

Then everything goes black and all I can smell is smoke.

I jolt up in bed; the memory of the crash so real I can still smell the smoke. It takes me a moment, but as soon as the fear from that dream clears from my mind, I realize my mistake. It wasn't the dream that had me smelling smoke. My whole loft apartment is filling with it. I jump from the bed, grab my phone, and call 911, rattling off my address before I even realize why it's filling the room so quickly.

My stomach drops.

"No!" I scream.

I grab my bag, rushing to the back stairway, and press my hand against the wood to check for heat, making sure the exit—the only one—is safe. I turn the handle, the smoke even thicker in the stairwell, but I run down as fast as I can without tumbling to my death. When I reach the bottom, and see the front of my bookstore in flames, I trip, falling hard to my knees. It takes me a few unsteady tries, but I get out the back door and run around the building to watch as the flames grow. I drop my purse and clutch my phone as I pray that the fire department is quick, watching the flames lick and dance closer to destroying everything I hold dear.

I don't realize I'm screaming and crying until I feel two strong arms pulling me from the ground.

"Shh, Carrie," Luke says with sympathy, and I turn to bury my face in his chest.

"How did you know?" I wail.

"Volunteering night," he answers, rubbing my back. I pull away long enough to see him wearing his fire gear, and it only makes me sob harder. "The boys will put the fire out, darlin'. It hasn't spread to the top yet, so let's think positive, 'kay?"

I shake my head against him and continue to cry, my

mind lost somewhere in the nightmare that woke me up and the one that was waiting for me.

"Holy shit! Caroline!" I lift my head off Luke's shoulder just in time for his sister to collide with us. He silently shifts his hold so that he has both of us as Lucy wraps her arms around us. The two of them create a Hazel family circle around me as I burst into another fit of tears. I have no idea how long we carry on—Luce and me—but he holds us strong the whole time, watching as his fellow volunteer firemen battle the fire inside my bookstore. By the time the all-clear is given, Lucy has moved to sit next to us on the curb across the street and Luke has shifted my body so I'm sitting across his lap, Lucy's hands grasping mine. I finally stopped crying shortly after the paramedics checked me over, but I can't help the deep depression that had settled into my bones watching my life go up in flames.

"It's gonna be okay, Carrie," Luke says again when I hiccup.

"It will be, Caroline. It will," Lucy agrees, tightening her grip on my hands.

"It's all gone." I continue to look at the charred remains of the front half of my store and feel my chin wobble.

"It's not, sweetheart," Luke tells me, trying to get my attention off the store with his hand on my chin, but I pull away from his grasp and continue staring. "We'll get you settled. Insurance will handle the damage, and the fire only got to your kitchen and bathroom. I'll get in there tomorrow and get out everything I can, and you can stay with me and Luce until they finish rebuilding."

I don't speak. I can't. The Sequel was so much more than just a store. It represented everything I had overcome. And now it's gone—even if just temporarily.

I don't remember Luke driving me back to his and Lucy's house across town, but by the time he pushed a pill into my mouth and poured a drink of water down my throat I'd already started crying again. I didn't even question him, trusting him without doubt. By the time I felt my lids getting heavier, Lucy was lying on one side of me and Luke on the other, all three of us stuffed in her double bed. I wasn't the only one who'd been scared tonight. I might've lost a part of The Sequel, but I can only imagine what my best friends thought when they didn't know whether I was hurt or not. I curl into Lucy's side and feel Luke's arms tighten around me.

You would never know that we hadn't known each other our whole lives, being as close as we are. I met Lucy when I was nineteen in school in Austin, and we instantly bonded over the fact that we'd grown up in neighboring towns. We shared a dorm for a month before John moved me into an apartment with him, but Lucy and I remained close. She decided to move back home with me after I opened up The Sequel in Wire Creek. She wasn't wrong the other night on the way to the PieHole when she told me some people share a bond as close as family without being related.

This, right here, is my family, and even though I'm heartbroken about the store, I still have them.

The rest will figure itself out.

I hope.

I finally stopped crying shortly before I fell asleep, but not once did my best friends let go of me all night.

6

CAROLINE

"Rich" by Maren Morris

⭐

Eight days later, the insurance adjuster had finally made it out to what was left of The Sequel. Luke wasn't saying much about what he'd heard about the investigation from his friends at the fire department, but I knew it was looking like someone had set fire to my store intentionally. I couldn't think of anyone who'd hold a grudge against me enough to try to kill me, something they'd clearly been hoping would be the outcome. Needless to say, Luke was being more protective than normal, and that was saying a lot. I honestly didn't mind one bit though.

It had taken five washes and a ton of fabric softener to get the scent of smoke out of my clothes, but at least it had finally come out. All of the furniture would have to be replaced, something the insurance adjuster would hopefully deal with. Everything inside of the store was ruined. If the fire didn't get it, the water did. All in all, it could've been so much worse. I was alive. I just had to pull myself from the ashes again.

"You hangin' in there?"

I look up at Luke, falling into his side when he offers his arm. "Yeah. Just sad to see it like this. Who would do this, Luke?"

"Don't know, sweetheart. Could be some dumb kid for all we know. They'll get it sorted, just have to trust the boys leadin' the investigation. You're safe and that's all that matters."

"It could've been worse," I agree, saying my earlier thoughts out loud for the first time, still looking on as the insurance man pokes around the bottom level of my building.

Luke shivers and I look up at him. "You're still breathin', so yeah, it coulda been a whole helluva lot worse."

"It's gonna take a while to rebuild, Luke. I don't want to keep imposing on you and Lucy."

"It's not imposin', Carrie, and you know it. Family isn't a burden. You'll stay until things are back up and runnin' here and not a minute earlier."

I nod but plan on finding a way to get out of their house before that. I know he doesn't see things my way, but all I've been is dependent on someone else my whole life until opening up The Sequel. I don't want to fall back on that just because I'm now homeless. I already talked to Sheila at the motel in Law Bone and she's worked out a deal to help me with a long-term-rent-type situation at the motel. I would've preferred to stay in Wire Creek, but we don't have a motel, so that was out. Pine Oak was definitely not an option. So, Law Bone it is. I'll find a way to break it to the Hazel duo in a few days.

"I'm goin' to head back to your house, if you don't mind stickin' around with this guy. It just . . . it's just seein' it like this. You know?"

Luke gives me a small, sad smile and nods. "Yeah. I'll be back to pick you up when he's finished and we can head over to Hazel's together."

After letting Dan, the older man checking things out, know that I'm leaving and that Luke is there for any questions he might have, I head back to Luke and Lucy's place to get a nap before heading over to Hazel's for the night.

Whether out of pity or a general need for someone, Luke asked me to work at Hazel's until things are back up and running at The Sequel. Since all he wanted me to do was act as his office manager of sorts, handling all the paperwork and orders he hates dealing with, I said yes. To be honest, it was something I jumped at in order to keep my mind occupied, more than anything. I'm good with numbers—actually, damn good with numbers—so handling his books was something I could do in my sleep.

It didn't hurt that, when I finished work for the night, I could get a drink while waiting for Luke to close up.

Lucy was only helping me out at the store on her off days at the hospital where she was a full-time registered nurse, so she isn't out of a job, thank God. However, now that I was working weird hours with Luke and sleeping during the day, I felt like I hadn't seen my best friend in weeks, not days.

I haven't been asleep for long when Luke gets back and lets me know it's time to head to Hazel's. I change out of my wrinkled sleep shirt and into some short shorts, a Hazel's tank top, and a new pair of sandals. The scent of the fire was too heavy on the old boots I'd normally wear and I had to toss them. Just another thing that was taken from me.

"You sure you're good to handle payroll?"

I smile at Luke as he drives. "Yeah, Luke. It's like asking if a genius can handle a color-by-numbers sheet."

He chuckles and shakes his head. "Sometimes I forget there's a feisty little smart-ass in that tiny body of yours, Carrie girl."

"Lukie Dukie, I'm just a big bag of mystery, you know."

He laughs under his breath, the radio playing some current pop country song. I look through the darkness and let my thoughts wander to my plans. I should've known Luke saw right through me earlier, though, and the second I start thinking about how I'm going to tell him and Lucy about leaving, he opens his mouth and I groan inwardly.

"I know you talked to Sheila about stayin' at the motel."

"I wasn't goin' to keep it from y'all," I tell him immediately.

"I know you weren't."

"I just didn't know how to tell y'all."

He clicks his tongue. "You could have just said it, sweetheart. Even though I meant what I said earlier, I understand your need to exercise your independence. You've come a long way this year and you deserve what you need to be happy."

"I need to prove to myself that I can keep survivin' on my own, Luke," I tell him, honestly. After all, that's the root of it.

"I know you do. If what you want is to stay in Sheila's motel until you rebuild, at least you'll be close to Hazel's and I can still make sure you're okay. I might not like it, and Luce is damn sure not gonna like it, but I understand where you're comin' from."

I twist the straps of my purse and mull over my words. "Can I . . . do you . . . will you still want me to work at the bar?"

Out of the corner of my eye, I see him turn my way, but I keep twisting the leather strap in my hand, not wanting to see his face if there's disappointment written on it. I almost jump out of my skin when his hand covers mine.

"Don't ask stupid questions, Carrie," he drawls in a

gruff tone. "You've got a job at Hazel's for as long as you want it. You know I hate that numbers shit, and you add a little brightness to that place. Family, yeah?"

"Yeah," I whisper, a lump forming in my throat.

"Yeah," he parrots, pulling into the parking lot of the bar and shutting his truck off.

I climb out of the cab, even though I know it drives him nuts when I don't wait for him to open my door, and follow him around the back to enter through the employee doorway. He'd normally just walk in the front, but since this is the easiest way for him to dump me in the office, I know he only does it so he can fool himself into thinking I don't see just how crazy things get here at night.

"Let me know if you need anything. Just shoot me a text and I'll come sort you out."

"Yes, Dad," I say sarcastically with a roll of my eyes.

A few hours later, I feel like I'm about to find out what it's like to have my eyes permanently crossed. Luke Hazel is a shit bookkeeper. Reading his handwriting was almost traumatic, but I finally sorted out his payroll and wrote the checks for all sixteen employees so he could come sign them later tonight. Having had enough of his office's four walls, I open the door and step into the smoke-filled air. My eyes roam around the room while I stand there and enjoy the music. It was so muffled by his office's heavy door that I could hardly hear it in there. I'm on my second glance around the room when I see him.

The shadowy stranger.

My dark cowboy.

I take a step forward before I realize what I'm doing, stopping instantly.

No way. As much as I want to, and boy do I *want to*, I know I'd be testing fate by giving in to another night with him, and I think fate has proven to be against me lately. I blindly reach for the knob behind me at the same time I see his back straighten and his head turn my way. I gasp when I feel his eyes on me. I could walk over there and offer him my body again, but instead I turn and rush back into Luke's office.

There's no place in my life for a man like my dark cowboy, as much as I wish otherwise. I'd love nothing more than to get lost in the feelings I know he can drown me in, but my life is crazy enough without adding more insanity to it.

Maybe another time—another place—but not now.

Not when everything feels so out of control.

This must be what it feels like to miss something so deeply you crave it . . . even if you never really had it to begin with.

7

CLAYTON

"Hometown Girl" by Josh Turner

⭐

"**A** little higher on the left," my sister says for the umpteenth time. I do what she wants and lift the banner up—again—to the left. "No, my left."

I turn on the ladder and look down at Quinn. "Your left is the same as my left, Quinnie."

"Oh, then the right."

Fighting the urge to roll my eyes, I adjust my hold and move the banner again. From my perch, the thing is right as rain, but no damn way am I arguing with my hormonal sister. Tried that once and I swear to all things holy, the devil came out of her body and tried to pull me down to the pits below.

"Quinn, you've got that thing so high, no one's gonna be able to see it!" Leigh calls from just outside the barn, coming into the large open area with one hand on her hip. "Why do you have Clay up there anyway; we decided the other night to put it above the door—outside."

"You've got to be shitting me," I mumble under my breath. I close my eyes, count to ten, then do it all over again because I'm still seconds away from blowing the top of my head off.

"Need some help?"

I look down, hoping that Maverick can tell without words just how close I am to wringing our little sister's neck, but keep my mouth shut out of fear that I'll lose my temper if I open it.

Control.

I don't just like it—I need it. Without it, I feel like I've lost the reins on everything around me.

Quinn and Leigh continue to bicker about the best place for the stupid-as-fuck banner while I continue to level Maverick with my seething gaze. His eyes dance, that lighthearted happiness that he developed in the past few years now pissing me off while I'm stuck up here.

"Come on down. I'll take care of it and you can go do whatever the fuck Tate's been doin' for twenty minutes with the fuckin' drinks."

I look over at my brother in-law and laugh when he steps away from the cart we pulled in here early this morning and looks at the drink table in confusion. Why so much shit is needed for a joint baby shower, I'll never know. Especially since this is something I never thought I'd experience personally, much less as an uncle.

"Why does he look so damn confused?" I ask Maverick, climbing down carefully and handing him both ends of the banner.

"Quinn said she wanted everything set out in the shape of fuckin' rattles. Can you believe that shit? Since when does she give a damn about all this stuff?"

"Since *she* and your wife have been planning what our baby showers would look like from age ten, Maverick Austin Davis-James."

I burst out in a loud bark of laughter at the sound of my baby brother's legal name. I understood his reasons for not wanting to keep our family name when he married Leighton, instead choosing to take hers, but hearing Quinn sass him with that mouthful never fails to crack me up. "You heard her, Mr. James." I laugh, slapping him on the shoulder before walking away to help Tate figure out how the hell a bunch of cans are supposed to look like baby rattles.

An hour later, I make myself a promise that the next time either one of them winds up pregnant, I'm moving to Alaska until the birth so I miss all this party shit. Or fuck, I'll just buy them all the stuff they need if it means I don't have to hang streamers, arrange food and drinks into shapes, and, worst of all, put a bunch of melted chocolate into diapers so they can play some fucked-up game of Sniff the Shit.

Thank God I'll never find myself in this position.

Shaking my head, I walk away from the last table I sprinkled a bunch of pink and blue confetti on, dusting my hands off on my jeans. The party isn't set to start for another hour, and I'm about to use every second to find a secluded, not fucking pastel corner in which to enjoy some silence. Maybe then I won't jump on the back of Dell, my palmetto, and hightail it back to the ranch.

Stepping out of the barn, I adjust my hat so the sun isn't so harsh on my eyes after being inside for so long. Sometimes I still can't believe the changes Maverick made to the old James property since he came back to Pine Oak. He's built himself one fine rodeo school: even from this distance, I can see some of his students out in the training arenas, working with their teachers despite the fact that it's Saturday. I come over here from time to time to watch Maverick in his element, beyond happy that he's been able to retain such a big part of his life after being forced to give up riding professionally.

"Somethin' else, isn't it?"

I nod, watching the boys in the distance instead of turning to look at the very man that was on my mind.

"Thank you for all the help today, big brother. How close were you to losin' your shit in there?"

"You don't want to know," I answer honestly.

Maverick grunts out a laugh.

"You doin' all right?" I ask, knowing fine and well he'll understand what I'm asking.

He kicks a rock off the cement drive we're standing on, and I give him the time he needs to mull over his words.

"Still weighs on me, Clay. I'd be lyin' if I said otherwise, but every time I feel our baby movin' in her belly, a little of that fear gets beat back. Never thought this was somethin' I would have. Not after all the shit I did to fuck it up back in the day. I love my wife bigger than life, but I love our baby somethin' even bigger. That pushes me through the dark thoughts."

I hum, looking away from the boys working damn hard to be the next best thing the rodeo ever saw, to look at Maverick.

"Somethin' else on your mind, brother?" I ask, frowning at his words.

"Shit, Clay," he says with a long exhale. "I keep thinkin', what if I'm just like the old man was?"

My jaw goes slack as I look at him in shock. "You fuckin' with me?"

He lifts his hat off his head, the wild, thick, black-as-night hair that all us Davis kids have not tamed in the least, even with the sweat wetting it from being under his black Stetson for hours. He runs his free hand through his hair, frowning at me the whole time.

"That man fucked with my head for so long, Clayton," he says solemnly. "What if I don't know how to be a good father to my child because of him?"

Grasping his shoulder, I turn him so we're face-to-face. "You hear me now, Maverick. Buford Davis was a shit father up until he was faced with his own mortality, but he is *not* us. You're gonna be the best father a kid could have. The fact that you're worried at all should tell you what you need to know. A man doesn't feel the fear of bein' a bad parent if he could even have an ounce of what it takes to not give a shit about them inside of him. You carin' about it at all means it could never happen. You get me?"

He swallows thickly but nods after a beat of silence.

"That kid's gonna be smothered with so much love it'll never know what life is like without it."

Maverick's eyes close and he drops his chin so I lose his gaze, but not before I saw what I said take root. My brother, while he might have been broken when he left, has become one hell of a man with the love of a good woman.

"What do you say we go find the whiskey Tate stashed behind the back of your big fancy-ass barn and toast the fact that I'm about the be the favorite uncle in this family?"

"Fat chance." He laughs after clearing his throat. "You aren't takin' top seat as uncle if I have a say in things."

We both laugh, but inside I feel my heart get big as fuck when Maverick gives me an unguarded, carefree smile. Those shadows normally pulling his scowls deep are nowhere to be found. Then we grab Tate and warm our bellies with some of the best liquor Texas ever did see.

- ★ -

I'll remember this day for the rest of my life.

If I survive it, that is.

I look over at the other men who were forced by their wives or girlfriends to attend, thanking the good Lord that I'm not the only one about to puke. Logically, I know it's just chocolate, but that doesn't mean shit when all your eyes see is a pile of brown goo inside a diaper.

"Come on, Clay!" Jana, Leighton's longtime bakery manager, hoots from the far corner. "Get that sniffer in there and hurry up before you lose this whole thing!"

Did I mention I'm on her team? She's been bellowing from the sidelines since the horn sounded and our time started. I'm down to my last two piles of shit to identify before I can get the fuck away from this insanity.

"If you don't get that snout into that diaper, you're gonna owe me an hour-long massage."

The prize.

Shoulda known she was frothing at the mouth for the gift card to some fancy spa in Austin. Seemed like every woman in town—because there's no doubt they're all here—is after that damn thing.

"I'll buy you your own dadgum massage if you'll pipe the hell down, Jana!" I yell over the laughter around us.

I look down at the diaper again and close my eyes before bringing it to my nose and sniffing.

Snickers.

Scribbling the word down, I move on and quickly repeat the process. I wisely keep my eyes shut so I don't fight my stomach to keep the whiskey I've consumed down.

"Done!" I bark, standing from my seat so swiftly, the old wooden chair topples over. I don't even look at the people cracking up at my discomfort. Stomping over to the two women who thought up this torture, I slap my paper on the table in front of them. "I'm not babysittin' until those rugrats are potty trained."

Quinn laughs her ass off. Leigh just smiles sweetly up at me.

I'm opening my mouth to tell them just how serious I am when Leigh looks over my shoulder, her smile growing. Then I hear a voice that's been haunting my dreams for almost two months now.

"Hey . . . uh, I'm sorry I'm late," the sweet-as-pie voice says from behind me.

Takes everything in me to not react when there's one hell of a war raging inside of me from just hearing that breathy apology. I clench my teeth so hard, my jaw hurts, but I don't turn.

"That's all right, honey. I know you've been going through a lot lately so I'm just happy you came out."

"She wouldn't have missed it," a new voice I don't recognize says.

"Lucy loves babies." My heart thunders in my chest when I hear her speak again.

Leighton stands and walks past me, I assume to greet the late guests. Quinn slaps my thigh and I look down at my sister.

"Get out of my way, you big giant."

Realizing I'm blocking her ability to heave out of her seat, I reach down and help her stand. She shoves me aside the second she's up with more strength than a tiny woman should have, and follows in Leigh's wake. I steady my breathing and turn. I should have known nothing I could do would matter. When I saw her across the smoke-filled bar the other night, I felt that like a punch in the gut. Now, seeing her this close is enough to have my cock going from zero to sixty. She doesn't notice me, or if she does, she isn't making it obvious. Her eyes flicker around the crowded barn, looking at what seems like everything and anything at once. If I thought it was hard to ignore this pull without being face-to-face, it's going to be next to impossible now. And I'm not even sure if I want to ignore it.

Fuck, I need to get out of here and figure out what the hell is going through my mind.

"You remember my big brother Clay right Caroline?"

I look away from the dark-haired beauty who has me licking my lips and praying for an apple pie to look at my sister. I know Luke called her Carrie that night, I heard it clear as day, and the name has stuck with me since. Just as the thought comes, I remember the name she was screaming in my ear that same night. Looks like we were both playing a damn game.

She looks up at me, her cheeks turning pink despite her olive skin. Her dark brown eyes search mine, but I don't see recognition. One dainty hand comes out, timidly, and she gives me a weak smile. What happened to the feisty woman who came on my cock so many times I felt the vise grip days after I snuck out of that hotel room?

"N-nice to meet you," she says softly.

Reaching out, I drag the tips of my fingers down hers and across her palm before engulfing her hand inside of mine. I know the exact moment she figures it out. Her plump lips part on a gasp and her hand spasms in mine.

"Pleasure," I rumble, my voice just as thick as my cock.

"Davis," she breathes.

"Yeah," Quinn chuckles, drawing the word out and looking at her like she's lost her mind. "My oldest brother, Clayton *Davis*, the family name and all."

My eyes stay on hers as the silence turns awkward for those watching. Putting her out of her misery, I regretfully release her hand and take a step back, tipping my chin down in a quick nod. "I'll leave you ladies to catch up."

Still looking at Carrie—no, Caroline—I raise a brow and hope to God she sees the promise in my gaze. This isn't over. Just touching her again was enough to make that thought clear as day to myself. No more denying this connection.

I might've been prepared to never give in to that again, but there isn't a force strong enough to keep us from colliding. And that's just what we're doing. I've felt that tug twice now in her presence as the connection between us pulled and pulled. We aren't going to ignore fate if she wants us to cross paths. I would have probably gone on my way without looking for this woman who's haunted my memories for two months, but I'm not a stupid man and I damn sure won't look a gift horse in the mouth now that this is proving to be inevitable.

We'll finish this later.

Caroline and me.

In private.

8

CAROLINE

"Flatliner" by Cole Swindell & Dierks Bentley

"**W**hat the hell was that?" Lucy hisses after Clayton *Davis* disappears through the open door that we had just entered a few minutes before.

I shake my head, not even sure where to begin explaining how I know the eldest Davis, and in front of his family no less.

There's no way.

Just my mind playing tricks.

I've been under so much stress lately it wouldn't be a stretch to think my mind conjured up the one person I haven't been able to stop thinking about. Between the sleep I've been losing since the fire, seeing that the motel I call home now has the thinnest walls, and the residual sadness I feel every time I handle more red tape from the insurance company dealing with The Sequel, I'm about as close to going insane as it gets. My life is up in the air—where my future had been is one big question mark, and now, on top of that, I'm hallucinating.

"You and Clay know each other?"

I blink at the question, not really sure which of the pregnant ladies in from of me asked, but hoping neither really expected me to answer. If what I felt when my hand touched his looked half as time-stopping as it felt, I wouldn't want to know the details if it was my brother or brother-in-law.

"That was intense," Lucy chimes in, not helping this situation in the least.

Even if that wasn't the same man, even in my naïveté I can recognize the connection that we felt. My palm tingles at the thought and I look toward the last place I saw him, oddly having to fight back the desire to run after him and demand answers.

Quinn steps into the path of my gaze and looks at me with fascinated shock, her green eyes as bright as gems, twinkling with mischief. "Jesus Jones. You and Clay?! I mean, you're beautiful, honey, so I don't doubt you turn heads, but he's just so . . . *Clay*!"

I sputter, shaking my head in denial so fast that I surely look like I'm impersonating a bobblehead doll. "No!" I exclaim, fidgeting with my purse strap as anxious, nervous energy starts to get the best of me. I can feel my hands grow clammy at the thought of being on display, and I have to fight to keep my back straight instead of hunching like I normally would when the spotlight is turned toward me.

"Oh my," Lucy gasps in a breathy tone. "She's lying."

I turn to my *ex*–best friend and continue shaking my head. *God, shut up, Luce.*

"She's lying so bad, I'm shocked her nose isn't a mile long," she keeps going with a laugh, sticking her bubble-gum-pink-tipped finger in front of my face, and I swear right then and there that her death will be slow and painful.

"This is better than pie." Leighton giggles happily.

"No, this is better than a '51 Ford ready for a complete rebuild," Quinn adds with a dreamy sigh.

"Or a sale at Target!" Lucy exclaims, clapping her hands and bouncing on the balls of her feet.

I drop my gaze, looking at my sandals as my face heats. It'd be pointless to continue denying what they just witnessed seeing, as I'm the worst liar in the whole state of Texas.

"You have to tell us everything," Quinn whispers, leaning into my side to push her shoulder into mine.

"Well, maybe not everything," Leigh snorts.

"Screw that, I want all the juicy details. He might be my brother, but he's been livin' like a monk since that stupid bitch he dated last and girlfriend, you'd think he was asexual the way those two *didn't* carry on in public. No sparks close to what we just saw between y'all." She waggles her perfectly sculpted brows.

"You might as well just tell her, Caroline." Leigh snickers. "You can't shock her easily. Trust me, I've tried."

Quinn continues nodding, her brows still going up and down suggestively. "Just wait until this one"—she points to Leigh—"starts tellin' you about the monster cock."

"Q!" Leighton gasps, but she smiles a second later, so she must not be offended. "Anyway, you gotta give us somethin', honey. The way he's always ridin' those horses, I bet he can work those hips like no one's business."

Oh my God. This isn't happening.

"Would you three shut up," I hiss, already seeing a few people listening in on our huddle. Thankfully, someone up there is on my side, because the girls stop the instant I ask them to.

"This isn't over," Leighton promises. "And, Caroline, you're goin' to need to get over that shyness of yours now that you're one of us."

One of them? What does that mean? Just because . . . no. A one-night stand doesn't mean I'm going to start coming to Sunday dinner. I haven't seen him in months. If he'd wanted more after that night, he wouldn't have disappeared before I woke up. I open my mouth to tell all three of the giddy women in front of me just that, but stop when a voice starts talking in a cheerful bellow.

"Who's ready for some presents!" Jana screams. I vaguely remember her from Leighton's bakery. Her question causes me to look up from the deep study I had been doing of the sandals Lucy made me wear today just in time to see her jump down from the chair she must have climbed up on to make her announcement. She pushes through the people between her and us in a rush before grabbing both pregnant women. I could kiss her for being the proverbial bell that is saving me.

"Those two aren't going to be satisfied with your terrible lyin', you know. Even if you really don't know him—which I know you do, no matter what you say—a blind old bat could've seen the sparks flyin' off the two of y'all," Lucy stage-whispers, drawing a few more eyes our way.

"That's what I'm afraid of."

A group of older women push between us on their way to get a better view of the presents being opened. I excuse myself and get out of their way. Only in a town as small and nosy as Pine Oak would a baby shower be an event that could rank right up there with Macy's Thanksgiving Day Parade. Well, the fact that two of the town darlings are the guests of honor doesn't hurt either. Oddly enough, I forgot how much I love the closeness the residents in Pine Oak appear to enjoy.

"Who was that anyway, Caro?" Luce says after we move to the back of the room.

I sigh, ignoring the fact that neither Hazel twin listens when I tell them how much I hate nicknames, and look around to make sure no one is listening. "*That* was the dark cowboy."

Her blue eyes all but bug out of her head and she

whips around to look in the opposite direction, blond curls fanning around her as she turns her gaze toward the doorway leading out of the barn. Well, at least I *think* this is a barn. On the outside that's exactly what it looks like, but once you step foot in here, it looks like some kind of western-style grand ballroom—complete with chandeliers made out of antlers.

What are the odds that I would run into him here? The dark cowboy I shared a faceless night of passion with couldn't have been a stranger passing through town? No. *My* dark cowboy—the very man that I've been using the memory of for two months now to keep me going whenever I start to get depressed about everything going wrong in my life; the man who showed me how powerful being with someone who cared about your pleasure was like; the one who ruined me for life—*he* was the same man I'd had a crush on for a whole year before I started dating John in high school and moved past the silly lust I thought I'd felt for the eldest Davis.

Davis.

Of course.

It makes sense, now that I'm not letting my hormones drive the show.

He never did correct me, nor did he confirm that actually was his name. I'd just taken what Luke said and assumed. Maybe I had subconsciously known it was him all along, using the illusion of anonymity to escape the unhappiness in my past that I had been overcoming since moving to Wire Creek. Nevertheless, I can't deny that my dark cowboy is, in fact, Clayton Davis and not some stranger anymore.

"Well." Lucy hisses, looking back at me and pulling me from my thoughts, "you should sneak out of here while they're distracted with the presents and find him."

I snort. "That is never going to happen."

"Why not?" she whispers harshly, drawing the attention of a few people standing near the back of the barn. I look up, meeting the steady emerald gaze of Maverick Davis and quickly look away from the intense curiosity I see in his eyes.

I take a step back, farther away from the crowd, and grab Lucy before leaning closer toward her to whisper softly, "Even if I was the brave kind of woman who'd run after a man, you know I'd clam up the second I catch up with him."

"What happened to the woman who went back to the motel with a man she didn't even know a thing about? Hmm? *She* was brave. *She* didn't clam up. She took the bull by the horns and enjoyed the hell outta that ride. That woman *is* you, Caroline. Don't pass up a chance like the very one in front of your face."

"What chance?" I sharply question. "I just happened to run into him here because this is his family, Luce, not because fate, the good Lord above, or Clayton Davis wanted me to find him again."

"Yeah? You think so? And how, pray tell, do you argue that this isn't one of your romance books comin' to life?" she continues like a dog with a bone. "I see all those dog-eared pages of yours, honey, and I know you believe in serendipitous moments just like this one. This is your fantasy in black-and-white comin' into full-color focus. Go get your hero."

"I'm not havin' this argument with you, and there isn't anything in the world that would get me to chase after that man."

I mean it, too. There isn't a damn thing the universe could throw at me that'd make me brave enough to go after a man like Clayton Davis. He's the epitome of perfection. Pair his good looks with just how well I know he can use *everything* he was blessed with, and you have the whole package—the whole package that a woman like me just doesn't know how to handle without looking like a fool.

He's been inside of me, for Pete's sake! I don't even think I could look him in the eye now. I can just see it, me staring up into those dark green eyes with drool dripping down my chin. There's no way I could hold a conversation with him in the light of day after I've had the part of him that makes my heart skip a beat just thinking about it touching the deepest parts of me.

I shift, my thoughts conjuring a throbbing between my legs. Lucy tries to get my attention again, but I ignore her, fighting the urge to grab my phone and google "how to move to the moon."

She pokes me in the ribs for the second time, and I finally pull my attention off the floor to look at her, ready to tell her to shut up if she starts on me again, but the words die on my lips when I see the expression on her face as she looks at something just over my right shoulder.

I pray my gut is wrong. That she just saw a spider or something. But I know there isn't anything my cheerful friend would look at like that except for the very person I feared would jump at the chance to confront me if she recognized me here today.

"Caroline?"

Well, damn. I close my eyes and try to prepare myself for seeing my mama for the first time since I was eighteen years old and ran away. I haven't heard that voice in almost five years either. Not since the last time I called the same telephone number that I learned in kindergarten and begged for the woman who should've loved me enough to save me, to help. She hadn't called me Caroline then, though; no, she had a new name for me by the time I had been broken enough to make that call. A whore. That's what I became to her.

My chin wobbles and my watery eyes shift away from Lucy's shocked face toward the open barn door, which taunts me with the promise of a quick exit. There's no question of staying or running now. Staying in here, away from the chance of running into Clay, means facing the woman who played a huge part in the nightmare I lived for years. Seeing her would bring back all the pain I had been healing from. Staying would be painful and I'm just not strong enough to deal with it. But going . . . going would bring me to the person that I've been dreaming of for weeks.

I would take Clayton Davis and door number one any day—even though that option scares me in a whole different way than the confrontation I'm escaping does. I never want to go back down the road the woman behind me represents again.

"Go," Lucy mouths, reading my mind. I nod and see her face soften with love before I run out of the barn. My legs pump furiously as I sprint toward the huge house in the distance and the safety I feel with each measured step away from the party calms me.

I keep churning my legs, my heart thundering as I cry silently for the girl who needed that woman so badly, blinking as the tears threaten to spill over.

When I come to the end of the rows of trucks and cars parked between the barn and the house, I suck in a painful burst of air when I realize I somehow completely missed a huge animal, which seems to have come out of nowhere. I slam into the horse with a painful jolt, my butt hitting the ground a moment later and my elbows digging painfully into the gravel a beat after that. The tears finally come and I make an embarrassing sound between a gasp and a wheeze as a sob bubbles free.

Some gravel hits my bare legs when the man atop the

horse that almost killed me jumps down. The water blurring my vision makes the sun look even brighter as he reaches my side. I look to my lap and push up to my elbows with a grunt of pain, avoiding looking at the man who witnessed my humiliation, but I don't need a visual to confirm just who is cursing low under his breath. I know from the awareness zipping across my skin alone who it is. How is it possible that, after only one night, my body is desperate for more of his touch?

Could this day be any more humiliating?

Probably not.

"You okay, sweetness?"

I squeeze my eyes closed at the endearment, curl my legs up, and press my forehead against my knees. I can't handle that word coming from him right now. Not when I'm vulnerably raw. Not when I've been hearing it in my head for weeks and weeks accompanied by the memory of his harsh breaths against my skin as he emptied himself inside of me.

"Please, just go," I beg, my tears coming even faster now.

"Caroline!"

At the sound of my mama's shrill voice in the distance, I whimper and try to make myself disappear by tightening my arms around my legs.

"What the hell?" he mutters.

The fear of ghosts past clawing closer, I look up and hiccup a sob before opening my mouth. "Get me out of here." I hold his worried eyes and beg him with everything in me to take me far away from here. Everything else that happened from the moment I slept with him up until the embarrassment I felt at coming face-to-face with him again vanishes.

It makes no sense logically, but once those frantic words leave my lips, I know he is the one person who can banish this feeling of uncontrollable desperation. I could rush back to Lucy and have her take me away from my mother instantly, but just looking into his worried eyes, I can feel the balm of calm that his nearness brings within me. I felt it during that night in the dark, and I feel it now—something inside me begging for him. He should be the last person I plead with to save me right now, but the second the words left my mouth, I felt with no doubt that he was the only one.

And, as if to prove that this really could get more humiliating, his hands go under my armpits, dislodging my hold, and pull me up off the ground as if I weigh nothing. Once he has me back on my feet, he bends and I see the top of his cowboy hat moments before he throws me up onto the back of the beast that took me down.

If I weren't seconds away from pure panic, I would catalog every moment that happened next to replay mentally for the rest of my life. It was a move straight out of the pages of a romance novel. Clayton Davis, cowboy in shining armor, heaves himself right up behind me and adjusts both of our bodies so that we fit on top of the horse together. I'm more in his lap than actually sharing the saddle with him, but with my butt pressed tight against his crotch and my thighs spread wide on top of his own, a whole new rush of feelings start inside me. One strong arm curls around my belly before I can even blink and he clicks his tongue. Suddenly we're blazing toward the fields behind the barn at lightning speed. I curl my hands around the arm holding me and pray I don't fall to my death as he guides the powerful horse away.

We burst through the field, not slowing in the least, and I have to force my nails out of the thick muscles of his forearm when it becomes clear I'm not in any danger of falling.

"Where," I choke on my words, clearing my throat. "Where are we going?" I call over my shoulder.

"Away." His one-word answer rumbles against my back, his arm tightens around my belly, and he continues to lead the horse with one hand holding the reins.

I look over the horse's head and almost throw up. "Please, Clayton! Stop!" I cry out as we get closer and closer to the fence line.

He immediately calls out a command and we slow before stopping completely just a few yards from the fence I was sure was about to kill us. I slump in his grasp, my position uncomfortable and borderline painful now that nothing is distracting me. He drops the leather reins and his hands move on my body, igniting fire in their path as they glide, now distracting me for a whole new reason.

Before I realize his intention, he's lifting my body and turning me in his strong arms as if I was a child.

I flail, thinking surely the horse is going to dislodge us both if he takes even a tiny step. Not wanting to fall, I loop my arms around his neck and hold on for dear life.

"You've got to stop tossin' me around like it's nothin'," I protest.

"Never been on a horse?" he asks, ignoring me and drawing my attention from the ground under us and to his handsome face. Without the darkness to hide in, I see him—really see him. Just as I'm sure he sees all of me. Every unremarkable bit of me.

That strong jaw that I had admired the night I found him as my barstool neighbor, the only part of him that I ever got a good look at, is proud in form and sprinkled with the same dusting of facial hair that I remember burned my sensitive skin as it rubbed against it.

My belly churns as I study the man who had, until now, been a faceless stranger. There isn't a flaw to be found. Perfect nose, full lips, and eyes brighter than a lush summer field right after the storm clouds clear and sun shines bright on the rain-soaked grass.

And those mesmerizing eyes are studying me just as fiercely as I am him.

"Thank you," I finally say, grateful that my mind wisely didn't blurt out how perfect I find him. "You're correct, I've never ridden before." Silence continues as his eyes probe mine. "Horses scare me," I explain, nervously trying to fill the void his mute perusal of me is creating.

The quiet ticks around us. I'm entranced as much by it as I am with the man holding me. That is, until the horse takes a step to the side and I turn into a mess of arms and legs as I attack my savior while basically trying to climb inside his body. His chest moves in what I hope is laughter, and he adjusts his grip on me while allowing me to settle. I somehow manage to turn myself completely within his strong arms and wrap all of my limbs around him like some kind of deranged spider monkey. I realize my mistake the second his hands settle on my butt and the heat of his hold radiates through my thin shorts.

I swear, I stop breathing right then and there.

I lift my chest back from his, that rush of heat on my bottom making me feel fearless and the shyness that normally hinders my every move in life falling to the wayside as I look into his eyes.

"I'm sorry," I gasp. "I'd get off you, but I'm terrified to move."

His lips tip at the corners in the tiniest of fractions and his eyes get warm.

"Not complaining," he rumbles softer than a man his size should ever be able to speak.

"If you could just help me get down and then maybe point me in the direction of where we came from, I'll get out of your hair. Or . . . off of your body, I guess."

He shakes his head. "That's not gonna happen, darlin',"

he answers, his tone leaving no room for me to disagree. Even if I wanted to, though, the expression on his face is enough to kill any complaint I might have voiced. I wasn't argumentative to begin with, but the second he stops talking and inches his face closer to mine, I'm held captive. "I like you lookin' at me like this a whole lot more than I like you doin' it with fear in your eyes. And I like this softness in your eyes a fuckin' helluva lot more than seein' you with tears, baby."

Oh. Wow.

"You want me to take you farther away from who-ever put those tears on your beautiful face? Or do you want me to bring you back to your friend so she can do it? Either way, Caroline, I'm not leavin' your side until I know you're okay."

Call me weak. Call me the very thing the woman I was running from had accused me of being years ago. But don't call me a coward anymore, because right now I'd do anything in the world if it means I get to keep having this man look at me like I'm the most important thing to him. Doesn't make a lick of sense, seeing as we don't really know each other—apart from in the biblical sense and all—but that doesn't seem to matter. My heart feels like I'm finally safe.

"Please don't take me back there," I whisper.

His head moves in one strong, sure nod. He takes one hand off my bottom as the other shifts so one huge palm is now directly between my cheeks, fingers spread wide to support me. I gasp, unable to keep from wiggling, when two of his fingers brush against the most sensitive area under my shorts-covered center. He doesn't bring attention to how close he is to my entrance; instead he holds my gaze, his face softening even more when a puff of air escapes my lips.

"Are you gonna be okay if I let Dell move again?"

"Dell?" I frown.

"My horse."

"Right." I look around us but jolt when I realize just how far off the ground we really are. Especially now that I'm not just on a horse, but even higher after I just used Clayton's body like some weird human pole.

"I won't let you fall," Clayton promises, his voice low and calming.

It could easily happen though.

"No, it couldn't."

My eyes widen when I realize I said that out loud, thankful he didn't realize I wasn't talking about the horse in the least.

"You're safe with me."

I take a slow, deep breath. "Don't let go of me," I tell my dark cowboy.

"Not sure that's gonna be possible, sweetness," he oddly answers, then makes a clicking sound. He doesn't look away from my eyes, not when we start moving at a slow walk. Not when we start to trot a little faster. He holds me captive while I trust not only him, but also the animal carrying us. I should be terrified at what his words make me feel. I shouldn't allow myself to think they mean something that should be impossible, but with my body plastered against his and his breath mingling with mine, I find myself melting into this man who is as much of a stranger as he was two months ago.

Only now that stranger has a face *and* a connection to my life through my friendship with his family. That means today won't be the last time we see each other, even if those seven words don't mean what my heart thinks they do. This isn't the end of Clayton and me.

9

CLAYTON

"Body like A Back Road" by Sam Hunt

I let Dell lead the way, knowing he'll take us back to the ranch eventually. I say a silent prayer that he does what he normally does when I let him take control during our rides and wander the long way through my property—enjoying the freedom of his hooves—because I'm not ready to let the woman in my arms go. I've never felt this connected to someone. I felt it the first time I had her in my arms, ignored it, but I won't make that mistake again. I'm sick of living a shadow of a life because I let my fucked-up past cloud my way toward some sort of normal future. Even if nothing comes of this, I'm going to try.

"I'd convinced myself what I felt that night was just the whiskey," I admit. I smile when her cheeks heat, my words hitting the bull's-eye.

Who would've thought a woman blushing could be so erotic? But with a vision of just how far that blush will spread, all I can wonder now is if her small tits turn pink with a blush when she comes—something I never got to see that night because of the darkness she seemed to need.

"Might've been," she whispers so softly I have to strain to hear her, and then she lays her head against my shoulder, relaxing just a bit in my hold. She probably doesn't even realize she's doing it, but that move right there shows me that she trusts me to lead.

"You make me feel like I'm comin' alive, sweetheart. I've got no words to explain it better than that, but what I know is there ain't no way on this green earth that it's the whiskey that is doin' the work. Wasn't the cause then and damn sure ain't now."

"Heat of the moment, maybe. An adrenaline rush," she weakly argues without conviction.

"I'm old enough to be able to control my cock in the heat of the moment. Even if I was feelin' some adrenaline, it wouldn't make me feel like I was out of control of my own body. You feel my heart poundin' in my chest now? You explain that as heat of the moment when the only time I feel calm is on the back of one of my horses."

She turns her head away, and as much as I love the feel of her relaxed in my arms, even when I know she's afraid of horses, I wish I could look into those rich chocolate eyes of hers—so dark that I could get lost in their depths—to try and figure out what's going on in that beautiful head of hers.

"Did you know who I was?" she asks, her mouth moving against my neck causing a chill to roll down my spine. My hand half on her ass and half on her pussy twitches violently with the sensation of it.

"No, I didn't. I knew you were a gorgeous woman who looked about as lost as I was feelin' when I walked into Hazel's that night. Knew exactly who you were back at Mav and Leigh's though."

"You wouldn't have tried to find me if we hadn't crossed paths today."

It isn't a question.

She's not wrong either. Something we both don't need me to verbalize, but I don't like her thinking I was just using her as some fuck toy either. We'd both been looking for something that night, but I don't make a habit of spending the night getting lost in a woman before vanishing, and I've felt bad about that since. My loneliness drove me to her, and it kept me from finding her after, but it won't keep me away from her now. There's a reason we crossed paths to begin with, I know that with absolute clarity.

"It's okay," she continues, a little softer. "I understand it better now."

I frown, seeing the roof of my house over the horizon. "Understand what, Caroline?"

"Why a man like you wouldn't have tried to find a woman like me."

"What the fuck does that mean?" I sharply ask, making her jump slightly.

She sighs. The sound holds notes of sadness, but she doesn't lift her head from my shoulder. Her lips continue to speak against my neck. "It's funny the things you remember. Those memories that you hadn't thought about in years comin' out of nowhere at the oddest times. I remember once, durin' one of the famous Davis boys' bonfires, somewhere around the time I turned eighteen, I was sittin' on the back of your sister's tailgate watchin' everyone let loose around me when I saw you with some tall Barbie doll–lookin' girl with the biggest boobs I had ever seen. The first thing I thought was how someone so thin could stand upright without topplin' over all the time. Stupidest thing to think about in that moment, but I did anyway. After that, though, I couldn't look away from y'all. Not even when you pushed her against Ronny Billings's truck and pulled her jean skirt up to her chest and started thrustin'. I kept watchin'. I don't even know why I'm rememberin' it so clearly now, but I was transfixed by you even then. Though I think that was also the same night I stopped walkin' around with my head in a cloud of fantasies."

Jesus Christ.

I don't remember a thing she's talking about, but I have no doubt it probably happened. I was careless with how I took my pleasure in years back. Those nights might've started out as a way for us to sneak beer in high school, but if she was eighteen when she saw me doing that, I was well past high school age and at that point, the bonfires had turned into an easy way for all the boys I grew up with to fuck young, tight, and eager-to-please pussy. I was no better than they were and I didn't stop being careless until I got burned by the wrong woman.

"I'm not the man I was back then," I defend myself, wanting her to believe my words more than I care to admit.

"I didn't say you were, Clayton." She takes a deep breath while I revel in the way her saying my full name makes me feel. "I was just explainin' why I know I'm not the type of woman a man like you would be goin' for. Well, I guess you might think I was that type of woman, since I gave myself to you just as easily as that girl did back then, but even if you did think that, you wouldn't have looked for me."

"Hey," I grunt with a harshness that even makes Dell pause slightly before continuing his lazy trot toward the stable.

"I wouldn't have looked for you either," she continues as if I hadn't spoken, unaware of the intense emotion she's igniting in me.

"Why's that?" I ask thickly.

"Because while I might *think* I'm not the kind of woman you want, I *know* I'm not the woman you need."

This girl. She can't be serious. Even if I didn't know deep in my bones she's worth the effort of trying to figure out her riddles, I'd still keep trying to get the answers if it meant I get to keep feeling like something I've been missing for a long damn time was just found.

"Oh, Linney, it's gonna be fun provin' you wrong." Her body jolts in my arms and I smile. "First things first, how about you tighten those sweet legs of yours around my body and hold on while I get us down from Dell. Then, if you don't have anywhere else you need me to take you, you let me start showin' you who I am now and not who you think I might be?"

" 'Linney'?" she questions, one brow arched.

"Really, darlin', that's all you heard?"

"My name is Caroline."

"I know your name, Caroline Lynn Michaels."

Her eyes widen and she clears her throat. "Well, then you know Linney isn't it."

"I know you're sweet as pie when you're all heated. Anyway, I can get you that way. That woman isn't prim and proper Caroline. That woman is wild-as-hell Linney."

"I'm not sleepin' with you," she sputters after I get us down and hand Dell off to one of the stableboys, not an easy feat, but she hardly weighs anything, as tiny as she is. Her face gets red the second she realizes we aren't alone anymore and, with a squeak, drops her head back to my shoulder.

"Jorge doesn't speak English, sweetness, but even if he did, he's paid to work, not to worry about what kind of sleepin' is goin' on between his boss and the beautiful woman wrapped tightly around him." I mean to put her out of her misery, but I can't help but tease her a little. It's way too satisfying to see her embarrassment painting her cheeks.

She mumbles something against my skin, her position muffling her words so badly I can't understand her. Her legs loosen around me next, and I regretfully release my hold and help her stand. I look down at the top of her head, noticing for the first time just how tiny she is now that she isn't wearing boots. Not just her height, but her build too. Without her boots, I'm guessing she's got to be close to a foot shorter than my six foot three. Every delicate inch of her makes me want to do nothing but wrap my arms around her, protect and worship her until she makes me stop.

Not once in my life have I felt this way about a woman who wasn't my sister or Leigh. My family. If I feel this strong of a pull to Caroline without really knowing a thing about her besides us being compatible, I imagine it could swallow me whole when I finally do get to know her.

"Dinner, Caroline. Let me cook us some dinner tonight and we can get to know each other a little better. Then maybe you'll listen to why I wouldn't have gone lookin' for you and you can fill me in on why you wouldn't have done the same."

"I'm not sleepin' with you," she repeats.

"Didn't invite you to," I joke, bending down to her eye

level when she gasps. "But when I finally do get the privilege to have you again, there ain't gonna be any sleepin' then either, sweetness."

I press a swift kiss to her shocked lips before taking her hand and guiding her toward my house. The same house that makes me feel like I'm drowning in my solitude is looking a lot better now that I'm picturing her inside it with me.

- ★ -

I flip one of the two steaks on the cutting board and rub my own mixture of seasoning on the meat while Caroline shifts nervously on the barstool in front of me. She hasn't said much since we got inside. Every time I catch her looking at me, she ducks her head and blushes. It's cute as hell how shy she is. It's been thirty minutes of us playing this game while I prepare our dinner, and so far the only thing she's willingly asked me about is the ranch.

Safe topic, I reckon. Nothing that requires much input from her and not something that leaves the door open for me to press for more on her.

Not that I don't mind talking about how well the Davis ranch does breeding horses, especially if, by doing so, I make her more comfortable with me. But I'm not a patient man when it comes to something I want, and make no mistake, I want this woman.

"Tell me why you were runnin' back at the party," I ask her softly, continuing to handle the steaks. Hopefully by keeping my attention off her while I probe, I won't freak her out with the question that's been on the tip of my tongue since she collided with Dell and me.

She sucks in a harsh pull of air. The sound makes my hands freeze before I look up from my task to study her. She doesn't like attention, something I don't need to know her better to figure out, but with that pained sound, I want her to see the sincerity behind my asking so she can't doubt that I genuinely want to know what upset her. When she doesn't answer, I give her what I hope to hell is a reassuring expression of compassion before I turn and walk the four feet to the large farm-style sink to wash off my hands. I feel her stare follow me the whole time I clean my hands, dry them off, and walk back to the island. This time I stand next to the food I was prepping so I can press my hands down on the counter and wait. I keep my face calm, and I hope she senses she can trust me and open up.

"You aren't going to finish gettin' the food ready until I talk about what happened, are you?"

My lips twitch.

"I probably should just tell you all the ugly parts of me so you'll understand what a waste of time pursuing this would be. Save you from gettin' upset when you realize you're wastin' your time on someone broken," she mumbles.

"Darlin', you're not broken. You're still standin', which means you're just a little dinged up, maybe even a little bit bent, but you'd be hard-pressed to find someone who isn't."

She frowns a little, her eyes searching mine rapidly. "You really believe that?"

"Sure do. You aren't ever truly broken until you can no longer keep movin' forward and they're lowerin' you into the ground. It's what you call the ugly parts of someone that prove to others just how strong they really are."

I was expecting her to look away, but when I stop talking those dark eyes watch me with such intensity I almost feel like *I* should look away, but I hold her gaze and let her take whatever time she needs to weigh my words. To find the truth in them, even if she isn't ready to fully believe them. You don't change your beliefs at the drop of a hat, but all it takes is one moment of doubt that there could be another way for things to start coming into focus. I've seen bent. I've seen fractured. But if the people I know who've been both can find what they need to be happy and move on, so can this beautiful woman who has me wrapped in her spell.

"My mother was there," she finally says, as if that explains it.

I frown. "Who's your mama?"

"Misty Michaels."

Well, shit. I keep my face as clear as I can but inwardly cringe, curse, and kick shit—trying to keep the disgust I'm sure she was waiting to see from her. Well, sweetheart, that isn't gonna happen. There aren't many people's names I could hear and instantly want to curl my lips, but Misty Michaels is one of them. Regardless of what I think of Caroline's mama though, I damn sure won't condemn the woman in front of me just because the woman who birthed her has her nose so high in the air you'd think she could smell the angels passing gas. I could've taken one look at this girl, sweet and shy with just a little fire flickering inside of those brown eyes, and known she wasn't a thing like her mama.

"I take it y'all aren't close?"

She laughs humorlessly. "Well, let's see . . . If your mama had called you a whore after you had just finished beggin' her to help you, would you continue to be close to her after?"

"My mama ran off because she enjoyed fuckin' cowboys and gettin' high more than she liked her kids, so no, darlin', I wouldn't expect you to be close to someone who doesn't deserve that privilege."

Her eyes go wide and her back jolts straight. I might not recall the younger version of her, but her mama was in Pine Oak long before I was born, so there isn't a chance Caroline hasn't heard at least some rumblings about my mama. There aren't secrets in this town. That doesn't mean I should've laid it out there like that, but I stopped giving my mama the power to upset me a long damn time ago, so the habit is impossible to break now.

"I'm sorry. About your mama," she says in a meek whisper, relaxing her back and looking down at her hands as she worries them on top of the island. "I remember Quinn missin' y'all's mama a whole lot when we were growin' up."

I nod, even though she can't see it. "She's made her peace where our mama's concerned, Caroline. You'll get there too when you're ready."

"Did you? Make your peace, I mean."

What a loaded question that is. "I accepted her place in my life a long time ago, but I was also older than my siblings when she left, so I didn't feel the sadness Quinn did or the hope that she could somehow become the mama she shoulda been, like Maverick did. I held my anger close to my chest, but I stopped allowin' her to hold those strings a few years ago. She played no part in makin' me the man I am now, and I can move on with my life knowin' I'll never abandon the people I love like she did."

"You . . . are y'all . . . is she in your life?"

I shake my head. "Maverick is the only one who keeps a small connection to her, but that's a story for another day."

"You haven't forgiven her," she muses, finally giving me those eyes again.

"No, but the difference is I've forgotten her."

She moves her head in the smallest of nods, shocking me when I expected her to argue the importance of forgiveness like my siblings do. I have a feeling that whatever her mama did to her, she doesn't feel the need to forgive either.

"She doesn't deserve my forgiveness, Caroline, but I didn't spend every Sunday with a sore ass because of the hard pews in church without learning why it's somethin' we should offer. It just isn't somethin' I can give her, so instead I've given her my disregard. I can move on with my life without lettin' what she did continue to fuck me up. We don't pick our parents, but we get to decide what to do with the life they gave us."

"I wish I could push it all aside that easily and that she didn't affect me still."

"What did she do to you back at the baby shower?"

She glances across the room toward the huge bay window behind the kitchen table that overlooks the back pasture, where a few of my horses are enjoying the freedom inside the fenced-in property, amid nothing but God's green earth and blue skies. There's nothing more beautiful than the land I've always been proud to call mine. Well . . . almost nothing.

"She said my name. That's it. She called my name and I didn't even need to see her—just the sound of her voice brought back all the things I never wish to remember again. All those memories I worked so hard to forget."

"Wanna talk about any of that?" I ask, knowing when it's wise to not push for more until she's ready to tell me, but wanting her to know I'll listen when she is.

"Maybe on our second date," she mumbles, more to herself than me. My smile grows when, after realizing what she said, her mouth snaps shut, her cheeks turn pink, and her eyes widen. Goddamn, she's one hell of a breath of fresh air. There isn't a part of her that isn't transparent, and after dealing with the kind of women who wear masks to get you, I find it incredibly alluring to know what I'll get with her.

"Fuck, you're cute," I tease sincerely, hoping to put her out of her misery. "Second date it is, Caroline Michaels." My smile grows and I shake my head with a laugh. I can't remember the last time I felt this lighthearted, especially considering that never happens when my mama was just in the forefront of my thoughts.

"How are you single?" she blurts in a rush, not looking the least bit shy now that her tongue is loosening up. Or maybe she's getting more comfortable with me, God willing, and no longer feels unsure about me wanting her here.

"Honestly?" She nods. "Spent a while screwed up because of my mama, but after I got past that, I was burned pretty damn bad and I haven't found a woman worth lettin' myself get vulnerable for again."

"That sounds like a doozy of a story."

"You want my ugly now? Or should I tell you about it on date three?"

She giggles softly at my teasing, but the sound still carries, hitting my ears and causing a rush of pleasure to burst through my body, knowing I made it happen. It's hard to believe she has such a hold on me, but there's no denying the powerful chemistry between us. Who knows if it's our bodies remembering each other or something deeper, but we're damn sure gonna find out.

"Who says there'll even be a date three?" she smarts off with a tiny smirk.

"Said I was still single because I haven't found one in the past . . . not that I haven't found someone since."

She sputters and I feel my cheeks get tight as my smile grows. She straightens in her seat before speaking. "I think I'll take that story now, if you don't mind, and then maybe we can figure out if date two and three are goin' to happen."

"Fair enough, darlin'."

I walk to the fridge and grab a beer, looking over my shoulder and holding the bottle up to silently ask if she'd like one as well. Her dark brown hair moves around her face like a sleek curtain when she gives a tiny nod. I reach in the fridge to grab another one before walking back to my spot. I keep my eyes on hers as I twist the top off, placing the open bottle between us for her to take. When she reaches for it, I keep my hand in her way long enough for hers to graze mine, wanting to know if I feel the sparking burn of awareness I felt back in Mav and Leigh's barn. She licks her lips at the same time that sensation lights a fire across my fingertips, and I know I'm not the only one who feels it. She takes a small sip before placing her bottle softly in front of her and folding her hands on top of each other to wait. I make quick work of opening my own before taking a deep pull.

It probably isn't wise to tell the woman I'm hoping to get to know better about my past relationships. Especially when the one she's asking about is the very reason I've sworn never to get close to a woman again. I probably would've kept living like I have been until the day I died, too, had I not run into Caroline today.

"Five or, hell, maybe closer to six years ago, I was datin' someone seriously enough that we had that discussion most couples have at some point about their future. She wanted my ring on her finger and didn't have any problems lettin' me know it. You can imagine it wasn't pleasant when she heard how I felt about gettin' hitched. I explained that I didn't want the same things she did and likely never would." I take another large swallow of beer, and she keeps staring at me with open interest.

"My future was here on the ranch. I had responsibilities bigger than she understood and plans to make this place somethin' different than my father had. My pops was still around then, and I hadn't taken full control yet. He wasn't the hard man he had been my whole life at that point, seein' as his health was gettin' worse, but he wasn't willin' to give up his control over the ranch. He didn't agree with my vision for things and I knew better than to argue with Buford Davis. But I knew one day I'd be in charge and until then, I was goin' to focus on makin' sure this place was the best it could be. On top of workin' from sunup to sundown, I was also still runnin' the books for the auto shop. My plate was full and my plans didn't include addin' a wife while I was spread so thin, and, to be honest, it was gonna take someone a lot different from her to change my views on marriage. I made clear that I wasn't gonna give her a ring anytime soon—if at all."

"But you stayed with her even though you couldn't see that for y'all's future?"

I nod. "I did. I'm not exactly proud of the fact, but despite how I felt about marryin' her, I was still immature enough to enjoy what she did give me. Not too long after that talk, she brought it up again, only this time she mentioned babies. I think she knew after that she was tryin' for somethin' I wasn't ever gonna give her."

"Marriage or babies?" Caroline asks, tilting her head slightly.

"Both, I reckon. I wasn't ignorant to the negatives of both in my life at that point. I hadn't ever had any good examples of relationships enough to see marriage as somethin' worth havin'. The second I found out how much she wanted babies, though, I knew we were drivin' on two separate roads that would never meet."

"Because you don't like kids?" she asks with a frown.

This is the most unconventional first-date conversation, I'm sure, but nothing about how I met this woman has been ordinary, so I shouldn't be surprised. And, if I'm honest with myself, she should know about my history with Jess before someone in town fills her in, especially if we're gonna continue exploring this thing between us. Seeing that I plan on continuing, I want her to hear it from me. There's no doubt, with her mama bein' who she is, that she'll find out sooner rather than later, and I want her knowing my side of it before the bullshit rumors hit.

"Long story short, I found her sittin' on the floor in my room one day not long after that with a pile of condoms in her lap and my bedside drawer wide open. Who knows how long she'd been pokin' holes in those condoms, somethin' I probably never would've known about if I hadn't come home to change the pants I tore open on some barbed wire. Lady Luck did me a favor. We had words. She tried to lie her way through the impossible until she changed tactics and broke down. Tried to explain herself and her actions, but how the hell can you justify that kind of shit? She went on and on with that bullshit until she finally dropped the act and got pissed instead. One second she was cryin' all over me, the next she was rantin' and ravin' about how she had been flushin' her pills for months, but when that didn't work—because I wouldn't ever fuck her bare—she started the condom shit. I don't think she ever cared enough about me to respect what I had told her I wanted, or maybe she didn't give a shit about me at all and only wanted what bein' a Davis gave her. She craved my name and the money that came with it more than she wanted my baby, but figured gettin' one was her ticket to try hookin' both those things at once."

"Wow," Caroline breathes the second I stop speaking. "That's some crazy stuff, but I'm sorry that happened to you. No one should force you to do somethin' you don't want to do."

And she just continues to shock me. I expected her to push me on why I had felt so strongly against marriage and children—that's what everyone else does when they find out why Jess and I split—but she heard my story and accepted my words with nothing but support and understanding. If this isn't just more proof she's someone worth . . . *more*, I don't know what is. If we come to be something more than two people exploring each other, I'll have to give her that, but it feels damn good to have her accept and support my feelings with no further explanation needed.

"We all have ugly in our past, sweetness. You just have to realize it was really life teachin' you a lesson. When you find something that finally proves all that ugly was worth survivin', it doesn't look so bad when you see what kinda reward you get in the end."

"You don't even know me," she gasps with wide eyes, correctly reading between the lines. I'd go through that bullshit again just to have one more taste of her. I have a feeling that after she lets those walls down and really lets me see her, I'm not going to feel any different.

"And you don't know me. What I do know, though, is how I feel when I'm around you. I know what you feel like when you're comin' undone. How you curl into my side when you're exhausted, your body trustin' me without thought. I know you hate your feet bein' under the covers while you're sleepin'. And that I've never felt like I was comin' and goin' at the same damn time and not been pissed I couldn't control the chaos of it." I walk around the island and brush my fingertips across her neck until I'm cupping her head delicately and tipping her face up to look at me. "One night of being bad with you, Caroline, and I felt more with you in the darkness than I've ever felt with anyone else in the light. We might not know every little thing that makes the other tick, but you can't deny our chemistry alone is enough to make explorin' the rest worth it. I feel the pull to you like someone lassoed me around my chest and yanked."

"Just because we're compatible in bed doesn't mean we'll be the same out of it." Her argument is weak, since she's staring up at me with hooded eyes and flushed cheeks that I know have nothing to do with her being embarrassed or shy. She feels it, that same yank right in the middle of the chest that is impossible to ignore anymore.

"How about we just figure out the rest together?"

"And I'm supposed to just . . . what? Trust a man I don't know blindly?"

"You know me, Linney. Your body already trusts me," I murmur as she jerks her head from my hold when she realizes she's been leaning into me. "You feel that trust. You know my family and you know more about my past than even they do."

She snorts, the sound cute as hell. "If we're being honest, then yeah, I reckon I do know you. I know what you feel like between my legs and in my mouth. Other than what you told me tonight, I don't know much more about you than how amazin' it feels when you fuck me."

I cough on the swallow I had just taken. I don't know what was more of a shock, what she said, or that she used the word *fuck*. I knew that feisty princess was in there.

"Well, aren't you a little whiskey in a teacup, darlin'? The most delicate thing you've ever held in your hand, but on the inside, there's a fire just waitin' to burn right through you. Tell me, Linney, tell me just how amazin' does it feel when I *fuck* you?"

"I don't know where that came from," she squeaks, a mixture of mortification and disbelief in those big round eyes. As the silence settles around us, she makes another tiny peep through her parted lips before looking away from me.

With a smile, I reach out with a gentle touch and take her fidgeting hands out of her lap and guide her to stand in front of me. She continues to give me the top of her head until finally, looking up with no encouragement from me other than the soft circles my thumbs are making on the top of each hand, she looks me straight in the eyes.

"I enjoy the hell out of seein' your skin turnin' pink because you say somethin' cute, Linney, so no more of that backpedalin' because you think I'm not gonna like it when you speak your mind and sass me." I bend, her eyes widening as I move. "Just so there's no mistake, I find it sexy as fuck when you speak freely."

She bites her lip while contemplating me. "I'm not used to bein' able to say what's on my mind, Clayton," she whispers, the way she says my name—my whole name—hitting me in the gut before makin' it roll with flutters. Jesus. "I never been with a man who allowed that."

Once it stops feeling like the ground under me is shaking and I mull her words over enough to read between the lines, the pieces start to click together. And when I start arranging the things I do know, I don't like what I see.

A small accepting frown tugs at her mouth and she nods, seeing understanding starting to bloom in me. "I don't want to talk about what I'm sure is goin' through your mind right now, but I can admit that you aren't the only one who feels the pull, and if you really want to keep gettin' to know each other, I promise I'll tell you everything you're wonderin' about another day. Might not be on date two, five, or even ten, but if things start becomin' more between us, I promise I'll give you all of my ugly."

Tucking a piece of her dark hair behind her ear, I nod. "You keep givin' me the fire that burns inside that teacup, I'm gonna be fine waitin' for you to be ready to give me more, darlin'."

She slowly leans into my hand, still hovering at the side of her face, and this time the move isn't something done subconsciously. "I don't understand the connection I have to you at all, but I like how you make me feel."

"And how's that?"

She shrugs and smiles a small, sweet-as-fuck smile that makes me fight the urge to wrap her up in my arms and never let go. What the hell is this woman doing to me? I might not have the answers to explain it, but when she opens her mouth to answer me, I vow right then and there that I'm not going to let my past be a reason to cloud my future anymore.

"Safe. You make me feel safe, Clayton Davis."

10

CAROLINE

"All On Me" by Devin Dawson

- ★ -

"**W**hat's the latest on the insurance stuff, Caro?" Lucy asks around a mouthful of fries.

"Yeah, Carrie, they seem to be takin' their sweet-ass time," Luke joins in, reaching across the table to nab one of my two pickles while he talks. I slap his hand away when he comes back for the other.

"Caroline," I scold, saying my name slowly while looking between the two of them. "We've been best dang friends since I shared a dorm with you, Lucy, but still years later, you two refuse to stop callin' me childish nicknames. Caroline. C-A-R-O-L-I-N-E. One is mature, elegant even, while those nicknames make me sound like a badly pronounced Spanish dish or a five-year-old."

Luke shrugs, lifting his hand to wave the pickle I

hadn't noticed him successfully sneak while I was ranting away. I roll my eyes and reach for it, but he just laughs and pulls his hand farther away.

"That explains why you have a problem with callin' me a nickname a five-year-old would have, seein' as you're always actin' like one yourself, Luke."

Lucy giggles, and I narrow my eyes at her. "You—"

Her hand shoots up, interrupting me before I can go at her too. "Calm down, *Caroline.* You need to get out of that thundercloud you've been stuck in."

I grouse under my breath, but don't argue with what she said. Not because I don't want to—oddly, I do—but because she isn't wrong. Not only am I out-of-my-mind frustrated with the lack of progress with my insurance settlement, I'm a whole different kind of frustrated because of a certain tall, handsome, and dark cowboy of mine. And that's just what he is . . . *mine.* In the week since our awkward run-in at Quinn and Leighton's baby shower, he's made it impossible to doubt that.

I take another bite of my burger and think about Clayton. We haven't been able to find time to actually go on a date, but it hasn't stopped him from calling me whenever he has a chance, texting me when he doesn't, and making it known I'm not far from his thoughts. Every time his name pops up on my phone, I get a rush of happiness. I'm quickly becoming obsessed with those calls, but I miss the rush of being near him. I'm a giant mix of depressed happiness because I miss the man who is quickly ingraining himself in my life, but is too busy to do more than talk through a phone.

"She doesn't have anything to say to that, Luce, because she knows she's been bein' a little shit lately." Luke takes a bite of his burger before pointing it at me. "I figured she was just bein' pissy now that she found out how much work fixin' all my accounting was gonna be, but nope, she's flyin' through that mess like I didn't have two years' worth of shit in piles all around my office, so I've got no answers for you unless it's y'all's lady time."

"I'm right here, you know, you can stop talkin' about me like I'm not," I tell him with a frown.

Lucy thumps him over the head. "How many times do I have to tell you, Luke. Women don't all menstruate at the same time, so just because you can't miss when I'm on mine seein' as I live in the same house as you doesn't mean Caroline's cycle is at the same time."

He stops eating and looks deep in thought, like the mystery of a woman's uterus is some big secret he's just figuring out. His bad mood lightens up a little when he starts volleying his stare between Lucy and me before looking down in the general direction of our bellies and doing the same.

"So it's *not* your lady time then?" he finally questions, looking adorably confused now.

I glance around the tables closest to ours quickly, making sure no one heard him. "Would you shut your trap, Luke? I don't need all of Wire Creek knowin' about my time of the month. For your information, I'm in a bad mood because I got some bad news about the rebuild and I'm havin' a hard time shakin' myself from the funk that delay is puttin' me in." Not a lie. Also, not the whole truth.

"You're so on your lady time," he jests.

"I'm goin' to kill you slowly if you don't stop talkin' about me bein' on my period!" I hiss in a harsh whisper.

His face splits into a smug grin the same time someone clears their throat behind me. I glance over at Lucy in horror, hoping she'll help me disappear into thin air, but she's not paying me any attention. Just like her brother, she's now looking past me. Except, where Luke looks more curious than anything, Lucy is giving her best impression of that Snapchat filter that has the huge mouth—smiling so big and weird you'd swear she's in pain because of it.

"Linney."

My shoulders hunch and I close my eyes. I've never in my life liked my name shortened. However, the affection that I hear in the nickname Clayton gave me does nothing but fill me with happiness. It's something no one but him has ever called me—a short version of my middle name—and maybe because it's all his, I love it. But even with the rush of hearing him call out to me, his timing sucks. This can*not* be happening. Clayton's voice sounds behind me again, repeating the nickname he hasn't stopped calling me since last weekend. Even with the rush of pleasure I get from a nickname when it's coming from his lips, humiliation still chokes me at his embarrassing timing.

"Hey!" Luke exclaims, oblivious to the fact that I'm dying right in front of him, causing me to open my eyes to find him pointing at me. I see Clayton move to stand next to my side of the booth out of the corner of my eye, effectively blocking any chance I have at bolting. "How come *he* gets to call you something other than Caroline and we can't? You just met him and you've known me and Luce for close to a damn decade but won't let us."

I don't correct him. It wouldn't matter if I tried, because Luke wouldn't understand something I can hardly put my own thumb on. I haven't even told Lucy about the stupid brief crush I had on Clayton in high school, before I met my last boyfriend years ago. Having something special with Clayton Davis is beyond words. Never, not once, has anyone shortened my name and it not been like nails on a chalkboard, but the man who was my first crush many years ago lights something inside of me when I hear him rumble that nickname, and I'm in no hurry to lose this feeling. I'll be dammed if I'm going to explain that to Luke and Lucy, though. The secret is mine and Clayton's, no one else's.

Lucy elbows her brother and I decide now would be a good time to escape, but since I can't leave with the hulking cowboy blocking my way, I do the next best thing. I close my eyes and go with the good ol' theory that if I can't see them, they can't see me.

"What is she doing?" Luke questions.

I hear Lucy chuckle but keep my eyes closed. That is, until my body is moved by the solid weight of another person pushing his body into the booth next to me. I jolt, sucking in a shocked breath that does nothing but fill my lungs with a scent that is all man—outdoors, fresh air, and just a hint of soap. Before he pushes all the way into the booth, my eyes open and all I see is Clayton's smirking face, one side of his mouth tipped up and his eyes amused.

"Now what is she doing?" Luke stage-whispers to his sister.

"Reckon she's figuratively shittin' her britches, big brother," Lucy jokes, not even attempting to keep her voice low.

"Better than literally doin' it, but if that's the face she makes when she's takin' care of business, I think she needs to go get checked up at the doc. Somethin' ain't workin' right."

I whip my head around and gape at them. "Would you two *shut up*," I express venomously.

Luke holds up his hands in surrender. "What? All this could've been avoided if you'd just let the whole nickname thing go earlier. We wouldn't even be talkin' about your shit right now. It was you who started down this path, little one, don't get mad that I'm just tellin' you the truth."

"This did *not* start because of me. It started because

of your sick enjoyment of embarrassing me because, for whatever reason, you find the fact that I'm shy to be some sort of freak-show act for your entertainment purposes, Lucas Hazel."

"I do not," he defends instantly.

"Yeah, Luke, you really do," Lucy confirms with a nod.

"Hey!"

She shrugs. "Not maliciously, I know you're just tryin' to get her to come out of her shell. Caroline knows that too, but you take it too far sometimes."

"I'm sorry, Caroline," Luke mutters, and I can see written all over his face that he really does feel bad.

"It's okay, Luke." I lift my hand with the intention of grabbing his across the table, but I jump when it's hijacked by long tanned fingers that grab me with soft care. Then, with my mouth hanging open, I watch my wayward hand being lowered into Clayton's lap as he holds it gently with his. I blink at my captive hand, flex my fingers, and wonder how I actually forgot he had sat down. My skin tingles where he's touching it and I find my fingers curling tighter, loving the contrast of his suntanned hand against my pale one.

"Linney," he utters in his deliciously deep voice, bringing my gaze from our joined hands to his bright green eyes. "Thought you were havin' dinner at the ranch with me tonight?"

"What are you doin' over in Wire Creek?"

"Had to grab somethin' from the feed store that ours

in Pine Oak was out of. Saw you through the window," he answers, pointing out the window to the feed store across the street.

"Oh," I lamely breathe.

"So, are we not havin' dinner at the ranch tonight?"

"We are," I confirm with a frown.

He studies me and I take a moment to appreciate how handsome he looks with his thick, dark-as-night hair sticking in a million directions. I look around, half expecting the ever-present cowboy hat to jump out and bite me. "Where's your hat?"

"Granger, one of our newer horses, got spooked today," he answers with a shrug, as if the fact that a huge animal getting spooked isn't something that requires any more explanation. But seeing as I know nothing about horses, my imagination is running wild, something Clayton doesn't miss. He gives my hand a squeeze and leans a little closer. "Sweetness, you worried about me?"

I shove him with my shoulder lightly. "You'd be worried too if you were picturin' some huge beast tryin' to stomp you to death before eatin' what's left of you, Clayton Davis."

He tosses his head back and laughs, deep and loud, straight from the gut. His hilarity booms in my ears, the rich sound making me smile. I don't even care that everyone is looking in our direction, not when I get to see this guarded man be so carefree. He's one of those people who laugh with their whole torso, too. His shoulders jump, the corded muscles in his neck flex, and his whole body moves. I drink the sight of it in until he finally stops, untangling our fingers to wipe his eyes. I have a few seconds of disappointment that he let go before he's lifting his arm up and over my body to hook it around me. His fingers grasp my shoulder, and a moment later he pulls me into his side.

And I willingly scoot my hips to get myself as close as I can without urging.

"You're one helluva breath of fresh air, darlin'." His lips press lightly against my temple and the arm around me flexes. "I knocked my hat off because I was in the middle of dismountin' him at the same time he was tryin' to two-step, and my hat landed in a giant pile of manure. Didn't feel like goin' up to the house to grab another one when I had other places I needed to be in order to finish up my day."

"Oh." Well, now I feel a little ridiculous. "Do you need to go, then?"

His brows pull in as he frowns in confusion. "Go where?"

"You said you had other places you needed to be."

His eyes dance—I swear it looks like his dark green orbs have come to life and are swirling with lighter flecks of gold that I've never noticed before. If he keeps looking at me like that, I'm going to have a hard time ever giving this man up.

"No, darlin', I'm already there."

"Y'all together now?" Luke butts in, breaking the hold that Clayton's words have on me.

"Yes," my dark cowboy tells him, not looking away from me.

"We're explorin' things," I correct, looking over at Lucy as I see the expression on his face change slightly. She appears to be about to burst with excitement. When I look at Luke, his face is blank while he assesses Clayton. "What, Luke?" I probe, not sure I'm going to like what's on his mind.

This is why I hadn't told him about . . . whatever's between Clayton and me. I'm not sure what title to put on it, to be honest, and since Luke's been in my life for a long time I knew he'd expect something more than what I could articulate. He saw me at my worst, saw how hard I've worked to move on. He and Lucy are the only two people in the whole world who understand how big a deal it is that I'm taking this step with Clayton. But they're also the two people whose opinions matter most to me, and I'm not sure I could handle it if they didn't approve. Which is probably why, in the week since he first cooked me dinner at his house, I haven't told either of them that I agreed to see what's between the two of us. I couldn't even explain my feelings toward the man to myself, let alone verbalize them to anyone else.

I squirm under Luke's scrutiny as his stare bounces between us, the silence heavy except for the sound of my heartbeat thundering in my ears. What if he sees something in Clayton that I don't—or can't—something that could mean my judgment is still warped and I need to give Clayton up. Could I let go of a man who is quickly burrowing under my skin? Could I really just walk away if one or both of my closest friends don't like him?

No, I don't think I could.

Actually . . . I *know* I couldn't.

After what feels like hours, Luke shrugs, smirks, and then goes back to eating what can only be a cold burger now.

"What did *that* thing you just did with your face mean?" I snap, my period-driven hormones and my lack of patience colliding in a burst of sass.

"What're you talkin' about?"

I look at Lucy. "Why does he always do that? Make you think the worst, but not speak a dadgum word before some stupid *I know everything* smirk comes across his face. Then, still not sayin' a thing, continue on like nothing happened and you start questionin' your sanity?"

Her shoulder lifts, indicating she's just as clueless, and her lips twitch.

"It's the most annoying thing in the history of . . . *ever*, Lucas. I can tell you want to say somethin', so why don't ya stop actin' like I can't handle whatever it is and just spit it out, bucko!"

Clayton's chest moves in silent laughter that I ignore in favor of glaring at the man across from me. Lucy chokes on a loud cackle before covering her mouth with her hand. Luke, though, holds my very annoyed scowl.

"You sure you wanna hear it, Carrie?"

"Caroline, you big dummy."

He rolls his eyes and points to Clayton. "You let him call you Linney." He leans back and crosses his arms as if that statement holds all the answers.

I shrug, making the arm around my shoulders tighten the smallest bit. "So?"

I watch Luke's emotions change like someone flipped a switch inside him. One second he's serious as a heart attack, and the next he's smiling a toothy grin, his eyes crinkling at the corners. The change is so quick, had you not been watching him closely, you would've missed it.

"I think that right there about says it all for me, but since your lady time always makes you feel the need to pick fights with me, I'll clarify so you can stop lookin' for reasons to jump down my throat. You, sweet Caroline, hate when anyone calls you some shortened variation of your name. I know it's because your mama always had some different name for you growing up and it makes your remember that shit. When others do it, your nose always scrunches up, your eyes get all slitty until they almost look fuckin' closed, and your nostrils start floppin' around like they're gonna take flight and leave your face. You have never, not in all the years that I've known you, been able to hear someone shorten your name without losin' your mind. Which is why we always keep doin' it—

not just because we want to erase the negative things your mama did, but because it's funny as hell to watch sweet, shy, little Caroline Michaels get pissed off. But when Davis does it, you look like a stampede of kittens just ran up to your feet and promised you a life of fluffy cuddles."

"His name is Clayton. Not Davis," I stupidly say, clearly still looking for a fight.

"Name's still Davis, too."

"Don't think I've forgotten you made me think that was his first name, Luke."

He laughs. "Change the subject, fine. Means you know I'm right. And Caroline, it's not my fault you were callin' out his last name all because you didn't bother to properly introduce yourselves the night you met."

My face heats, and I know he's going to win if I keep trying to argue with him. What's the point? He isn't wrong. Not even a little. And all four people sitting in this booth know it.

I turn my head and look at the man holding me close, his face so near mine that his soft breath dances across my cheeks. My gaze falls to his mouth when he smiles and, having decided it's time for me to be brave enough to at least confirm what Luke just said, I open my mouth. "I like it when you call me Linney, Clayton. Luke, as frustrating as he is, isn't wrong, and you should know it means somethin' to me and that I'd like it if you didn't stop."

The left side of his mouth twitches twice before his full smile appears. "All right. And just so you know, I like the fuck out of you callin' me Clayton. No one calls me by my full name, but even if they did, I wouldn't like it half as much as I do when you're sayin' it in that sweet whisper. That's all yours, Linney."

He's halfway through his mini speech when my focus moves from his full lips to those green eyes that even a nun could get lost in. I blame those stupid, beautiful eyes for what I do next, because it's so out of character for me, it's the only way I can explain it. My back straightens, my head moves, and I press my lips to his in a soft, quick, but no less amazing kiss. He sucks in a sharp breath when my mouth connects to his, the hand resting on my shoulder flexes, and when I pull away, the soft look of happiness in those green depths shows me that I can trust the guy who chipped away a big piece of the armor that had been guarding my heart.

"Now that all that's out of the way, want to tell me why you're eatin' here when we made plans last night?" he asks softly, voice low and forehead resting against mine a second longer before lifting away, keeping his face close.

"Because I was hungry?"

"Darlin', it's four in the afternoon. Are you tellin' me you're still gonna be hungry for dinner after eatin' one of Big Tom's famous burgers?"

"Have *you* had a Big Tom burger?"

He nods, smiling a tiny smirk.

"Then I think you know why I'm eatin' one at four in

the afternoon. When someone says they're goin' to have one of the best burgers in Texas, you don't pass that up."

His eyes crinkle at the corners. "Are you still goin' to want dinner when I pick you up, or should we do somethin' else?"

At the mention of him picking me up, something real close to embarrassment starts to burn up my throat, which makes no dang sense. I certainly didn't set my store ablaze and in turn, make myself homeless—but that's just what I am, homeless. I shouldn't be ashamed of it, but even though I didn't intentionally keep it from him, I still feel badly about it.

"How about we just leave from here?" I offer lamely. "Save you the trouble of havin' to drive an hour from here to Law Bone, when we're both in Wire Creek." Of course, in my quest to save him some gas, I don't realize my mistake until it's too late.

"Uh-oh," Lucy whispers loudly with a giggle, clearly coming to the same conclusion.

"Why would I be drivin' out to Law Bone tonight to pick you up if you aren't helpin' out at Hazel's when you live here, darlin'?"

I hear Luke laugh, but I don't look away from Clayton. "I was goin' to tell you," I rush out, proud that I don't feel my cheeks getting red.

He lifts his head more and looks at me with one brow up, waiting for me to continue.

"You see, there was a tiny problem with my place . . ." I

bite my lip and wince. "Okay, so maybe by tiny I mean real big, but that was before well, you, and I really didn't think to mention it last weekend when we were at your house after the shower and, to be honest, it kinda slipped my mind with the whole head-on-collision horse-crash thing and runnin' into my mama and well, *you* . . ." I stop talking, thankful that my mouth finally just decided to snap shut when my brain wouldn't stop the flow of verbal diarrhea.

"She had a fire at her bookstore. She doesn't normally work at Hazel's—she only does that now because her place is gone. Tried to get her ass at Luce's and my place, but she's a stubborn one, our Carrie," Luke mumbles around a slice of pie I didn't even notice had arrived.

"Caroline," both Clayton and I tell him at the same time, breaking our staring contest in the process.

"Jesus Christ, not you too!" Luke grunts in annoyance.

I look back to Clayton just in time to see a mean-as-heck expression on his face, aimed at one of my best friends for something as simple as using a nickname that he now knows I don't like. I have no idea why that's so hot, but it makes my belly flutter in the most insane way.

"I really was goin' to tell you—it just didn't seem like the right time," I defend weakly.

Clayton looks down at the table and shakes his head, but I know he isn't *that* mad, because there's a slight tip to the side of his mouth. He mumbles something, but it's so low I can't hear him.

"What?"

He slants his head my way. "I said, you're lucky I find just about everything you do cute as fuck, Linney, because right now I want to pull you over my knee and tan your goddamn hide for thinkin' there wasn't a 'right time' just once during this whole week to fill me in. Talked to you every day and a few nights until you fell asleep. Tons of times in there you could've mentioned that you owned a bookstore, which you just so happened to live above; that it burned down; and that you don't really work at a place that makes me uneasy just thinkin' about you bein' in."

"Aww!" Lucy gushes. "Did you hear that Luke?"

"I'm sorry," I offer lamely, ignoring Luke's grumbles about me being safe at his bar.

Clayton nods and reaches out to pulls me back into his side before placing another kiss to my temple. That move would make my knees weak if I was standing.

"We can talk about it later, darlin'."

Lucy pretty much holds a one-woman conversation for the rest of our time at the diner. Luke leaves right after he finishes his pie when a pretty redhead walks in. He throws some cash on the table without saying a word and takes off toward the back of the diner in hot pursuit.

I spend my time listening to Lucy talk to Clayton, his deep voice rumbling against me when he answers, but I don't say much, not when all I can think about is what will happen later when Clayton and I talk.

I should've told him, he's right. I make light of it because if I don't, I'll break down in tears thinking that someone might've intentionally set that fire, and I don't want to ruin this evening.

Tonight is something I've been looking forward to. Not just because it'll be another milestone I reach. Ever since John, I haven't dated. Clayton's the first man I've wanted anything more from. Not only that, but it'll be my first date with someone who isn't a teenage boy. Well, my first planned date after the unexpected first one. And now, like it or not, I get to start it by telling him I'm homeless, technically jobless, and one hot mess.

Clayton's body shifts, his hard thigh brushing against my leg, pushing the skirt of my knee-length dress up my thigh a little. I shove it down quickly and smooth it out but freeze when I see his free hand reach down to adjust his crotch. Glancing up, I see his eyes trained on my legs, and a rush of excitement bursts through my body. I might not completely understand how someone like Clayton Davis could be into plain Caroline Michaels, but seeing him affected by something as simple as the six inches of skin above my knee does something to me. I feel empowered by his reaction. Maybe this is what normal people do when they're exploring things—this push and pull of powerful lust is exchanged between them—but I have never in my life experienced it.

Wanting to feel that rush again, I wiggle my bottom and curl my hands into the fabric of my dress, pulling it up a little. He stops talking the second I tug the hem higher; then he clears his throat and continues. I look back at his lap, disappointed that he didn't touch himself again, but no less determined. My hand doesn't even shake when I release my skirt and place it on his thigh. As my fingers inch closer to the bulge in his jeans, I don't feel a bit of shyness. The sense of freedom its absence inspires is overwhelming and I feel a rush of lust. I keep watching my hand as it creeps closer to the hardness pushing his denim up and almost come out of my skin when his hand drops on top of mine and yanks it to that very spot, his hips flexing as he grinds against my palm.

Oh, *wow*.

I press my thighs together and close my eyes. Memories of him moving just like that inside of me become overwhelming.

"What are you doin'?" Lucy questions, the sound of her voice shocking me like a bucket of cold water over my head.

I rip my hand from his hold, missing the hard heat against my palm instantly, and fiddle with my skirt before looking up at her. I'm not embarrassed or ashamed when she winks at me. No, I feel like I'm on top of the world— even if my best friend did just witness me rubbing my kinda-boyfriend's crotch shamelessly.

"You ready?" I ask Clayton, smiling at Lucy while I do so she knows I'm not ignoring the question she doesn't really need an answer to.

"Yeah, Linney. I'm more than ready."

It's been so long since I haven't been afraid that I

promise myself right there as we shuffle out of the booth with greasy food scenting the air that I'm going to give this little adventure everything I have and trust whatever is in store for us. Good or bad.

Because I have a feeling there isn't anything better in the world than being cared for by this man next to me.

11

CAROLINE

"Think A Little Less" by Michael Ray

"**Y**ou'll text me later?" Lucy asks while hugging me good-bye outside the diner.

"Maybe tomorrow mornin', Luce." She shuffles her feet a little and makes a low noise of excitement in my ear. When she pulls away, she looks ready to burst with excitement, making me laugh softly. "Because it will be late, Lucy Hazel, not because I'll still be with Clayton." I whisper, hoping the man waiting just behind me doesn't hear.

Which of course he does, because that's how lucky I am.

"Try tomorrow afternoon, Lucy. And it will definitely be because she's still with me," he corrects, and I jerk around to gawk at him.

"Clayton!" I gasp.

"Linney, we both know you aren't goin' anywhere but to my bed tonight."

"But," I start, but close my mouth when I realize I really don't have an argument to offer. Turning back to Lucy, I shrug. "So, I'll talk to you at some unknown hour tomorrow, okay?"

She snorts and gives me a blinding smile before taking off to her car with a wave. I watch her get in and pull away before I turn to the man at my back. He's leaning against his truck with confidence. When I take a step toward him, he straightens but doesn't move aside from that, letting me set the pace. Still riding the high from inside the diner, I step toward him and wrap my arms around his middle and press my cheek to his chest, hugging him tight and smiling so big it hurts my face. His strong arms fold around me and his chin rests against the top of my head.

I'm just about to tell him how much I like feeling him against me, but when I start, my eyes light on the last person I ever thought I'd see again staring at us across the street, and the words die on my lips. I know Clayton notices the change in me because I jerk in his hold, but shockingly, the fear over seeing my old boyfriend doesn't last but a second. Not with Clayton holding me safe.

"You all right, darlin'?" he rumbles against my cheek, not letting me go.

I clear my throat, pull my eyes from the man across the street, and look up at Clayton with a smile. "I will be."

I can tell he wants to press, but for whatever reason he keeps his silence before kissing my forehead. He then opens the truck door for me and I climb in. I watch as he shuts the door and quickly scans the area around us. I don't look, not wanting to know if I really saw a blast from my past, but judging by the harsh lines that appear on Clayton's face, I don't think John was only a figment of my imagination.

The second he climbs into the driver's seat and jerks the truck into reverse, I know he saw John. The drive from the diner to Davis ranch isn't a terribly long one, but with the tension between us getting thicker, it feels like it's cross-country. The ride only makes me more uneasy, aware that I need to tell him about my past sooner than I wanted. I need to trust what's growing between us—that the strong connection we've felt from day one is worth taking a chance on. I need to start opening up.

"That was my ex," I whisper to the window, watching the pastures full of cattle pass by.

He lets out a rush of air, and I feel the energy around us get even thicker with tension.

"I was with him for a long time, Clayton." I speak slowly. "It . . . it wasn't good."

"When?"

I finally look over at him, confused by his one-word question. "When what?"

"When did he become your ex?"

"A few years ago, give or take some." I know exactly how long it's been. How long I've been afraid because of what he did to me in using my fear against me to make my normal, timid nature so much worse. Call me a coward, but I'm not going to go into the depressingly long length of time that it's been since I've been able to get to this place—to move on—if I don't have to.

His hands tighten on the wheel and a muscle jumps in his jaw, but he doesn't talk, and I have a feeling there's something more here. Something that I'm missing.

"John," I start, but stop immediately when Clayton starts cursing a violent streak, his nostrils puffing out like those of an enraged bull. Not wanting to be the reason he's mad, I slouch in my seat, unsure if I should continue. His hand leaves the wheel and reaches for mine, taking it in a firm grip and not letting go.

"Finish what you want to tell me, Linney. It's not you I'm pissed at."

"You know him well?"

A strangled laugh comes out of his mouth. "Yeah. I know John fuckin' Lewis pretty damn well."

"I don't have a good past where he's concerned. Are you sure you want to hear this?"

He pulls into the ranch's driveway, not answering me until we've parked close to the front of his beautiful home. He cuts the engine, gets out, and walks around the truck's hood to open my door. He unbuckles my seat belt and turns me with a gentle grip on my knees before opening my legs and stepping between them, dragging his palms up my thighs to rest under my skirt. I have to push the fog his touch puts in my mind away to focus, because only then does he speak.

"I know him, know him well enough to have a pretty good idea of what you're gonna tell me. I don't like it, but that isn't for you to worry about, darlin'. I don't want you ever feelin' like you need to keep somethin' from me because I won't like hearin' it. He's the ugly you talked about?"

I nod, my chin wobbling and drawing his attention immediately. His fingers tense, but he keeps going.

"I know you didn't want to talk about this yet. You promised to give it to me when we got serious, but darlin', I don't need more dates to tell you I'm already there. I'm not goin' anywhere because of the shit you went through in your life. No matter what you have to say to me, we're still gonna be explorin' us. I don't want to push you when you aren't ready, but Linney, there isn't a thing I wouldn't do to keep you in my life."

God, this man. How is it possible that we've only just started when I feel like my soul was made for his? I shift to get closer and drop my forehead to his chest, feeling his strong heartbeat. His thumbs rub my thighs, soothing and reassuring me.

Trust him.

The thought rushes through my mind and I suck in a breath, lift my head, and give him my ugly.

"I left Pine Oak when I was eighteen. I spent four months before that with John wonderin' what he saw in me, but not ready to question it and lose him. Don't get me wrong, it wasn't perfect, but he made me feel important and gave me hope that I could have something different from the life I was facing if I stuck around under my mama's control. So when he promised to get me out of my mama's house and a whole bunch of other things that he just *knew* he could give me once we got to Austin, I believed him. I believed all of him. I know now that I naively gave him my blind trust because I felt like he was the only way out." I inhale and hold the breath deep in my belly for a pause before blowing it out slowly. "It wasn't all bad. I met Lucy and Luke because of it. I also lost a lot of me in the process though. A lot of me that I didn't find again for almost six years. He drank excessively, yelled more often than not, and, toward the end, used his fists."

Clayton's quiet, but I can see my words are costing him. I give him a look, asking silently if he wants me to keep going. At his nod, I do.

"He got mad about some beer one night and sent me out to get it. Long story short, I got into a pretty bad wreck on the way back. A drunk driver slammed into me and I spent a few months recovering. But it was because of that accident that I was finally able to get away from him. I spent a week in the hospital before Lucy and Luke picked me up. I knew I had my chance and we had it all planned out. They were taking me to their place to finish my recovery and Luke got all my stuff back. It wasn't until a few weeks after moving in with them that I realized just how good my chances of making a clean break were. The man who hit me worked for some big auto chain and his company wanted to settle out of court. The settlement money was enough for me to come back here and open The Sequel, and I lived in the apartment above it for five years, until the fire."

"You haven't dated since?"

"No. I haven't felt safe until . . . you. I don't think you'd hurt me, if that's what you're thinkin'. Not like him."

"Fuck me," he breathes, his forehead dropping to mine. "I don't deserve someone as sweet as you, Linney. I really don't. But that's not gonna stop me from keepin' you. Words are weak, darlin', it's actions that mean somethin' when it comes to a man's character. I promise I won't ever lay a hand on you. My temper can burn bright, sweetness, but *never* do you need to fear me causin' you harm like that. We might fight, talk to each other with heat, but I'll never hurt you. Fuck, Caroline," he says, his hands framing my face with such gentle reverence I gasp. "How anyone could harm a hair on your head, I'll never understand."

"I know you wouldn't hurt me. I saw that in you from day one. Why did you look so mad back at the diner?"

He looks away, his hands going back to my legs but this time on the outside of my skirt.

"Clayton?" I probe when he doesn't answer.

"I'm gonna ask that you trust me now, sweetness. Trust that it's nothin' you need to be concernin' yourself with. Me wantin' to protect you will always be limitless in its reach."

"You're askin' me to give you somethin' I've only given to two people."

"I'll never make you regret trustin' me."

I search his eyes but see nothing except sincerity. He has no idea how much power he's asking me to give him. But my dark cowboy won't twist my trust into something ugly. He's a good man—always kind to others, humble in his pride, fierce with control, and worthy of respect. My heart feels the safety within his promise. My mind recognizes our connection without doubts.

It's time to drop the rest of the weights that hold me captive. My breathing is rapid, but I feel sure about my decision. I lift my hands and press them against his chest. He closes his eyes on an exhale when I drag them up to wrap around his neck. When those emerald orbs finally lock back on me, I press against him and bring him close enough for me to press my lips against his.

His fingers dig into my flesh the second my mouth opens, and I lick the seam of his lips, a groan coming from deep inside of him rumbling around us. When our tongues slide against each other, he pushes his hands under my skirt again and goes straight to my hips. With one strong pull, he's got his hips flush with mine, and the thickness of him presses tightly against my sex. I whine, wiggle, and pray that he gives me some friction. Our kiss changes when he starts to smile against my mouth. If anyone were to see us, toothy grins pressed together, I can only imagine how insane we'd look.

For the first time in my life, I don't care what anyone else thinks—I'm just happy this man makes me feel safe, shows me how to be bad, and breathes new life back into me with every small step of us exploring. If this is how strong we are after such a short time, I can hardly wait to see what comes next.

12

CLAYTON

"More Girls Like You" by Kip Moore

— ★ —

"**Y**ou look good. Haven't seen you without that ugly-ass serious mask on in a long time."

I look away from Midnight, one of the best stallions on my ranch, and raise my brow at my brother. I just finished riding the property, letting Midnight go all out and take complete control of our ride. I forgot how fast the old horse could go when he wanted to show off.

"What the hell are you talkin' about?" I ask Mav after giving my horse one last brush.

"You've got the girls goin' nuts. I swear to Christ, you're gonna put one of them in labor the way they're actin' like you datin' is the most excitin' thing goin' on in their lives. They keep freakin' out that you're gonna get spooked and ruin it."

"You're fuckin' kiddin' me right now with that shit?"

He grunts and shakes his head. "Just repeatin' what they keep yammerin' about. Figured you should know that your love life is gonna make you an uncle sooner than you reckoned."

I flip him off before guiding Midnight back into his stall. I do a quick check of the feed to make sure everyone did their work today. Not that I need to worry about how things are run here. I've been stepping back more, and it's been refreshing. I trust my staff here implicitly, and by doing so, I free up more time to be with Caroline.

I never thought there'd be anything in this world that would have me wanting to spend less time on the ranch, but three weeks with her and I'm finding my happiness is directly connected to her and no longer to the ranch. She brings out a protective side to me that has only ever been shown to my siblings and the ranch. We spend as much time together as our complicated schedules allow, but it's never enough. For the first time in my life, I wish I had some sort of normal career where I could take her on the kind of dates she deserves instead of us "dating" here at the ranch for dinners, movies, and just generally spending as much time together as possible. I've been getting her in my bed most nights, something I did the second I found out she was staying at the fucking motel in Law Bone. In the past few weeks, she's only spent a handful of nights there, and each of those nights I spent unable to sleep, worrying about her. Between my responsibilities here on the ranch and her helping out at Hazel's, we get little time even for our unconventional, ranch-bound dates.

"Heard you ran into Jess the other day," he says, twisting his Stetson between his hands.

"Don't remind me."

"Also heard she's been running her mouth 'bout y'all bein' back together."

I stop in my tracks and look over at Maverick. He places his hat on his head and walks over to stand next to me.

"You're gonna want to get on top of that shit. That woman was evil when you were fuckin' her, but you and I both know she's not ready to believe it's over forever, regardless of how much time has passed."

We walk in silence toward the house, his words weighing heavy in my gut.

"Does Caroline know about Jess?" he finally asks.

"Yeah. Told her that night of the baby shower when she had dinner here the first time."

He mulls over my words while straddling his ride home, not starting it up yet. "The girls know about Jess tryin' to get back with you. They know she's cornered you once and tried a few more times unsuccessfully. They're worried about you dealin' with that as a brother, but they're worried about what could happen to Caroline if

Jess manages to tear y'all apart. You've got my wife and our sister actin' like worried hens and it's startin' to piss me off."

I clamp my teeth together as my breathing speeds up.

"Don't like hearin' that, do you?" He turns the key on the four-wheeler, shattering the silence. "You should probably let her know that your ex is sniffin' around again before she thinks you're keepin' it from her for some reason other than protectin' her feelin's. There won't be anything good that comes from her findin' that out from someone else." With that, he hauls his ass back to his own house.

I never regretted selling him back Leighton's family land when they got together. I didn't need it, the Davis ranch being as huge as it is. But it's times like these, when he takes advantage of being so fucking close by coming by to stick his nose into my life, that I question the sanity of my choice. Even the five hundred acres of our combined land don't provide enough distance when he gets a hankering to start handing out advice.

It's been a long-as-fuck week for Caroline now that the rebuild is under way on The Sequel, and the last thing I want is to bring this shit up tonight, but I know Maverick's right. I'm not blind to why Jess started this bullshit again. She's always made it clear she wants to get back together, and it's my fault for not being more definite in my refusals. Now that she knows I'm seeing someone, it's worse than ever, and seeing how Caroline's mama—Jess's boss at the salon—was with her the last time she tried coming on to me, it won't be long until it gets back to my girl. And the *last* thing I want is her thinking that I was keeping that from her.

Fuck.

I pull my phone out of my back pocket and pull up the last text she sent me. She stayed at the motel last night, not wanting to drive in the storm we had roll through after leaving Hazel's. I didn't sleep for shit and my mood has been terrible, but when her text pinged through early this morning, I almost came in my pants. All day I've been dealin' with the promise built off that message, and I finished my work twice as fast as normal.

Her small, perfect tits fill the screen of my phone and I groan when my cock throbs. We've been playing this game for a week now, teasing each other every chance we get, but never going further than heated kisses and feeling each other up like two horny teenagers. I've been craving her body since I last took it close to three months ago, and that need has only gotten worse since we've gotten together. When she sent me her first sexy text, I almost died, but when she sent me the first naked picture of her body, I was pretty sure I actually had. There is something hot as fuck seeing my shy and timid Linney opening up to me like this—giving me something that I know she's never given any other man.

And now it's likely going to be even longer before we get down to business again. I don't see her wanting to ride my cock after I tell her my ex-girlfriend grabbed my crotch in the middle of town yesterday.

Regretfully, I close out the picture of Caroline's naked chest and stomp through my house to shower. Thoughts of my good girl being bad make my jeans get painfully tight around my erection.

Ten minutes later, I've just started palming my cock when I feel it.

That zap of energy that sparks from top to toe when Caroline is near.

We could be back in that pitch-black motel room and I would know exactly where she is.

I keep stroking myself, waiting to see what my good girl is up to.

When I hear the curtain move, the rungs gliding almost silently against the pole, I smile to myself and release my cock, letting my hand join the other one pressed against the tile, letting the hot water roll down my neck and body. My ears strain to listen in an effort to try and figure out her next move.

But it never comes.

I'm half convinced I was imagining her, but I can still feel the hum of awareness on my skin, so I wait. Then, from my position leaning forward against the tile, I see the very tips of her purple-painted toes in the space between my braced feet.

Jesus fuck.

She's been less and less shy with me over the past few weeks, but never this forward. We have dinner together as often as we can, always ending up on the couch, but it's been me who'd make the first move to pull her into my lap and kiss her until we were both wound the hell up. I've been waiting for her to let me know she's ready for more, something I told her a week after finding out about her punk of an ex. I wanted her to make sure she was ready, because the next time I get my cock in her tight pussy, I won't ever let her go. "I know you're there, darlin'," I admit, and my smile grows when she screams and those tiny feet jump back.

"Dang it, Clayton!" she gasps breathlessly.

I push off the side of the shower and turn, expecting to find her covering as much of her body as she can, but when I finally see her I almost swallow my tongue. My cock jerks, and my smile drops with my jaw.

There she stands, every inch on display. I don't know where to look first. Her hands are on her hips, long tanned legs are spread apart, and her fiery temper is on display, all while her pussy is bare and begging for my tongue. I can't eat apple pie anymore because of that sweet pussy. Licking my lips, I move my gaze up, over her flat stomach and right to her tits—perfect little handfuls of flesh that heave with her heavy breaths, her rosy nipples hard from my attention. By the time I force my eyes off of her chest, any annoyance she felt at getting caught sneaking up on me is gone.

My girl wants to be bad and she isn't afraid to show me.

Her lightly tanned skin is flushed red with arousal, her eyelids growing heavy as the same need I feel takes her over.

"You tryin' to sneak up on me, Linney?"

She bites her lip and nods.

"Are you sure you want to take this step? I told you, once you give me this gift again, I'm not gonna give it back. We're gonna stop explorin' and start plannin' a future."

"I know," she whispers, stepping a little closer.

"Baby." I drawl the word out lazily, taking my own step forward when her eyes close at my endearment. "Caroline, I mean what I say. We've been goin' slow for almost a month, darlin'. You ready to admit what's happenin' here?"

Her eyes open and there isn't a lick of doubt in those beauties. "We were gonna happen the second you tried to kill me with your horse."

I grab her as her giggles echo around us and pull her naked body into my arms. "Sweetness, we were gonna happen the second you sat your ass down on a barstool and told me you were a good girl."

"Hey! I *am* a good girl!"

Her tiny hands hit my shoulders and I close mine

around her hips and lift her effortlessly off her feet. Her legs wrap around my back and I feel her lock her feet above my ass. My cock, having no trouble letting her know he wants to say hello, settles in the middle of her sex. Her back hits the shower wall and I flex my hips, dragging my thickness through the hug of her wet lips—their dampness having nothing to do with the shower.

"Yeah," I breathe, needing to be inside her more than I need air. "I know you are, darlin'."

She leans forward and starts peppering kisses all over my chest and up my neck. My hips rock steadily as my cock slowly glides through her wetness. I need to be inside of her, but not until I hear what I need to hear.

"Tell me, Caroline."

Her kisses stop, mouth on my jaw. When she looks up at me, I don't miss the meaning in her eyes. It tells me she's just as lost in me as I am in her. The shyness that I normally see is nowhere to be found.

"I'm ready to be yours," she says with confidence and hunger. "Please, Clayton, make me yours."

All rational thought vanishes as I take her mouth in a bruising kiss. I press her against the tile with my hips so that my hands are free to roam that gorgeous body. Her legs tighten and her mouth gets greedy. When I palm her tits, the small weight of them perfect in my large hands, she moans into my mouth and starts to rut against my length. I can feel the wetness of her arousal coating my cock, and I start moving with her until we're frantic for more.

It isn't until I lift back and enter her with one long thrust that I realize why she feels so fucking good.

"Condom," I breathe heavily.

"Pill," she answers, her head falling against the wall with a thump as she starts to roll her hips. With a deep breath, I realize just how much trust I have in her, no doubt filtering in whatsoever at her assurances of using birth control.

My eyes cross. "Goddamn, Linney, you keep moving like that and I'm not gonna last."

She hums but picks up speed.

"You want me to move, baby? Want to be bad with me?"

"Please," she whines. "You're so deep. I'm so full."

I bite her collarbone and pull my hips back so just the tip of my cock is kissing her entrance. She makes a low sound of protest as she digs her nails into my shoulders, her eyes pleading.

"You want me to fuck you hard or love you slow?"

"Hard first, slow later." Her feet tighten on the top of my ass, trying to get me back inside of her. "Clayton!" she begs.

I lean forward, nose to hers, and smile wickedly at her. "Tell me to fuck your pussy then, darlin'. Give me the words."

Her brown eyes go wide, but she doesn't stop trying to

push me back in. She wants to say it, but that little bit of shyness left when she's with me holds her back. So, I give her a teasing shallow thrust and arch my brow. Her chest heaves and those nails bite in again.

"Fuck me, honey. Fuck me hard."

"Motherfucker," I gasp. Hearing her say those words sends shock shooting right through me.

Then I fuck my girl until my ears are ringing from her screams and I've drained almost three months of frustration and want into her tight body.

We don't get out of the shower until I wash every inch of her and she returns the favor. I came so hard I'm sucked dry. My cock shouldn't be hard this soon, but I already want her again. Hell, I wanted her again as I was groaning out my release. But I know that before I allow myself to take her again, I need to get our talk over with. I'm not sure what she'll do when I tell her my nasty ex is sniffing around, but I'm not going to take her again while the shadow of Jess is hanging around me. I hope like fuck that after I tell her, she'll still want me to love her slow, like I promised.

"Let's get in my bed so I can feel you in my arms, Linney?"

She glances up from drying off her legs and frowns. "Why does your voice sound like that?"

"Like what?"

"Like you've got the weight of the world on your shoulders." She stands and regards me before her eyes open wide and her jaw drops. "Oh my God! Am I bad? Was it . . . not good?"

I sigh and point to my cock, my still-hard cock. "Darlin', my body is already beggin' to get back in you and I don't think it can be missed that I almost fucked you through my shower wall."

"So I'm not bad then?"

Having had enough of this space between us, I grab her gently by her shoulders and pull her to my body. My cock jumps the second her soft belly presses against it. "I've never felt anything better than what I get when you give me you."

Her whole body goes soft and she smiles up at me. Her hands on my chest start to roll across my skin until she's looping them around my neck. "Then what's on your mind, Clayton?"

"I need to tell you somethin' that happened and I would rather do it with you naked in my bed so I can keep my word and love you soft after."

A small worry wrinkle forms on the skin between her brows, but with a deep breath she nods and lets me lead us to my bed. She climbs in first, sitting on her knees and watching me as I drop the towel I had knotted at my hips. Not once does she hide her naked body, and I know that means she's more worried than she lets on.

"Come here, Linney," I request softly once my back hits the headboard. Her eyes go from my face, down my body, and up again before that worry between her brow grows. She sucks in a wobbly breath, but scoots forward. I take her face gently between both hands.

"What's goin' through your mind?" I question her.

"You've got me worried."

My thumbs rub against her soft cheeks before I lean in and press a soft kiss to her lips. "I'm sorry, darlin'. I don't want you worried, I just didn't want to put off talkin'."

Her tiny hands shake as they move from my shoulders to my neck, one on each side as she studies me. "Is this about John?"

Fucking John. I should've assumed he'd be her first thought, seeing as she hasn't brought him up since I asked her to trust me when it comes to that douchebag.

"No, I haven't seen him since that afternoon in Wire Creek."

"Oh."

"You been worried about him?"

She shakes her head. "Not really. He hasn't called in a while and I think he got the picture that we're together, so I don't expect him to now."

"What do you mean he hasn't called in a while?" Jesus Christ, I didn't even think to ask if he's been in contact with her since they split up.

She shrugs. "He called a few times after we were done, but stopped for a few years. He called me more recently, but the last time was the night I met you."

"You'd tell me if he did, right?"

Her head moves in my grasp as she nods. "I would, but he won't, since I changed my number the next day."

Somewhat pacified, I drop the subject.

"What's goin' on, honey?" she asks with concern when I don't say anything.

"You know my ex?"

"The one who tried to trick you into more?"

"Yeah. That one." I shift my hands, wrapping my arms around her body to pull her closer, needing to feel more of her skin against mine. Her hold on my neck slips for a second before she adjusts her arms and her fingers press into my hair. "I've run into her a few times since we started this thing, but other than runnin' her mouth, she hasn't done more, until two days ago. When I saw her, she cornered me, and before I could get her to move, she grabbed me in a way only you should be grabbin' me."

"Where?" Caroline asks, her eyes no longer worried now that they're burning with rage.

"It didn't last long, but I know people saw before I could stop it and I didn't want you to hear it from someone else."

"*Where* did she touch you, Clayton?" she asks again.

"Fuck," I breathe, dropping my head against the wooden frame.

"She touched this part of you, in the middle of town?"

I nod, clenching my jaw when she stops moving and I lose the sensation of her wetness caressing my body.

"And what did you do when she touched what isn't hers anymore? When she touched what's mine?"

I look back at her, shocked by the brazen words, still expecting to see her anger but there isn't any to be found. Her eyes are dancing but no longer spitting fire. Curiosity, maybe, but her trust in me is clear as she waits for me to explain.

"I grabbed her wrist and told her never to do that shit again, but whether she actually heeds that is another story."

Caroline nods, lifting one hand to run through my hair as she studies me. She repeats the process again as the silence ticks on before leaning forward and pressing her lips to mine in a quick kiss.

"Does she know you're seein' someone?"

I nod, my grip tightening just a hair, her body pressing more firmly against mine. "I told her, and seein' as I said I was buildin' the future I hadn't wanted with her with you, I'm thinkin' she got the point. I made sure she knew that not only do I dislike her disrespectin' the woman I'm buildin' a life with, she doesn't have a chance of makin' that life with me."

Her eyes, which were locked on my lips while I spoke, jumped to mine. "What?"

"What part, darlin'?"

"I'm not sure," she gasps.

"Caroline," I murmur with a smile.

"Well," she starts, scooting her bottom closer and rubbing against me, smiling when I groan. "I'm not happy that happened, but I think I like knowin' that you said all that to her. She doesn't deserve your kindness after what happened, even if it makes me a bitch to say so. I mean, I understand if you told her that to get her off your back and all. We haven't really put titles on us or anything, I mean. Is that what was botherin' you? That I might think you wanted for us what she hoped to get from you before y'all broke up?"

"I think it bothers me more that you think I wouldn't want that."

She deflates in my hold, just a tiny bit. "You were clear when we talked about it how you felt about marriage. Even if we were at that point where we'd be talkin' about it, I know where you stand."

"Stood, Linney. I'm not standin' there anymore."

"What?" she breathes.

I smile, leaning my face closer, and take her mouth in a deep kiss. She grabs ahold of my hair, pulling slightly, and sighs into my mouth. I kiss her slow, moving my tongue against hers in lazy glides. Her hips start moving against mine in a dance of pure torture. Each time she presses forward, I thrust up off the bed, and it doesn't take much of that for us to become too breathless to continue kissing.

"One of these days," I tell her as I roll her onto her back, "I'm gonna have a talk with you about our future." My hips lift and I reach between us to guide my cock into her body. "And darlin', I'm gonna have one hell of a different way of explainin' my thoughts for our future than I did back then. Until that time comes, you just let me love you slow and fuck you bad."

13

CAROLINE

"Close" by Ryan Kinder

— ★ —

The second he starts moving inside of me, I know this is different from any other time. Our night at the motel had been fueled by lust and the mystery the darkness created. It had been frantic, both of us knowing we only had that night. Earlier, in the shower, it was just as rushed, but driven by the need, our tantalizing past few weeks. This though . . . this is a profound kind of coupling. With every slow thrust I can feel the words he knows I'm not ready to hear. But, as I look up into his clear eyes, I hope he can see what I'm not ready to say.

I'm quickly becoming dependent on what's building between us, and after hearing what he just said, I know I'm not alone.

I could go the rest of my life with nothing more than

what he's giving me now as long as I continue to feel wholly and completely adored by him. I might not have tons of experience with relationships, but I do know what we share is special. He hits a spot deep inside me and I push my head back on a moan.

With each lazy thrust into my body, I feel him battering down the remnants of the walls I've put up. With each precious kiss, he promises me a future without hurt. When he looks deep into my eyes and plunges into me, I clamp down and come so hard it steals my breath. And when he starts picking up speed, taking me harder, I drag my nails down his back and feel my orgasm bleed into a second. With my moans echoing his, his come shoots into my body, and I know I'm going to give him every bit of myself until he has it all.

I close my eyes with a smile, my legs falling from their tight hold on his hips, and rub his back lazily.

"You hungry?" he questions when my stomach's grumbling breaks the afterglow.

I hum my answer, but don't move to actually do something about it and let him go. We both groan as he slips free.

"Come on. Let me feed you, darlin'," he jokes with a smile when my stomach continues talking.

He tosses me one of his shirts with a handsome smirk, watching me closely as I cover up. I can only imagine the blush covering my body under his watchful gaze, but it isn't from feeling shy. When he groans a complaint over losing the sight of my naked body, I feel the heat of arousal and pride knowing I can make a man as perfect as Clayton Davis come undone like that.

I push my hair out of my face and smile up at him. He says something under his breath about never letting me wear clothes again before pulling his jeans over his own nakedness. He has to tuck his still-hard length down before zipping them up, leaving the button undone.

"That can't feel good," I muse, pointing out the impression of his erection clear through the worn denim.

"It's not, but if I don't get us both fed, I won't have the energy to do anything about it later."

"You sound like I'm a sure thing," I joke.

"Prayin' you are, darlin'. I'd live in that sweet pussy if I could."

I gasp, swatting his abs. He only smiles bigger and pulls me to my feet, kissing me hard. When we finally manage to leave his bedroom and get some food, it's almost nine at night. I have no idea how two hours passed so quickly, but I shouldn't be surprised by his stamina. I know from our first night together he can go until I pass out from his lovemaking.

"I think I'm goin' to sell when the rebuild is finished," I tell him after taking the last bite of my sandwich.

He doesn't look away, frowning slightly.

"I've been thinkin' about it a lot these past few weeks and, well, I don't really want to be livin' forty-five minutes away anymore. I used to think bein' that far from Pine Oak was a good thing, but now, not so much."

His face gets soft when my explanation sinks in. "What are you thinkin'?"

"The buildin' next to the hardware store is openin' up. The lady who owned it doesn't want to deal with the trouble of ownin' a business now that she's gettin' older, so I was considerin' opening back up there."

"Miz Jordan's? The florist?"

"Yeah," I answer quietly, looking at my plate knowing he's likely thinking the same thing I did when I found out that was the only place in town available for rent.

"Darlin', that's right next to your mama's salon."

"I know."

"Not that I don't think you could handle it, but Caroline, that woman bein' that close to you makes me feel a whole lot of unease."

I nod, looking away from the intensity in his gaze and pushing some of the chips left on my plate around with my fingertip.

"I love the idea of you bein' closer, darlin', especially if that means you're goin' to be doin' it sooner than later, but I'd be lyin' if I said I was okay with puttin' you that near to her."

"There's nowhere else, Clayton. I've looked. I wanted to know all my options before I brought it up to you. I want to come home, not just because of us, but because I don't feel safe in Wire Creek either. Being here, well, I don't need to constantly worry."

He frowns. "I thought they ruled the fire an accident."

"According to the report, but I'm not sure."

He steps around the island and pulls me into his arms. "Why do you think it wasn't an accident, Caroline?" I can see the concern written all over his face and in the tense set of his shoulders.

"I think someone's been tamperin' with things. Materials are goin' missin' and yesterday Joe, the contractor, told me some of the electrical he had finished was pulled out. How would that even happen?"

"I'm not sure," he says thickly.

"We only passed inspection because Joe worked through the night to fix the issue, but somethin' in my gut is tellin' me I shouldn't go back there. I wanted to talk to you before I put a for-sale sign in the window and start lookin' for somewhere else to open up again. Whether that's here in Pine Oak or maybe in Law Bone, either way, I don't want it to be in Wire Creek anymore."

"Don't buy the Jordans' old place. It might look like the only option now, but havin' you that close to your mama isn't gonna happen."

"I'm goin' to have to look at Law Bone, then, and the only thing I found there was clear on the other side of town. Not that I'm lookin' for a new space based on the distance to your place, but . . . uh." I stop when he flashes me a wide, toothy smile. "What?"

"Linney, I think we need to start basin' your search off how far it is from the ranch, so don't get embarrassed when you say it because, darlin', I agree."

"Now that I'm going to sell, Clayton, I need to find somewhere to live that isn't a motel. I can't use the ranch as my base when I might find somethin' to rent that's on the other side of you, but close to a potential space for the store."

He throws his head back and laughs. "How many nights have you been at that shitty motel, darlin'?"

I shrug. "It's been two months since the fire and I started stayin' there not long after that. I don't know exactly how long though."

"Let me rephrase that. How many nights since we started explorin' us have you *actually* stayed there?"

"That's different, Clayton. We haven't exactly had tons of time to get together between me bein' busy durin' the day either sleepin' or monitorin' the build, and you've got a busy schedule of your own here. By the time I get a few hours in at Hazel's and get here, it's been so late I either fall asleep or you insist I stay."

He steps closer, smiling down at me with the most open expression of affection. "Darlin', it might've started out that way, but I haven't wanted you anywhere else for weeks than in my bed. You want to make up one of the guest rooms as yours, do it, but I think it's time we both admit this is your home."

"Clayton," I breathe, not knowing how to respond to him.

"I've got an idea about the store, but I need to check

some things out before I get your hopes up. Until then get the place in Wire Creek on the market, check out of that goddamn hotel for good, and get your sexy ass where it belongs."

"It's too soon," I weakly argue.

"Then put your clothes in one of the guest rooms instead of mine!"

"But—" I start, only to stop speaking when his hand covers my mouth.

"I wouldn't be sayin' it if I wasn't sure, Caroline. You don't need to be in that motel. You didn't want to stay with Luke and Lucy, and I think we both know that under this roof is where you belong."

"I . . . okay," I agree, not letting myself look for reasons to keep arguing against this.

"Okay," he parrots with a grin that makes my heart pick up speed.

"If you change your mind though—"

"No way in hell that's gonna happen, sweetness."

"This is insane."

His chest rumbles as he laughs low and deep. "I think we're pretty good at doin' things with a little insanity, darlin'. That's half the run of our ride together. I never know what's comin' next and I'm not findin' it a bad thing to give up control if I've got you with me doin' so."

There aren't any more words after that as his mouth

takes mine in a doozy of a kiss. By the time he has me passing out from exhaustion, there isn't a single concern on my shoulders anymore, and I go to sleep with a smile on my face all because of the man who is slowly becoming my everything.

14

CAROLINE

"Happy People" by Little Big Town

- ★ -

"**L**et me get this straight," Quinn says, folding another baby blanket and placing it on Leighton's coffee table. "Clay, my allergic-to-anything-resembling-commitment brother, is not only in a super-committed relationship, but also livin' in sin with his girlfriend?"

Leighton snorts, throwing some tiny yellow baby socks at her best friend's head. "You make it sound so scandalous, Q."

"And you aren't shocked?"

"Well, no, not really," Leigh answers, looking down at her lap, but not before I see the smirk on her face.

"It's only been two months!" she exclaims.

"So what?"

I stop petting Leighton's giant cat, Earl, and chime in.

"We've technically known each other our whole lives. I had a crush on him before I started datin' John. I guess it's just our time now." At my words, they both look over at me with jaws wide open.

"You had a crush on him back in high school?" Leigh questions with a smile.

"You hussy!" Quinn laughs. "He's six years older than you."

"What?" I blush. "He's the most handsome man I've ever known."

"That's so sweet." Leigh sighs dreamily, wiping her eyes as they fill with tears.

I gape at her in shock when she starts crying harder. Hoping to find some sort of help from Quinn, I'm utterly flustered when I see her crying as well. "Uh," I hedge.

"What the fuck is goin' on?" a voice thunders behind me.

At the sound of her husband, Leighton waves him off and sniffles loudly. "Stop growlin', cowboy."

"Did you hear?" Quinn cries toward her brother.

"Hear what?"

"Caroline moved into the ranch house."

Maverick stops in his path and turns slowly to assess me. I haven't gotten very close to the middle Davis child, but I also haven't spent tons of time around him since Clayton and I stated dating. The few interactions we had were brief, and he studied every move his brother made with me. What I hadn't gotten in the months since Clayton and I started dating was his younger brother smiling freely in my direction. It's so shocking I can't do anything but stare at him.

"Well, I'll be," he finally says, his grin growing even wider. "I bet that bitch Jess isn't too happy about this news."

I shake my head.

"What's *that* mean?" Quinn questions, sniffling loudly.

"Just what I said, Hell-raiser."

"Why would what Jess thinks even be relevant right now?"

"You must not have been hearin' the gossip flyin' around town. I know Leigh told you about it because she said you were goin' on and on about how nasty Jess is."

Quinn looks at Maverick like he's grown a second head. "She mentioned Jess was sniffin' around Clay, not details! I've been stuck at home on bed rest for a whole week, asshole. How am I goin' to get the good gossip when I can't even waddle my ass into town?"

Leighton laughs, finally dry-eyed. "I forgot to tell you what I heard when I was at the PieHole last week. Sorry, Q. I got distracted when you started talkin' about your cervix and everything."

Quinn's eyes go from Leighton's to her brother's, over to mine, then back to Leighton's when no one goes to explain further. "Well! D, don't just sit there. Give me the goods!"

I sigh but don't say anything.

"It really isn't a big deal. His ex put her hands on him in the middle of the day smack-dab in the center of town. Jana told me that he grabbed her hand off his crotch the second he realized—a second too late, I should add—that she was goin' to touch him there. She didn't hear what he said, but rumor has it that it was somethin' about her bein' a used-up slut that he wouldn't touch with a ten-foot-long cattle prod, even if he wasn't madly in love."

"I think you're embellishing it just a little, Leigh," I add, rolling my eyes to hide the fact that my stomach is going nuts at the mention of love.

"She isn't far from the truth," Maverick says, sitting down next to his wife and rubbing her stomach. She looks at him and smiles before placing her hand on top of his.

"How is that woman still even sniffin' around? They've been broken up for years and I know he isn't stupid enough to have gone back even for a quickie, seein' as she's been with half the town."

Leigh hums in agreement when Quinn stops talking. "Did he ever say why they split in the first place?"

They look at Maverick first, but he doesn't glance away from his wife's belly, ignoring them completely.

"Uh," I stammer, "I love you two and all, but if you haven't heard it from him before now, you aren't gonna hear it from me."

I might've gotten back the friendship that was broken when I left town after high school, but my loyalty will always be to Clayton now.

I ignore the annoyed glances they both shoot me and meet Maverick's gaze. I'm not sure what I expected, but a wink followed by a low chuckle damn sure wasn't it.

"You know!" his wife snaps accusingly. "You hadn't even come back to Pine Oak when he was datin' her."

"Didn't have to live in Pine Oak to talk to my brother, darlin'."

"Well?" Quinn probes, looking at her brother.

"Yeah, right, Quinnie. And don't y'all be givin' his girl any shit for bein' faithful to her man. If Clay wanted y'all to know his personal shit, he'd tell you. You both know damn well you wouldn't say a thing if the roles were reversed, so give her the respect of doin' the same."

They stay mute as he leans down to kiss Leighton's belly before pressing another kiss to her lips. After rising from his seat, he walks by his sister and pats her head. Leaving the room, he shuts the back door softly. The girls share a look, then glance at me in shock.

"I think," Quinn breathes, "you just got a Maverick-size stamp of approval."

"She totally did," Leighton agrees with a smile.

Earl licks my hand and meows, clearly sick of me not petting him anymore. I lean back, fighting a grin. Five minutes later, he's not too happy with me when

Leighton shoos him off my lap so I can help her carry all the newly washed and folded baby items to the nursery. Quinn, knowing she'd be pressing her luck if she got off the couch since she's ready to pop, doesn't come.

"You seem happy," Leighton muses in the nursery.

"I am," I confirm with a smile.

"I haven't said it, but I'm really happy that you and Clay are together. It's not just that he's good for you—you're good for him. He's always been super private about his personal life, but I hope you know that both Quinn and I are here if you ever just want to talk to your girls about things. I respect the fact that you might never do that too, just so you know. We might be nosy, but Mav wasn't wrong."

"I'll keep that in mind, Leigh."

"A little advice from one girl who fell for a Davis to another: just don't ever tell Quinn about your sex life or you'll never hear the end of it. That girl is as weird as it gets when she finds out about that stuff."

I chuckle. "Noted. Don't ever tell Quinn how good her brother is." My eyes widen when I realize what I just said. "What are the chances you'll forget that?" I ask Leigh.

Her whole belly moves as she laughs softly. "Not even a little bit, but don't worry, I won't say a word. I've got a cowboy of my own, so I know how to keep quiet."

When we go back into the living room, Quinn is

asleep on the couch and Earl is curled up in a tiny space between her belly and thighs. A large cat, some breed Leighton called a Maine coon, there's no way he can be comfortable with his back half hanging off the couch, but he's purring away regardless.

"I'm goin' to let y'all rest and head home," I tell Leigh, feeling my heart skip a beat at the idea of home being the ranch. "I promised Clayton today I'd finally let him teach me how to ride."

I give her a hug, promising to call later, and walk out to my car. It'd be quicker if I knew the four-wheeler trails, but I don't mind the short drive. It's hard not to love it when every turn gives me the most beautiful views of Pine Oak's backcountry. Miles and miles of green pastures.

Every stretch of the road on the Davis property is lined with a stark white fence. Clayton explained that when his father had been running things, they had cattle roaming their lands. The Davises raised some of the best, but it was a business Clayton never saw for the future of the ranch. Since they no longer use the majority of their land for cattle, they farm out unused parts of those pastures for hay so that they can gain that resource for the horses.

Clayton tells me he owns pastures that have some of the best views in all of Texas, but since you have to travel by horse to get there, I haven't seen those yet. He's been working so hard to get me comfortable around the big beasts, but there's just something about those huge black eyes watching your every move that makes me uneasy.

I honk at Drew, the ranch foreman, when I see him working on one of the fence rails near the turnoff from Maverick and Leigh's road to ours. He pulls his hat off and waves it in the air before wiping his brow and bending back over to continue his work. Not far after that, I see two other hands do the same, and I give them a honk of my horn as well.

Right before the turn into the ranch house, I see a few cows in the distance, smack-dab in the middle of the road. The rancher who owns the land on the other side of the road has so many head of cattle, they're always dotting the landscape, but this is the first time I've seen wayward cattle making a break for it.

I continue down our drive, reaching for my phone in my purse. I pull up Clayton's number and give him a call, climbing out of the car while it rings.

"Linney," he answers in that deep way of his that's almost breathy but too manly to be called such. The sound goes straight through me, bathing my whole body in warmth.

"Hey, honey." I smile into the bright sun, walking up the porch steps and into the house. "I know you're busy, but I wanted to let you know some of the Larkins' cows are makin' a break for it. I saw them when I was turnin' in farther down the road."

"I'll give Todd a call."

"I figured you would. Are you goin' to be home for supper tonight?"

I can only imagine how tired he is, seeing that he left before sunup this morning to deliver some horses to a buyer out in Tulsa, Oklahoma. He made it sound like no big deal, but I can't imagine making a five-plus-hour drive one way and not being wiped by the time I got home.

"I should be at the ranch in about an hour, darlin'. Why don't we head into town for something?"

"Are you sure you don't want to just have a relaxin' night at home? You've been on the road all day."

He laughs. "No, I want to take my girlfriend out. Might not be as fancy as what we'd get if we drive into Dallas, but I don't take you out enough as it is."

"Clayton," I say with a smile, "you know I don't need all that." And I don't. I know he's busy with things at the ranch and his hours are long and taxing. I don't want him working his tail off all day only to get home and think I need him to take me out in order to show me a good time. All I want is to be near him. There're no distractions when you're getting undivided one-on-one time.

"I know, darlin', but I'm still feelin' the itch to show you off."

I roll my eyes, walking through the house toward the stairs so I can go get ready now that it looks like we're not going to be staying in.

"I was just visitin' over at Maverick and Leighton's. I

know Quinn is on bed rest, but why don't you give Tate a call and see if he'll okay a trip to town for dinner? I'll ring Leigh and see if she and Maverick want to join. They don't have much time left before the babies are here. As much as I love our time with just the two of us, I think we should have a family dinner before the little ones come."

A noise comes over the line that makes me pause in pulling off my leggings. "I like hearin' you refer to them as family."

"Well, they are your family, Clayton. What else would I call them?" I laugh awkwardly.

"And seein' as we're buildin' our future, they're yours too, Linney."

"Clayton." I gulp.

"Don't go sayin' my name like that when I'm too far away to do somethin' about it. One day soon, we're gonna sit down and talk so you know exactly what I see for us down the road and I can make sure you don't have any doubts as to where I'm standin'. Get ready, baby, I'll be home soon."

He hangs up before I can say anything else, but since he's rendered me speechless, that's just fine with me. I'm not stupid: I know he wouldn't have moved me into his home if he didn't see a future for us, but knowing how his last relationship ended, I worry he might not want the same things for his life as I do for mine—a family. There isn't much in this world that would make me willingly give up what I have with Clayton Davis, but the fact that he doesn't want kids might just be one of them. Which is the very reason I've been dreading the moment he wanted to have this talk.

What will I do if he only changes how he feels about marriage but not children? Can I stay with a man who can only give me his love but not his babies? I'm honestly not sure.

15

CAROLINE

"Tennessee Whiskey" by Chris Stapleton

— ★ —

"**W**ould you stop?" Quinn snaps, yanking her husband's plate back toward her so she can continue to pick off it, having already polished off her food. "Do you want to be the reason your child starves, Starch?"

He smirks, his handsome face more boyish than those of the other men at our table. If I wasn't already tumbling head over heels for a certain dark cowboy, I might find Tate Montgomery attractive. He shrugs and I hear Leighton snicker from across the round table. My gaze moves to her and she winks before mouthing something about waiting for it. I frown in confusion before she points to the two Montgomerys.

"Grease, there's no way my baby is starvin' in there," he jokes, pointing to her very big stomach. I know he meant it harmlessly, but judging by the expression on Quinn's beautiful face, she doesn't feel the same way. "Now, don't go lookin' at me like that, Quinn. You know that's not what I meant."

"Oh really?" she asks, crossing her arms over her chest, which is no easy feat, seeing as she's top-heavy *and* belly-heavy.

"You know I love your body," Tate tells her sincerely, but she doesn't stop leveling him with a glare.

"You mean the body that keeps growin' as big as a house, keepin' your baby from starvin' because I'm storin' food in there for him, or somethin'?"

Tate looks up at the ceiling and I hear Leighton chuckle a little louder.

"Give it a break, Hell-raiser," Maverick mumbles around a forkful of barbecue. "You know damn well he didn't mean what you're implyin'. Just because you're in a shit mood, don't take it out on your man."

"He's the one who put me in jail!"

This time, Leighton doesn't keep her hilarity down. She starts laughing so hard, I can't stop watching her belly with worry that she's shaking her baby up in there. Surely it's not good for it to move that much. "He didn't put you in jail, Q! Don't be such a drama queen."

Quinn turns her narrowed eyes at Leighton. "You aren't the one stuck talkin' to herself while her husband is off playin' inside other women's vaginas."

My eyes widen and I feel my cheeks heat as heads

start turning in our direction. Maverick has his fork frozen halfway to his mouth, staring at his sister in shock. Leigh is hooting even harder now. Tate, having clearly heard this many times, just looks down at his plate with a smirk. When I look up at Clayton, he's wearing the same expression as his brother.

I try to ignore the stares as Quinn continues to grumble about her vagina-poking husband, but it's almost impossible when it feels like the whole place can't take their eyes off our table. I'm used to the curious looks when I'm out with Clayton or even the girls, but they're never as bad as when all six of us are together. When you factor in Quinn's shameless way of saying whatever is on her mind, it really does feel like we're on display.

"You get used to it," Maverick grumbles, and I look to my right to see him studying me with understanding. "Took me a while when I got back to Pine Oak. I forgot what it was like to live in a town where everyone treated other people's lives like a soap opera."

"How do you ignore the stares?"

He shrugs. "You just stop carin' what they think. Only person whose opinion matters to me is my wife's. They're gonna think what they want regardless of the truth, so you might as well just pretend they don't exist."

"But doesn't it bother you when you hear them talkin' about you and it's not true?"

His mouth moves, not into a full smile, but it's not a hard line anymore. "They're not ever gonna spread the truth when they can stretch it and fill in the less interestin' parts with lies. You just live your life and make sure you keep yourself happy. The rest of that shit can go to hell."

I lean back in my chair and look around. Just like Maverick, everyone eating with us is oblivious to the stares from the tables surrounding us in the packed restaurant. Just like when we're at the PieHole or even grabbing groceries, people have no qualms about gawking.

The Davis family is Pine Oak royalty, so it shouldn't be a shock, but for someone like me, who isn't used to it, it's a struggle. I never did look at the attention with such an untroubled and relaxed mind-set as Maverick does, though. In my mind, I'm still afraid of what they think, but in reality, what does it matter? I've got a great man, his family welcomes me with open arms, and other than the uncertainty of where I'll reopen The Sequel, life is perfect.

I turn to see Clayton regarding me in silence and feel the last tiny part of unease fall to the wayside. A wide smile forms on my face, and I direct all the newfound freedom I feel at him. It's his affections, after all, that have shown me how to complete the puzzle inside of me—that have allowed me to finally shed the past and start living.

The chatter at our table fades away when I see his eyes flash. I know we haven't said those three special words, but when he gives me this unguarded focus, I have no doubts that they're there.

I never stood a chance at keeping my heart from him. Not when he makes me feel like nothing is impossible.

"Hey! Earth to the lovebirds," Quinn yells across the table, breaking the moment with her snapping fingers. "Did you tell her yet?"

"Shut up, Quinnie," Clayton scolds, frowning at his sister.

"What?" She glances around, taking a bite of her husband's sandwich. "You didn't say it was some big secret."

"What are you talkin' about?" I ask.

Clayton sighs, glaring at her a second longer before turning to look at me. "I planned to surprise you later, but since my sister has a mouth the size of Texas, might as well do it now."

"Oh, come on! You didn't tell me not to say anything. How was I supposed to know?"

"I don't know, Quinn, maybe because I said don't tell Linney so I can make sure it's what she wants before you get excited?"

She waves a hand in the air. "Potato, potahto, big brother."

Clayton sighs, but smiles at his sister.

"Well, now that you two got that out of the way, how about one of you spill the beans so everyone else—including Caroline—can know what's goin' on?" Leigh jokes.

"I have a place I think would be great for The Sequel," Clayton tells me.

Of all the things I thought he'd say, *that* didn't even cross my mind. My heart picks up as happiness fills me to the point of bursting with the knowledge that even with how busy he's been, he's been looking for something better than the Jordans' place next to the salon.

"Really?" I gasp with excitement.

"The buildin' next to Davis Auto Works went up for sale a few years back. We bought it with plans to either use it for storage or expand, but never really had time to deal with either. I think you'll find it's perfect, but I wanted to run it by Quinn before I said anything. The last time we talked about it, we'd decided that D.A.W. didn't need anything bigger, and the setup we have now for storage works. I had every intention of listin' it but never got around to it. Feels like one of those meant-to-be things, sweetness," he explains with a shrug of his shoulders, downplaying just how huge this actually is.

"You want me to buy it from you?" I question, excitement bubbling through me even more. "I'd love to see the space, but I trust you. Given that it's in my budget and all."

His face gets soft and he gives me his knee-weakening grin. "Linney, you think I'm gonna take a single penny from you, you've lost your mind." Clearly seeing the argument forming, he raises a hand and closes it over my mouth. "Another one of those things we're buildin', darlin'. The Sequel is a part of you, and *you* are a part of me. You get that fire bubblin' over the teacup and I'm gonna have fun showin' you another way to toss that sass around."

My mouth moves, but he doesn't take his hand away, so the words just come out garbled.

"You gonna let me do this if you like the space?"

I shake my head and narrow my eyes.

"You need me to love you bad and change your answer?" he smarts off with a low rumble of his voice, eyes dancing with amusement.

I pause long enough to show him that I'm not unaffected by that in the least. He throws back his head, a booming laugh rocking his body before he drops his hand.

"You are *not* givin' me a buildin'," I finally say when he quiets down. "You can't just give someone somethin' as big as a buildin' and think that's okay."

He leans toward me till we're nose-to-nose and effectively kills any chance I had at arguing logic with him. "Caroline Michaels, you gave me back a life worth livin'. The way I see it, a buildin' isn't even close to big enough to make us even."

Everyone laughs when I lean back in my chair and shut my mouth. Even being the butt of their laughter, I don't feel the old feelings of nervous unease. Not now. All I feel is contentment so deep in my bones I don't think I'll ever be afraid of my own shadow again.

I'm finally living a life free of trepidation and wild

with adoration. Who would've thought that one night with a dark cowboy would heal my soul of fear?

I'm still riding the high of having my own space thirty minutes later when we leave the restaurant, Clayton and I following the other two couples. His arm is over my shoulders, pressing me tight to his side as we walk. I have one behind his back and one resting against his abs. When we stop next to his truck, I lift the hand off his stomach and bring it to his neck, pulling him down and pressing my mouth to his. He doesn't pause, deepening our kiss instantly. I hear the others talking as they move to their vehicles, but don't pull away. When Clayton turns us and moves my front to press more firmly against his, with both his hands on my bottom, I smile against his mouth and lift my head to look up at him.

"What was that for?" he asks, his voice thick with the same pleasure I feel shooting through me.

"Thank you," I answer simply.

His expression changes into one that makes my heart pick up speed. He's gazing down at me like I just gave him the world in the palm of my hand. His eyes are shining bright, the swirls of green so luminous that they look like the clearest emerald stone. His whole face is smiling. One hand leaves my butt, grabs the hand not holding his neck, and pulls it to his chest. His heartbeat hits my palm with a frantic tempo as his gaze holds mine.

I open my mouth to give him every last piece of me, but before I can, the magical moment is shattered. I hear my name called in a vile tone that belongs to one woman and one woman alone. Only unlike the last time, I don't feel the same panic that had me bolting—not with Clayton's arms safely enveloping me.

"Well, well, looks like some things never change. Left town a whore and come back as one. At least you're movin' up in the world now that you've wrangled a Davis man."

I can hear the slur in her voice, but I don't let that excuse her behavior. She'd say the same thing if she were sober.

"What the fuck did you just say?" Clayton seethes angrily.

"I'm talkin' to my daughter, not you."

"No, you're talkin' to *my* Caroline, not yours. She isn't anything to you."

Since I haven't turned yet, I see Quinn and Leighton with their husbands gaping at the scene my mother is creating. When I look up at Clayton, his rage making the muscles in his jaw clench and jump, I frame his face in my hands and force him to look away from Misty Michaels.

"I need to do this without you actin' like my shield, honey." I see the refusal on the tip of his tongue but shake my head before he can voice it. "I *need* this to finally move on."

His chest swells with a deep breath and I know it costs him, but he nods sharply. I turn, his grip only loosening enough to allow me to face her before tightening again.

He'll give me his silence and allow me to fight my own battle here, but that doesn't mean he's won't make his support known.

I address her in a strong and clear voice. "What do you want?"

She sneers at me, teeth bared, making her weathered face look as evil as I know her to be. "That's no way to speak to your mother."

"You're right," I agree. "But you stopped bein' that a long time ago. So I'll ask you again, Misty. What do you want?"

Her head jerks back as her scowl deepens. "You little ungrateful bitch!"

Clayton's arm spasms, and I know he's close to losing his mind. I reach behind and pat his thigh. I can see a small crowd forming near the restaurant's entrance, but I don't care that people are openly gawking. I'm not going back to the woman who was afraid of what they thought. I'm not the one in the wrong here.

"I'm waiting. Say what you need to, but know this is the only chance I'll allow you the freedom of doin' so."

"I shoulda had the doctor suck you outta me the second he told me I was pregnant. Now I'm stuck with my whore daughter and her disrespectful tongue. You should be thankin' me for keepin' you."

I lean my head against Clayton's chest and laugh. "You have some nerve callin' me a whore when you can't even recall who knocked you up in the first place." I lower my voice, not wanting the whole town to know by morning what I say next. "I've been with two men in my life, *Misty*. One who almost broke me because I was naive enough to think he could follow through on his promise to help me get away, and one who healed me after the first did his best to ruin what you hadn't already. Seein' that the latter is also goin' to be the *last* man I give myself to, I'd say I'm pretty dadgum close to sainthood. You want to believe I'm a whore, then you do so, but when I crawl into bed at night with the man I love with every fiber of my bein', I'm gonna do that knowin' that my life is finally perfect and your opinion no longer matters."

I watch the woman who gave birth to me, the same one who never gave me any love afterward, sputter in shock. I've never spoken back to her. I didn't when I was growing up, still under the impression that I wanted and needed her love. I didn't when I was a teenager, seeking out the wrong company in an attempt to fill the void she created. And I didn't when I begged her to save me. I carried the burden I felt with her inability to care about me for nearly thirty years, but no more. Never again.

"Do me a favor," I finally say when she continues to look confused that I'm not breaking under her verbal abuse. "Pretend you had that abortion. When you see me, Clayton, or anyone else in our family, act like we're invisible. Look right through us, Misty, because we're goin' to do the same to you."

I turn awkwardly in Clayton's stiff grasp and hug my

arms around him. I can feel the power of his fury in the tension-filled muscles that are flexed hard. I ignore her, hoping she'll just leave. With my cheek against his chest, I hear her attempt to speak up.

"Shut your goddamn mouth." Clayton rumbles venom-filled words that seem to explode from deep in his gut. "You don't want to find out what happens if you continue this, Misty. Don't fuck with me, because I will end you if you even so much think about *my* Caroline."

I squeeze him tighter, not in fear or panic over the confrontation with the woman who used to make me feel those things, but to reassure him that I'm fine. When he finally relaxes his body slightly, I know she's left. I keep hugging him for another second until I feel a little more tension leave his body—only then do I look up at him.

"It feels good to forget," I whisper, knowing he understands what I'm saying when his anger vanishes instantly. I'd thought he was speaking out of his ear when he explained how he moved on from his own mama's hurt, but not anymore. She'll never deserve my forgiveness, so I'm going to forget her instead—just like he did his.

"Uh, guys?"

Clayton turns us together at Quinn's voice. She looks over the bed of his truck and gives a tiny wave. I scan the other three people at her side and frown when I get to her husband's pale face.

"I don't mean to interrupt what I'm *sure* was about to get interestin' and all, seein' that you just admitted you love my big brother at the same time you put your mama in her place so brilliantly, but my water broke five minutes ago and my vagina-pokin' husband has seemed to forget every year of medical school, because I'm not sure he's breathin' anymore."

16
CLAYTON

"The Fighter" by Keith Urban & Carrie Underwood

"**A**ny news?" Caroline asks, handing me the coffee that she got from the cafeteria.

"Nothin' since the last time Tate came out and said she was about to start pushin'. That was almost three hours ago, Linney."

She grabs my free hand and gives it a squeeze. "These things take some time, honey. She's in good hands. I know you're worried."

"I hate knowin' she's hurtin'." God, just the thought of my baby sister—someone I spent my whole life, until she married Tate, protecting with everything in me—being in pain cuts me deep. I glance over at Maverick, seeing the same worry etched in his face. I can only imagine his is amplified because his wife will be in the same position soon. "It's too soon," I finally whisper, feeling fear claw at me.

"She's only four weeks early, Clayton. I know they had her on bed rest, but they told her they wouldn't stop labor if she went early; they just wanted to give her as much time as they could. They're both goin' to be fine."

My hand shakes as I lift my coffee and take a sip of the black brew. I lean forward in my seat, elbows to knees, and hold the cup in both hands. This is why I crave control. Knowing what will happen, how I can manipulate situations to ensure the outcome I find most favorable, and avoid anything that can cause harm. There isn't shit I can do except let God's will work, and it's tearing me apart.

"How about we talk about what happened back in the parkin' lot of Pit's," Caroline offers in a soft voice.

Just thinking about what happened after supper makes me burn with a whole new rush of conflicting emotions. I'm so fucking proud of her for standing up to her mama, but I hate that she ever had to. I've never wanted to harm a woman before, but Misty has me itching to ruin her.

"Linney," I tell her softly. I knew from her violent reaction months ago from just hearing her mama call her name that her childhood wasn't a good one. I don't want her reliving that just because she thinks she has to give me more.

"I know I don't have to, but it's important to me that you know what I said was true. That what she thinks of me isn't what I am."

I turn my head, not moving from my hunched position. "You think I could ever think of you like that?"

She shrugs, picking at her coffee cup. "I spent my life thinkin' that just because she thought I was a whore, I must have been. It's why I never really dated—until John, that is. I didn't dress provocatively or give people a reason to think that, so as I got older, I realized it was just another way for her to make sure I knew my place in her life." She takes a deep breath. "I'm sure you realize after that confrontation that I was far from planned. She hadn't wanted to stick to Pine Oak, but when she got pregnant with me, there was never a chance she'd make it to some big city and be discovered. Her words, not mine. I have no idea why she kept me, but she did, and because of that she blames me for ruining her grand plans."

"And your father?" I question, sitting up and turning toward her.

She shakes her head, but when her eyes connect with mine, I see the clearness within them. They no longer hold pain, hurt, or care regarding her upbringing.

"She never knew who he was. She had a different man every week while I was livin' with her; I don't imagine it was any different leadin' up to her gettin' pregnant."

"It doesn't bother you?"

"It used to. I think that's just another reason I desperately sucked up any attention John gave me back then. He was the first boy who paid me any mind, and when he promised me a way out from under her thumb, I took it. And I continued to take it, because I believed that was all I deserved."

"Darlin'," I mumble, wrapping my arm around her and pulling her closer, needing that contact.

"I don't feel that way anymore," she continues meekly. "I know now that I was stuck mentally, believin' all the garbage she projected onto me. I might still have times when I get uneasy or shy over too much attention, but it's not like it was then. You have no idea what you've given me, all because you pushed me to look past that fear and explore somethin' I didn't dream I could have."

This woman brings me to my knees. Watching her become stronger each day has been nothing short of humbling.

"I don't need her. I never did. I'm the person I am now because I was too strong for her to break me. I survived her, I survived him, and now I'm bein' gifted you. I meant what I told her, Clayton. Until the day comes that you might not want me, you'll be the last one I give myself to. All of me, I'm yours."

I open my mouth to tell her just how much that means to me and how she's out of her fucking mind if she ever thinks that day would come, but before I can, there's a commotion that pulls my attention away from her.

"I'm a daddy!" Tate bellows with a huge smile, his

chest heaving as he stands in the middle of the waiting room with his hands on his hips.

I turn back to Caroline, but she shakes her head with a nod toward Tate. "Later. We'll finish this later, honey."

Knowing she's right but hating that she has—twice now—given me the words that prove how much she cares for me without me returning them, doesn't feel right. I need to wait to tell the woman who stole my heart weeks ago that I love her when I can take the time to prove it, and as much as I dislike it, that isn't now. I fucking hope she can see the truth in my eyes. I bend toward her and kiss her quickly before standing and grabbing her hand at the same time. We both walk over to Tate, Maverick and Leigh already at his side.

"He's perfect," Tate says with a beaming smile. Realizing that my sister just gave me a nephew, I feel like someone punched me in the chest. "She's the strongest woman I know, thought that before, but after witnessing her bringin' our son into the world I know just how true that is."

"A boy!" Leighton exclaims. She looks up at Maverick. "A boy, Mav!"

"Heard Tate, darlin'," he answers, his voice thick with emotion.

When he looks at me, I see the same overwhelming emotions I'm feeling in his gaze. I swallow what feels like a golf ball and nod. Mav's eyes close and I clench my jaw, but somehow we both manage to get ahold of ourselves, but fuck, it takes one hell of an effort for me to keep from crying like a goddamn baby. I'm so happy for our sister that I feel like I might combust.

I can't believe my baby sister is a mama.

"Y'all ready to meet your nephew?" Tate asks, looking every bit the proud papa he is.

I keep Caroline's hand firmly in mine while we all follow Tate down the hallway. We wait while he pops into Quinn's hospital room to make sure she's decent, but not even a second later he's back and ushering us in. Leighton is first, moving as fast as she can. If I wasn't feeling like I was about to break down and cry, I'd find her waddling that quick funny as hell. Mav follows, stopping to slap Tate's shoulder in silent support.

"Go on, honey," Caroline urges when I don't move from my spot in the hallway.

Before stepping into the room, I release her hand and pull Tate forward. His hug in return is just as tight as mine. "Congratulations, Tate."

"Thanks, Clay. Means a lot."

There's so much I want to tell the man who broke my sister's heart years ago, but I release him and nod instead. He's made her happy since coming back to Pine Oak, and that's all I've ever wanted for Quinn.

Leigh is bawling her head off when we step into the dimly lit hospital room, looking down at Quinn as she smiles at the bundle in her arms. When I look over her shoulder and see my brother finally lose the war over his emotions with wet cheeks and a warm smile, I stop trying to hold mine in and suck in a heavy, choppy breath. Quinn glances up from her son and smiles at me, her chin wobbling like crazy.

"Come meet him," she requests softly.

My vision gets blurry and I step to the side of her bed and get my first glance at the next generation of our family.

"He's an impatient one, but healthy as can be, with lungs stronger than you've ever heard. Doc checked him over and said that for bein' a month early, he's perfect." Quinn lays him down on her thighs, tucking the blanket around his tiny chin to give us a better look at the baby who looks like the spitting image of his parents. "Grayson Ford Montgomery just couldn't wait to meet the best family in the whole wide world."

"He's perfect," Caroline whispers, and I squeeze her hand.

"Oh, Q," Leigh cries softly. "He's the most handsome thing I've ever seen."

"Did good, Quinnie. Did real good."

My sister looks from Mav, when he finishes speaking, and blinks up at me with watery eyes. I reach out, roll my fingertip across Grayson's tiny forehead, and take a rough pull of air into my lungs. His lips purse and his nose scrunches, but his eyes stay shut.

"So proud of you, Quinn," I finally mutter, unable to

resist my new nephew's silky smooth skin and caressing his cheek with my fingertip again.

"Here," she chokes on a tiny sob, lifting her son up toward me.

Caroline jerks her hand away, but with the tiny life being placed into my arms, I don't dare look and see if I can read what's going through her mind. The second I'm holding the seemingly weightless bundle, I never want to give it up. Feelings so foreign to me are hitting hard.

"Jesus, Quinn," I breathe, staring down at Grayson.

"I know, Clay. I *know*."

He isn't even my own son and I already know I'd protect this child with everything I have in me. Knowing that, I can't even fathom how a parent could ever feel anything but unconditional love. I don't have to guess that both my brother and sister are thinking the same thing. We might not have had a mama who cared or a father who could until it was too late, but this boy and any children born into our family will never know that kind of pain. He's got two parents who love each other and will love him fiercely, but he's also got two uncles and the women in their lives who will do the same.

I bend at the same time I lift my arms up and press my lips to Grayson's tiny head before handing him back to his mama.

When I'm finally able to look away and at Caroline, I'm not sure how to read what I see in her eyes. For as long as I can remember I've known I'd never bring a child of my own into the world. The way I'd been raised hadn't shown me anything positive in the way of having my own children. Looking at the woman I can't imagine a life without, with the reminder of what my nephew felt like in my arms, makes me want to be able to see something other than what I've always believed.

17

CAROLINE

"Sunday Morning" by Parmalee

I climb into bed and pull the covers up over my bare legs. I can hear Clayton as he moves through the house, locking up and setting the alarm. He's been quiet since we left the hospital. To be honest, I'm glad for the silence. Watching him holding Quinn and Tate's son shifted something inside of me, something I hadn't been sure was there. Something I hadn't even been sure I had even wanted until I met Clayton. Knowing his past, I was completely unsure if the man I was building a future with wanted the same thing.

Children.

I never thought about that for myself.

Why would I? I was raised by a woman who hated me, hardly tolerated me, and had been one of the main reasons I desperately traded one nightmare for another. I went from living with her hate to just surviving another's. I never would have brought a child into that. Luckily, John had been meticulous about protection and I had never had to deal with that problem.

I've never experienced the positive love of a mother, and I'm not sure that's something I capable of, but seeing Clayton with a baby in his arms and a look of pure, tender love, I started to hope.

I know, though, that if that's something Clayton doesn't want, I will never have it, because there will never be another man for me. My heart only belongs to one man and without him, I'll never bring a child into this world. Knowing that, it feels like a dark cloud has settled over a special night.

"I could hear you thinkin' downstairs, Linney." I jump at the sound of Clayton's voice, so lost in my thoughts I didn't even notice him enter the bedroom.

He starts unbuttoning his plaid button-down, pulling it off and grabbing the white undershirt he had on underneath and yanking it off too. His belt clanks on the floor in the silence after he toes his boots off and then, in one fluid motion, he's got his jeans and boxer briefs off. I don't look away when he straightens and hooks his hands at his hips, studying me with silent consideration.

"We've got two choices, sweetness." His brow is furrowed, but other than that he appears calm. I know my dark cowboy better than that, though. He's holding his control close to his chest. "We can either finish what we were talkin' about in the waitin' room earlier or . . ." He looks down, shakes his head, and, with a heavy breath, glances back at me. "Or you can tell me what I saw in your eyes when you watched me holdin' my nephew."

"I . . . Clayton." My thundering heart jumps into my throat and I feel my lips press together tightly. He waits, but without being able to find the words I need to continue, I lift both my shoulders, silently telling him I need his guidance, because I honestly don't know if I can pick one over the other. Not when I could be getting his love in one breath and losing a piece of my heart in the next.

He steps forward and rounds the bed. I track his every movement until he's standing next to my side of the bed. When his hands leave his hips, I glance down and watch with wide eyes as they both slowly come toward me. He pulls the covers from where I have them tucked into my hips, baring my legs. He makes a sound of disapproval when I start to pull the shirt of his I stole—like every night—to sleep in over my panties, halting me instantly. When he takes my ankles in his strong grip, I close my eyes, not even shocked when he pulls me gently down the bed until my back is no longer against the pillows propped up against the headboard. Even in the heaviness of the moment, his strength is something that amazes me.

His hands push between my legs at the knees and spread them to the side. Then his heavy weight blankets me. Legs between mine, hard length against my panty-covered center, and naked chest over my cotton-covered one. My hands move of their own accord to rest on his back at the same time his arms go under my shoulders, pushing his fingers into my hair and cradling my head in his hands.

"Open your eyes," he orders, and I do so instantly.

His face hovers above mine, eyes searching but guarded. I don't have to guess what he assumed correctly I was thinking back at the hospital, but I know without a doubt that I need him to know one thing before I confirm it.

"I love you," I utter on a whispered breath.

I literally feel my words as they hit him, physically, as his whole body seems to grow larger and harder at once. The fingers tangled with my hair spasm. His chest pushes into mine as it puffs out. And the part of him that fills me with a beautiful pain swells against my sex.

"I love you," I repeat loudly and fiercely, fueled by his reaction. This time, his eyelids droop and his forehead falls to rest against mine. That wide chest of his starts to move rapidly when his breathing speeds up.

"I love you, Clayton Davis."

Then his mouth is on mine and his tongue plays with mine without pause. He kisses me so deeply that my eyes cross and I swear I can feel the earth move. There's so much passion in this kiss, my legs come off the bed to wrap around his hips and my arms tighten around his torso. I frantically try to get closer. We continue to pour

our feelings into that kiss, both of us growing more desperate with each caress of tongues and swallowed groans. When he rips his mouth free, it takes me a moment to shake the intoxication of it off.

"It shouldn't be possible to love you as much as I do, Caroline Michaels, but every single day I feel that grow into somethin' I reckon few ever are blessed to feel. I knew close to four months ago when you sat down next to me that there was somethin' powerful between us. Had no doubts a month later that connection was somethin' I was foolin' myself into thinkin' I could forget about when it snapped into place. And, my sweet Linney, it wasn't long after that that I realized I was made to love you."

He shifts his grasp, his hands coming out from under my head and his thumbs wiping the tears from my face. My whole body shudders as I suck in a wobbly breath.

"I need to know the rest, darlin'," he says with care.

"I'm afraid to give you the rest, Clayton."

He shakes his head. His handsome face relaxes and openly projects his affection. "Nothin' should ever make you afraid, Linney. Not when it comes to me and damn sure not when it comes to our love. I never want you feelin' the fear that keeps your thoughts from me."

My chest smooshes against his as I take a deep and calming breath. "I—I want that," I finally admit.

He holds my worried gaze, not reacting. "You want what?"

"What they have."

I finally lose the brightness of his emerald gaze when his eyes slowly flutter closed. A rush of air fans my face a second later. I hold myself still as my heart pounds in anxious beats.

"Please say somethin', Clayton," I plead when he doesn't move or speak.

"I don't want her here," he finally says, confusing me instantly.

"What?"

"She has no place in our bed, but I also can't let you go long enough to move our talk from this spot."

"Who are you talkin' about?"

"Jess."

My whole body jerks as his ex's name slams into my brain. Confusion as to why he's bringing her up now of all times blends into a hurt I feel slice deep.

"God, Caroline, you're killin' me." His hips press into mine as he shifts his body to rest his elbows in the mattress. "Look at me, baby."

I hadn't realized I stopped. Looking back into his beautiful eyes again, I see the pain inside of them.

"She was pregnant. Right after I finally broke things off, all her schemin' paid off. When she told me, I was going to step up. In my gut, I knew I didn't want that baby, but I would've been there and done my best to give it a good life. However, I wasn't gonna give her what she thought she could trick me into." A slash of pain goes through his features as he grows heavier on top of me, and I know where he's going, hating that woman even more. "When I refused her when she said we should get married right away, makin' it clear to her that would *never* be an option, she knew she'd miscalculated drastically. I never in my life thought she would kill my baby because of it though."

"Clayton," I gasp, moving my hands to cup his strong jaw. "Honey."

"It cut me to the quick, but even though I felt like a piece of my heart had been ripped out, I struggled with feelin' relieved as well. It's fucked-up, I know that, but with her selfishness, I wouldn't be forced to have her in my life because she had my kid."

"I'm so sorry," I tell him, my tears returning.

"I had a mama who couldn't love me and a father who didn't want to until he was dyin'. I didn't know my grandparents. The only real love I felt was toward my brother and sister. And with them, I saw what havin' shit parents did to kids. I grew up knowin' I didn't want to bring a life into the world without knowin' I'd be capable of what my parents weren't. That didn't change when she killed my baby, Caroline. I can't explain what it felt like holdin' my sister's baby in my arms, but even lovin' that boy instantly, if I didn't have you, I would never want that for myself. You make me *need* everythin' I never wanted."

A giant sob bursts from my lips.

"I told you we were gonna have this talk." He gives me a brief kiss. "I told you that what I wanted for our future would be different from what I wanted with her. I could live without anyone in this whole damn world, but you . . . I couldn't go on without you. I'm a man who knows what he needs, Linney, and that's you. I won't waste time when I know in my marrow that you're made for me to love. Ask me, baby. Ask me what roads we're traveling on."

"Wh-what roads?"

"The ones that collide together and form one indestructible path. One day, one day real damn soon, that road is gonna give you my name and give us a family that will never doubt what parents' love feels like. We both had a rough start, darlin', but there isn't anything we can't weather together. I knew it was time to cowboy up the second my good girl gave me her bad and together we made magic."

I'm crying so hard now, he had to stop talking softly halfway through that. I can see his smiling face, so full of love for me, through the tears swimming in my eyes. I blink frantically, but the tears keep coming. Not even when his lips drop to mine and we drown in each other's kisses do they stop. My sobs echo around the room as he undresses me, only slowing when he pushes himself into my body. By the time he's given me every thick inch, I finally stop crying. The passion between us is a soothing balm to my tears, which dissolve in the overpowering joy tipping me over the edge as I lose myself in the all-consuming sensation of the man I love loving me slow.

13

CAROLINE

"Humble and Kind" by Tim McGraw

— ★ —

You know the old saying when something feels too good to be true, it probably is? Well, there's no doubt to its validity in my eyes. Not after I wake up the next morning and the bubble of perfect love that had formed around Clayton and me pops. Only, when Clayton wakes me up this morning with worry hanging off him like a coat and tells me there's been another fire, the tears don't come. When I call Luke and hear him confirm what Clayton told me, I just feel a sad acceptance of what it means. There's no fear. No panic. Just the knowledge that whatever follows will be okay because I have Clayton to help me find my way through it.

The Sequel is completely gone.

What had been rebuilt and put on the market was just a pile of ash now.

There's also no doubt in anyone's mind that this fire was intentional. No matter what the report said about the first one, everyone now knows that one had been as well. What we don't know, though, is why.

"Talk to me, Linney," Clayton asks with a hint of desperate worry in his tone.

"What do you want me to say?"

"Jesus, baby, you just found out that someone intentionally set fire to the old store and you don't even look upset."

I shrug. "I'm upset, but not because it's gone. It was just an empty space. My dreams aren't tied up in there, and my happiness is not something I can only find in the pages of the books I sold. A few months ago, this probably would have felt a lot different, but then I went explorin' and I've got a path full of somethin' I never dreamed of. I'm stronger now. Too strong to let this break me."

"Fuck, I love you."

A small smile forms on my lips at his words. "The thing that bothers me now, even though I hate thinkin' that someone else might not be able to make a dream of my old space, is that I don't understand why *I'm* bein' targeted. Even though Luke said there was another fire across town at another business, I can't help but feel in my gut this is personal."

"What are you thinkin', darlin'?"

I sigh, shrug, and shake my head. "Do you think . . . Could this be John?"

A flash of anger crosses his face. "Do *you* think it could be?"

"I honestly don't know, Clayton. The John I knew years ago wasn't a good person, but he was an angry drunk who preferred to use his words and strength to hurt someone. He wanted people to know he was powerful in that way. Hiding behind a fire doesn't make sense. I just can't see him wakin' up one day and decidin' today is a good day to become an arsonist."

"Just because he didn't show it then doesn't mean he didn't have more malicious intent hidin' away and waitin' to come out."

"I know, I know. But it just doesn't feel like somethin' he'd do. If he's even still in town, he'd corner me somewhere before he'd hide behind a fire and not let me know he was the one who took more from me. The man I knew would've left no doubt it was him."

Clayton drops his head, looking down at his boots.

"What?"

A little pit of unease opens in my gut when he just shakes his head.

"Clayton. Tell me what's goin' through your head."

"Goddamn," Clayton grunts. "You knew him as a boy, Linney. You don't know him as a man."

"I was with him for close to six years. I might have

started with him when he was a boy, but he was a man when I finally left."

"And you haven't seen or really talked to him in close to another five, darlin'. People change, and you might not know the man that he is today."

I take a calming breath. Placing my palms on the counter, planting my feet on the rungs on the barstool at the kitchen island, I arch my brows at Clayton.

"I asked you to trust me," he finally answers my un-spoken silent demand that he continue.

"I do, but I don't need you keepin' somethin' from me because you think I need you to protect me from him. He can't hurt me, even if he is the one behind the fires. He'll never touch me again." The confidence I'm starting to get used to rushes through my body. I can tell the second Clayton realizes that while I trust him completely, I won't back down from this conversation.

"Son of a bitch," he grunts under his breath, studying my face before shaking his head and continuing. "I've had problems with him for a while, Caroline. A lot of those problems are ugly, and I wanted to spare you that shit."

"What did you tell me about the ugly in our past, Clayton? I got you and you got me; all of that stuff we've dealt with in our lives just helped us get to this point. So stop thinkin' I can't handle it and let me show you how strong your love helped me become."

"Fine," he grinds out unhappily. "I've known John

Lewis since his family moved to Pine Oak. He was a middle school punk then, as I'm sure you know, but his arrogance didn't turn dangerous until years later. I never liked him, but I didn't hate the man until more recent years. It started when Jess used him to attempt to make me jealous. Didn't bother me that she was carryin' on with him, but him tryin' to pick a fight with me got real old, real quick. He mighta had a drinkin' problem when you left him, but he developed a drug problem on top of that when he came back to Pine Oak."

"How long has he been back?" I ask, unable to stop the chill that trickles down my spine just thinking about him being so close to where I've settled, even if he never made an attempt at making me aware of that. Just thinking about how easy it could have been for him to inflict pain on me makes my heart race.

"Way I figure, right after you left him. Dates seem to match up."

"I never knew."

"Darlin', he was so strung out, I don't think he knew which way was up, let alone that you were only a half hour, forty-five minutes tops, away."

"Tell me the rest, Clayton. I can see all over your face that there's more."

He runs his fingers through his hair, his naked chest flexing as he does. "He was supplyin' drugs to some of the newer hands here on the ranch back then. I busted him myself when I came back from a night ride checkin' the property after a nasty storm to find him in my fuckin' barn dealin'. He was so high, but he was even more reckless. He took off before the sheriff got here, but not before his strung-out ass took out a fence *and* killed two of my horses on his way out. He didn't even slow, Linney. Blew right through them in his daddy's jacked-up truck. First time I've seen him since was that afternoon outside the diner in Wire Creek. I know he went to jail, heard rehab followed, but I'm not ready to eliminate him from the list of suspects who could be responsible for this just because he supposedly got help."

I shake my head, shocked by what he's telling me.

"I should've told you, but after you confided how bad things were when you were with him, I didn't want you havin' more reasons to fear that man. Not when I had hoped to protect you from that."

"You really think it's him?" A tremor hits me and I shiver, making Clayton push off the counter and walk over to me, pulling me from my seat and into his arms.

"I don't know, darlin', but I'm not goin' to assume it isn't." He presses a kiss to the top of my head and tightens his soothing embrace. "I'm sorry I kept that from you, but I'd do it again if I felt like I could keep you from shakin' like you are right now."

I shift closer and press my face against his chest. Clayton's scent fills my lungs and calms my racing thoughts. "Thank you for tellin' me, honey. I don't like hearin' it, you're right, but it makes me thankful I got out and got another chance at happiness. I'm not convinced it's him, but I'm also not convinced it isn't."

"I'm not gonna let anythin' happen to you. You know that, right?"

"Yeah, honey. If it's all the same to you, I'm goin' to hold off on startin' the process of openin' The Sequel here in Pine Oak. I know Luke doesn't need help at Hazel's anymore, but I'm goin' to give him a call and see if I can work in the—" I stop talking when I feel the man holding me growl, the sound in his chest vibrating against my cheek.

"You ain't workin' in that bar, Caroline. I respect Luke, and your friendship with him and Lucy, but I won't have you workin' in Hazel's when I know how rowdy that crowd is."

"Luke won't let anything happen to me, honey."

"Luke can't watch you *and* run that place at the same time. If you're worried about money, don't be. You never have to work another day if you don't want to."

I untangle myself from his hold and narrow my eyes at him. "I will not sit at home and do nothin' while you bust your tail all day, Clayton Davis. I'm not an idle woman, but even if I were, I won't be like *her*." I poke him in the chest, the thought of his vile ex and how she just wanted to use him for his money making me see red at his implication that I should be a kept woman and live off his hard work.

He wraps his hand around my finger when I poke him

one more time, and I almost melt into a puddle when he smiles that devastating grin of his. "Calm down, darlin'. You know damn well I don't think you're with me for my money. If you want to keep busy until you're ready to open the store here in town, you can take over the accounting for Davis Auto Works and here on the ranch. I hate dealin' with that shit, so you'd be doin' me a favor."

He had already successfully dashed my ire with that smile, but learning that he trusts me with something so important to him—his ranch and family business—a whole new emotion hits me, and hits hard.

"Clayton," I breathe.

"Don't go givin' me breathy Claytons now, sweetness," he warns, pressing against me and pulling me close by the hips so that I don't miss his erection.

"I really wanna be bad with you right now," I shamelessly admit, feeling a rush of arousal curl low in my belly and wrap around the base of my spine.

"Fuck, I love you," he rumbles, bending enough to pull me into his arms. My legs go around his body and my eyes all but cross when his hardness presses firmly against my aching core.

"I'd love to help take some work off your plate. I won't have you payin' me, but I meant it when I said I wasn't an idle woman."

"You keep givin' me this greedy-for-my-cock pussy and I'm pretty sure you'll be the one payin' me."

"You're naughty." I giggle, speaking against his neck,

kissing my way across his skin, and feeling the heat of his words bathe me in intoxicating pleasure. I rock my hips, wishing my lounge pants weren't in the way. "I love it when you show me your bad."

He hums, his fingers tightening on my bottom when I bite the thick column of his neck. Even with my pants and his jeans between us, my belly starts to flutter. My hips rock and roll quicker as his hold on me turns just a hair shy of painful. Thinking about his hands leaving bruises on my tender skin oddly only makes me hotter. His erection rubs me in the most toe-curling spot, and from that contact alone, I drop my head back, seeing the ceiling for just a second before my eyes roll back and close; then I come with his name on my lips.

"God fuckin' damn, that's the hottest thing I've ever seen, darlin'. You comin' from just rubbin' yourself against my cock, fuck," he groans, pulling me harder against his erection, pressing firmly against my sensitive sex and making me whimper. "My good girl doesn't need any help bein' bad anymore, does she? I'm about to love you so hard, you'll think I'm still inside you for days. So vividly that you'll take one step, feel what my hard does to you, and come from just the thought of me takin' you alone."

"Yes," I mewl. "Please."

"Go get in our bed. I want you waitin' for me, spread so wide, offerin' me that sweet pussy so I can eat my fuckin' breakfast in bed. I'm goin' to call Drew and let him know I'm takin' a sick day."

I jump down from his hold, my whole body alive and craving his promises. I don't even spare him a glance before I'm sprinting through the house, tossing my clothes as I go, and following his every command. Then, true to his words, he joins me a few minutes later and spends the day showing me just how delicious breakfast in bed can be.

19

CAROLINE

"Make You Mine" by High Valley

———— ★ ————

"**I**'m gonna kill her."

Lucy makes a snarling sound in her throat, backing up Leighton's threat without words.

I keep my mouth shut but grab Leighton's hand before she can leave the table at which Jana had told her, firmly and without room to argue, to "sit down and not move from that spot" not even five minutes after walking into her bakery. I feel the wide-eyed stares of the people in the shop around us, but it oddly doesn't bother me, proof that I really am becoming stronger. The only thing I care about in this moment is the nasty woman causing a scene inside my boyfriend's sister-in-law's bakery. His very, very pregnant sister-in-law's bakery. And that woman is going to find out just what the new me is capable of.

"You might think you've got him," Jess continues in a snarky tone. "Hell, you might even keep his attention for a little while, but he'll be back. He always comes back. No woman stands a chance at changin' that."

"You stupid bitch. Smartest thing he ever did was scrape you off, and he wasn't stupid enough to come back to you once since then. You can be damn sure he isn't gonna do it now," Leighton snaps with fury in her words.

"We have a history!" Jess shrieks, her beautiful face turning hideous and revealing her true nature.

I stay silent and study Clayton's ex. Jess really is lovely, I'll give her that, but she's the kind of woman who thinks that beauty is the be-all and end-all. The type that *only* has their beauty going for them and it really doesn't get them as far as they're convinced it does. Every time she throws more nasty words around, her shoulders start shaking with temper, her long blond hair swinging. Her blue eyes are cold, calculating, and full of vicious evil. She's taller than me and bustier than me, with curves I'll never have.

And I've never felt more beautiful.

"Your desperation is embarrassing," I finally say, low and steady, not backing down when that evil gaze homes in on me.

I stand and step in front of Leighton when Jess moves forward. Her eyes track my movements like a predator hunting its prey. Before Clayton, I would've curled into myself and backed down instantly under the weight of her stare and impending confrontation. Now, though, I'm ready to take this horrible woman on, and there's no way in hell I'm letting her close enough to Leighton to have even a slight chance of harming her or the baby.

"How does it feel to have my sloppy seconds?" she mocks.

I roll my eyes. "Bless your heart, honey. You really believe that, don't you? Insinuatin' a man as incredible as Clayton Davis could ever be sloppy seconds to any woman is pathetic and insultin'. You might think what you had with *my* man is worthy of bein' some second-hand, used-goods kinda love, but that handsome cowboy has never loved another woman until me. You were just a way to pass time until we found our way to each other."

She moves closer, stepping on my sandal-covered feet with her boots and making a shooting pain jolt through my body when she rolls her weight onto my toes. I don't give her the pleasure of flinching, though. I hold myself strong and true, unwilling to give her the upper hand.

"I was pregnant with his baby," she hisses, thankfully low enough that the people eating farther away can't hear.

Again, I don't react. Not even when I hear Leighton gasp as the secret Clayton kept from his family unfolds. I see Lucy start to stand in my peripheral vision, but I wave her off.

I might not care what the gawkers around me think anymore, but I won't allow Jess to hurt Clayton by bringing something so painful to light.

Moving my face closer, I sneer at her. "Correction, *bitch*, you tricked him and then *killed* his baby. Even if you ever had a chance at experiencin' the beauty of his love, you were dead to him when you showed him how nasty he already knew you were by doin' that."

I can tell she hadn't planned on me knowing the truth, but when her hand comes out and cracks against my cheek, I lose the upper hand.

"That is enough!" I hear Jana bellow from behind the counter.

"I'm fine, Jana," I call in her direction, pressing my hand against my cheek and not looking away from Jess.

"I'm gonna kill her," Leighton grumbles, repeating her threat angrily behind me, but thankfully, she doesn't move. I feel her knees bouncing against the back of my legs, so I don't need to turn to make sure she's still sitting. I'm not going to have another pregnant woman go into labor because she got too excited at the crazy that keeps invading my life.

"You can have that hit, Jess. I'd be mad too if I lost someone as amazin' as Clayton, but honey, you never did deserve him. I want you to really listen now. I'm gonna marry that man. In fact, he can't wait to get his ring on my finger. I didn't have to trick him into wantin' that. When the day comes that I'm blessed enough to share somethin' as beautiful as a child we created with our love, I'll be thankin' my lucky stars to have a gift that incredible. And we'll have that baby, Jess. It will be one that we both enjoy the hell outta workin' to get—without tricks and lies. We're gonna raise a house full of babies on that ranch. Babies we would have tomorrow, we want that blessin' built from our love that bad. Both of us. And sweetheart, I'm gonna keep lovin' Clayton so hard he'll feel that long after we've both left this earth."

"You stupid bitch. Clay doesn't believe in marriage." She cackles, the sound evil and malevolent, either not hearing me or really believing, after years of not having him, that Clayton might be pining away for her.

I press my hand against her breastbone, pushing her out of my face. After I get her a step away from me, I pull my phone from my back pocket and bring up Clayton's name. I hold up a finger in Jess's face and wiggle it a little before pointing down at my phone and tapping the speakerphone button. Ringing fills the shocked silence at the PieHole and this time I don't care that our audience is making an attempt to get a little closer and hear us better.

"Hey darlin'," Clayton answers, his voice soft and happy. I picture him smiling that heart-pounding smile and my own grows.

"Honey," I answer lightly, not wanting him to hear just how tense I am, but I should've known he'd hear it anyway. My cowboy knows his woman.

"What's wrong, Linney?"

"Nothin' I can't handle. You have a second?"

I hear him speak to someone, hear him moving around

a moment later before the click of a door shutting comes over the line. "Always got a second for you, baby."

"I don't want to keep you, I know you've got the doc out there checkin' on things."

"It's fine, Linney. Just finished with the last foal. I've got time before we move on to the fillies and colts."

"All right, honey." I pull the phone away and whisper to Jess. "Listen carefully." When her eyes flash, I pull the phone back up and address Clayton again. "You wanna get married, handsome?"

"You free in an hour, sweetness?" he answers immediately.

"I'm a little tied up right now, but I think an hour could be doable."

"I'll meet you at the courthouse then."

I laugh, feeling his love through the line wrapping me up in a cocoon of happiness. I don't even care if this didn't start out serious. I can't think of anything better than being his wife. I want this. As crazy fast as it is, I think I knew he was my forever the second he bought me a whiskey and promised to show me bad. "Only if you promise to start working on giving me those babies we both want right after our date at the courthouse."

The rumble of his deep chuckle comes through the line and I find my smile growing even bigger until my cheeks burn from the sheer insanity of my grin.

"My girl's got an itch to be bad?"

I hear Lucy and Leighton start snickering as heat

crawls over my skin. I might be ready to ignore the busy-bodies and nosy old biddies, but I bet any woman would blush hearing Clayton Davis make an announcement like that to a roomful of people. Difference is, I don't even care anymore. Let them know how much I love being a bad girl.

"I like the way you think, honey," I say softly, my eyes on the red-faced woman a foot in front of me. "But I think I'll take lovin' you slow before you love me bad."

"I love you, Linney," he drawls slowly in the erotic way that only Clayton can achieve with the deep raspy tones of his voice.

"I love you, Clayton."

"Linney?" he calls before I have a chance to say good-bye.

"Yeah, honey?"

"You let Jess know if she ever comes near you again, not even my woman callin' and givin' me her sweetness will be enough to keep her safe from my anger."

The woman in question jerks her head and gapes at the phone in my hand. I'm not even surprised that he knew about her being here. There isn't anything that gets by him, especially when it comes to my well-being.

"There won't be a safe place left in Pine Oak for her if she pulls that shit again," he says, the fury in his words unmistakable.

"You're on speaker, Clayton," I tell him, not taking my eyes off Jess.

"Good, baby. Maybe she'll heed my words this time

and not twist them up in her head to be whatever crazy shit she's convinced herself of this time. You enjoy your time with the girls, but when you finish you better get that sweet ass home so I can get my ring on your hand."

"What?" I gasp.

His deep, low laughter is the only answer I get before he disconnects the call with his parting shot still ringing in my ears. He doesn't just shock the nasty woman who interrupted my girl time though. He also floors me as well. I had been joking. I wanted to put his awful ex in her place, but the second the words left my mouth it became something else. I can't help but feel a little anxious over what will happen when I go home. I don't know if he's serious but hope he is, even if it makes us both crazy. When you know, you know. But the part of me that's completely owned by him can't stop the rush of pure pleasure I get when I think that he might have been planning for this if he really does have a ring.

"Holy cow," Leighton gasps breathily.

"Oh my *God*!" Lucy screams.

"I knew that sexy brooder would be a scorcher!" Jana bellows from her position behind the pie displays. "Just knew he'd give it real good."

With a pounding heart that has nothing to do with the showdown I just went through, I give Jess one last arch of my brow and let my whiskey-filled teacup boil over one more time. "Get out of my face, Jess. Get out of Leighton's place. And learn something from today."

I turn, my ponytail slapping across her face, and return to my seat at the table I had been sitting at before she stormed into the PieHole and started throwing her crap all over the place.

Clapping my hands, I look between Leighton and Lucy. "So, where were we?"

20

CAROLINE

"No Matter Where You Are" by Us The Duo

When I pull into the drive to the ranch, butterflies erupt in my gut. It's still early in the afternoon, so I know Clayton isn't going to be in the house, but that doesn't ease my nerves, but with the size of the Davis ranch, finding him is going to be like hunting for a needle in a haystack. I pull my car into my spot next to Clayton's truck and lean back against the headrest, closing my eyes, thinking about what could be waiting for me. The steady breeze from my air-conditioning cools my overheated skin in the process.

As anxious as I feel, I'm not going to be shy and timid about it. Not anymore. Even if he was joking, I have no doubt it'll one day happen for us. I'd be lying, though, if I didn't admit that I'd be disappointed now that the thought is in my head.

I want to be his.

I want him to be mine.

In the forever way that binds us legally and in the eyes of God.

I want to spend the rest of my life with Clayton Davis while he gives me bad and gives me the power to find myself with the confidence his love provides me.

A loud pounding pulls me out of my thoughts with a scream. My knees slam against my steering column as I almost come out of my skin. My eyes snap open and my hand flies to my chest as I look out the driver's-side window. My heart is still thundering in my rib cage, the lingering rush of panic from being caught off guard while I daydreamed still making it hard to focus.

Clearly having had enough of my wide-eyed staring, Clayton thumps his cowboy hat brim as he studies me through the window. With his hat farther up on his head, I can see his face clearly without shadows. His brows are pulled tight in confusion, but a small smirk is curling his lips. He shakes his head a few times, that smirk turning into a full grin, before reaching out to pull open my door.

I still don't move. I can't even blame it on the fact that he scared the crap out of me while I had been in la-la land. Nope. I don't move because he's looking at me in a way that has sucked the air out of my body and melted all my bones.

"Linney, love," he rasps, "you look cute as hell right

now, but I need you to stop lookin' like shock's got you trapped and get outta the car so I can get you in my arms."

"You scared me," I whisper, shaking my head in the smallest movements. So much for being a big brave girl. I was a fool to think I could handle a conversation of this magnitude without feeling a little trepidation.

"I noticed that, darlin'."

"You don't sound upset about it." I huff out a breath and cross my arms over my chest. Clayton's eyes move down and I follow his gaze to see that my flowy tank is giving him one heck of a show, the shirt's front now pulled low with my arms being crossed. The tops of my breasts and some of my white lace bra peek out of the wide scoop neck. I roll my eyes when he still doesn't look away, uncrossing my arms and pulling the material up. "A gentleman wouldn't have looked, Clayton."

"Sweetness, when it comes to you there isn't anything gentlemanly about the thoughts that constantly keep me company."

"Well . . ." I trail off, not having a good retort. "I didn't even show you much. You'd think I didn't keep you satisfied the way you're reactin' to a small glimpse of my boobs. Next time I'm tryin' to throw a fit, you could at least not be all swoon-worthy and distractin'."

"Linney, all it would take for me to react and be ready to feel your heat around my cock is you walking into a room. You don't need to give me a tease. But the lace was a bonus . . ."

"You're incorrigible." I sigh with a smile, turning off my car and getting to my feet between the car and Clayton's body when he doesn't move to give me more space.

His hands come up, fingers brushing against my cheeks. I rest mine at his waist and tip my head up to study my dark cowboy as he gazes at me. His eyes devour me, his hands not idle as he drags his fingertips down the column of my neck and down my bare arms until he reaches my elbows. Then he repeats his trail back up until he's holding me with his palms right under my jaw. He pushes his fingers lightly into my hair as best as he can with it up in a ponytail, and his thumbs rub against my cheeks with slow glides that awaken every inch of me.

"Hey," he whispers in a bold tone that makes his already deep voice sound a few degrees deeper. Velvet and sandpaper.

"Hey," I parrot back, sounding like I just ran a marathon. The way he's looking at me right now, *this* is something I've never seen from him. This, right here, is my dark cowboy giving me everything silently. Himself, his love, our future. All of it is shining bright down on us. The warm buzz that travels over my skin has nothing to do with the summer Texas sun high in the sky.

My fingers flex, doing nothing more than move against his stone-like muscles, as I make no attempt to gain purchase on his skin. My feet shuffle forward until I feel the toes of his cowboy boots. My hands go behind his back as I press my body against his and tip my head up. His back flexes under my touch, but other than that, he doesn't move an inch. Just gazes down at me, holding me gently.

"I got a lot I want to say about your call earlier, Caroline," he tells me softly. "You've got my head all twisted up, though, and I can't figure out if now is the time to say even half of the shit that's rollin' around without freakin' you out. But you brought it up, and now I don't think I *can* sit on it any longer."

The rapid tattoo of my heart has my breathing speeding up, but with his bright green eyes showing me nothing but the enormity of his love, I feel it—the fearlessness that only Clayton brings out in me.

"It's time," I rush without hesitation.

His face gets soft and he bends slightly to press his lips lightly against mine. He doesn't deepen the kiss, just gives me a brief peck before lifting his head a degree as he keeps his eyes locked on mine. "Yeah?"

"Oh, yeah." My breathy affirmation is met with his eyes flashing with pleasure, the corners of his mouth tipping up, and the laugh lines around his eyes coming out. He adjusts his hold, his hands falling down a little until his palms are resting against either side of my neck.

"You . . . God, Linney," he drones, shaking his head but still smiling. "First, you're okay?"

Knowing instantly he's referring to the fact that I had words with his ex, I nod. "I'm fine, honey."

"When I got word that Jess was at the PieHole throwin' her shit around, it wasn't pretty. I almost took off Drew's head when he reminded me I couldn't do a single thing with the doc out lookin' over the horses and two buyers out from Montana. I didn't give one a damn about my responsibilities here when you are and will always be more important than anything else. If you hadn't called me when you did, I woulda been there in a second, not givin' one fuck about how much money I'd lose walkin' away from those Montana folks."

"I'm fine," I stress, hoping he understands that I mean it.

"I know. I just can't seem to help myself when it comes to you, darlin'. The thought of you feelin' anything other than happiness and love isn't somethin' I enjoy too much."

I tighten my arms around his body and lean up on my toes to attempt to get closer than our height differences allow, wanting him to really see me clearly.

"Clayton Davis, you've given me nothin' but happiness for over four months now, and I have no doubt you'll continue to do so for a long while, but there'll be times that even *you* can't control everything. Life might toss us some ugly. But I'm ready to take it on now if it does. Trust that I'm not goin' to break just because some of that ugly tries to creep around us."

"Trustin' you has nothin' to do with me wantin' to protect you and keep you safe from all of that, Linney."

"And that, honey, is what makes me feel like I'm strong enough to take on anything. Knowin' that you care that much, that you'll be there to keep me from trippin', gives me the confidence to finally live free of fear and worry.

There isn't a dadgum thing on this green earth that has the power to douse that. Not anymore."

"You want the rest?" he asks after holding my gaze for a few minutes, the weight of my words rolling over us.

I nod, his thumbs rubbing against my jaw as I do.

He releases his hold on my neck, drags his work-roughened hands down my skin until he's got my wrists in his hold, and unwraps my arms from around his body. Silently, he places my palms on his shoulders and leans down. The brim of his hat drags over the top of my head while he continues to get so close I can feel the heat of his lips against mine.

"Hold on," he rasps, confusing me.

When he grabs me at the back of my thighs and lifts, I squeal out in shock before wrapping my arms around his neck and pressing my chest into his face in order to keep my balance. Miraculously, I manage to stop acting like a weirdo long enough to grab his hat as it's knocked off with the force of my freak-out. Keeping my legs tight, I lift my chest out of his face and release the arm holding his hat to place it back on his head. When the hat blocks my view, I pull it back off and plop it on my own head. Mindlessly, I use my free hand to run my fingers through his thick, unruly hair. His body moves as he laughs softly and my hand freezes in its third pass.

"You look good in my hat, darlin'."

I shrug, the movement making his hat fall down over my forehead.

"Though I should probably get you one that fits better," he jokes.

I lift my hand back off his shoulders to adjust the too-large hat. Not wanting the anticipation to get thicker, I ignore his joke. Mentally, I take one last swing at the walls I had used to protect me for my whole life and give the man holding me everything. I know he sees the enormity of my feelings written all over my face when his whole body jolts and his eyes darken. "You've got me now, handsome. Time to give me the rest."

He starts walking, not looking away from me and me not looking away from him. When he turns us from the house and toward the stables, I frown in confusion.

"Trust me?" he questions, not missing a beat, knowing me well.

"Always," I answer emphatically.

His chest expands with my answer like that one word was everything to him. He enters the stable that houses his personal horses. I don't ever make it my mission to come in here with all the black-eyed beasts, but I know enough about this place that when he stops at the last stall, chills break out.

Onyx.

I know very little about him, but I heard Clayton and Drew talking about him and what I discovered broke my heart. He's a pure black Arabian horse that Clayton saved. I don't know all the details, but something along the lines of Onyx's old owners sold him for meat in exchange for cash. When a shipment of horses was stopped on its way to Canada, one of Clayton's old friends called him for help in placing the fifteen horses on their way to slaughter. No one wanted Onyx, so Clayton loaded him up and brought him back to the ranch.

That was about three months ago, and according to what I've overheard, Clayton spends every spare second he isn't needed elsewhere working with Onyx. When I first came here I remember seeing Onyx from a distance as he bucked and bucked, going wild in his desire to be left alone and even though I feared him immensely, I felt drawn to the beast.

I feel the horse's eyes on me as Clayton brings us farther in, and I shiver in his arms.

"You doin' all right, darlin'?"

I nod, not trusting myself to verbally answer without fear in my voice.

"I wouldn't bring you in here if I didn't think Onyx was ready to finally meet you."

I jerk my wide eyes from the black beast and look at Clayton. "What?"

"Knew the second I saw Onyx he was meant for you. He's a fighter. Hell, he'd fight the wind if he thought it was tryin' to get in his way. He's beyond loyal to those he lets close though. You earn that from him and he'll protect you from everything and anything. Includin' that damn wind. I knew the second I found him that there was only one person a warrior like Onyx was built for."

Shocked by his words, I can't do anything but drink in my handsome man's serious expression. When I feel something nudge my back, I jump in Clayton's arms. His whole face grows soft and full of affection.

"Told you," he grunts, tipping his chin in the direction behind me.

I turn, finding Onyx close to my back, his eyes focusing completely on me. When I don't move, he bumps me again with his nose and makes a show of blowing air through his nostrils. Clayton turns us so that his back is to Onyx, allowing me to study the beast without turning my neck so harshly. Something in the way the horse is looking at me sends a rightness-filled calm through me. I lift one hand and slowly move it toward Onyx. His tail swishes, and before I have a second to let myself fear him, he bumps the tip of his nose against my palm. He does this twice more before I find myself smiling at his antics and rubbing my hand against the slope of his head. If he were a cat, I imagine he'd be purring loudly.

"He likes you," Clayton says softly, kissing me against my neck. "I've been waitin' for this moment, and darlin', I had no doubts that you two would click instantly. You haven't been around horses enough to understand, but you've just become the most important person to him and all you did was give him your trust. Onyx and me . . . we've got that in common. All it took was one touch from you and you became our everything."

I keep caressing Onyx, but feel emotion grow into a thick ball in my throat. "Honey," I breathe, not capable of more.

"It sounds like a pile of shit, but I promise you, Linney, I mean everything I just said."

"He's just a horse. A horse that just wanted to be petted."

Clayton laughs, his hilarity jolting my body. "Darlin', in the time that Onyx has been here, he hasn't willingly let a soul touch him. He tolerates what's needed to cool him down after a ride, and that's usually done with a lot of bullshit from him. I can feel him itchin' to buck even me, someone he likes slightly more than toleratin', right off when I'm walkin' him."

I lift my hand from Onyx and frown at Clayton. "You're basin' this all on the fact that he nose-bumped me a few times?"

"No, I'm basin' this on the fact that he came to you, asked for you, and even now is tryin' to get closer to you."

I turn to glance at the horse and see that Clayton wasn't lying. He's pushing himself as far into the opening in his stall door as he can get. When he realizes that isn't working, he becomes agitated. I reach out to press my hand against his nose again, gasping when he stills instantly and presses gently against my hand.

"Trust me?" Clayton questions again.

I look away from Onyx and nod, feeling a rightness click into place.

"I'm goin' to let you go so I can get the horses ready. You okay with that?"

My heart warms, knowing that he's kept me in his arms for the past five minutes because he knew I was fearful of being this close to an animal I don't understand well enough to not fear. I press my lips to his before nodding.

"Then let's get ready for our first ride together, darlin'. Those roads collided and it's time we check out the new path before us."

Oh, wow.

Reluctantly, I slowly lower myself with his help until I'm standing and watching as Clayton gets Onyx and Dell, his horse, ready. When Clayton opens Onyx's stall, the horse walks to my side instantly and doesn't leave his spot next to me. His solid mass presses against me in a soothing way. I don't even realize I'm running my hands over his coat, loving the feeling of his powerful softness, until he makes a sound that makes me think he's enjoying the attention. For the first time, I feel no fear being near one let alone two horses, but I have a feeling that has a lot to do with Clayton and my trust in him, even if I feel the connection to Onyx that he was speaking about. When I look at Dell, a horse I know has the most even temperament and calm nature, I shiver and push my side into Onyx, who huffs air out. Maybe Onyx doesn't scare me as much because, him being solid black, those seemingly all-knowing eyes aren't so noticeable. Dell, though, is the opposite of Onyx. Dell is pure white. The way his eyes contrast against his coat makes them look even more arresting.

"I know, big guy," I tell Onyx softly, still looking at Dell. "He creeps me out too."

Clayton chuckles. I ignore him and keep talking to the horse at my side. "I should tell you, I don't know a lick about horses, but I promise to respect you. Just . . . I don't know, try and not go crazy and buck me off you. I don't want to break my back and have to be put in a home."

This time Clayton bursts out in a deep belly laugh.

"What?"

"God, I have no idea what I'd do without you in my life."

"That's good. Maybe that means you won't ship me off to live in a home when I break my back and become a burden."

Watching him tighten something on the saddle before turning, I drink him in. His full lips are smiling, the shadow of his facial hair along his jaw making him look rugged and sinful. But it's the brightness shining from his eyes that holds me captive.

"There will never be a day that I won't have you in my arms when I wake, Caroline. I don't care what's thrown at us in this life, me needin' to care for you will never be somethin' I look at as a burden. I'll spend every second of every day showin' you that I deserve that honor." He steps closer and lifts his hat off my head, placing it opening side up on a shelf near us. "Even if you get thrown from a horse and break your back—even then will I love every second that I'm blessed with you in my life."

I feel my chin tremble and I know if he keeps going, I'm going to burst into tears.

"You ready to take a ride with me, darlin'?"

I swallow thickly, my chin still fighting with my emotions, and nod.

Clayton moves to help me mount Onyx. Knowing that he wouldn't be putting me on the back of this horse if he wasn't confident in the animal's abilities eases some of my nerves. I listen intently as he continues to explain everything I need to know as Onyx waits patiently for me to climb onto his back.

"Left foot in the stirrup and pull your body upward. Take your time and swing your other leg around. Just hug his back with your legs and slip your other foot into the stirrup. I'll hold his reins, but he's well trained, darlin', and I suspect he'll be statue still while you get sorted."

"He's not gonna just take off with me danglin', right?"

I'll give Clayton credit, if it weren't for the slight twitch of his lips, I wouldn't know how bad he wants to laugh at me.

"Trust, darlin'."

"Trust. Right. I do."

"Then get your hot ass in the saddle, baby. We've got plans."

It takes me two tries to get myself up and into the

saddle. True to Clayton's words, Onyx doesn't even flinch, letting me get myself positioned with my back straight and orienting myself to balance with my weight centered to my bottom like I was told. Clayton walks around and makes sure my legs are in the proper position, giving me a few tips as he does.

"When we start ridin', keep your toes up, ankles stable, and your heels pointing downward. You let Onyx lead."

"What do I do with these?" I ask, holding up the reins he just placed in my left hand.

"That is how you steer. A gentle touch against Onyx's neck will signal the movements that you want. Move across his right side to go right and left side to go left. Keep them in your left hand, right hand on the saddle. We'll work on all of this another time, but even though I know he'll guide you without help, following me, I still want you to know what to do on the off chance that he decides to show off."

"Okay." I gulp. "Right for right and left for left. Seems easy enough."

"If somethin' happens and you need him to move quick, grab the reins in both hands and gently pull or squeeze in the direction you need him to go. It's not often that it happens to our horses, but if you need to emergency steer him, that's how."

I nod, filing that information under *let's not think about what could happen that would require emergency steering*, and give Clayton a nod. "How do I get him to turn on?"

His lips twitch again. "Squeeze with your legs and let him know you're ready."

"That's it?"

He nods. "Yeah, baby, that's all it takes."

"You'll be close?"

"Always, Linney. Always."

21

CLAYTON

"I'm Gonna Love You" by Jamie Lawson

She's a natural.

You'd never know she's never ridden or that before this, she'd been afraid of every horse she encountered. Her smile is huge, carefree, and full of life. The only time I've ever seen her looking more beautiful is when she's under me and gasping out my name.

We've been riding about ten minutes, but five into it she let go and I quickly changed our course so I could watch her longer.

It didn't take me long to get everything I needed in order. I texted Leighton shortly after I got off the phone with Caroline earlier and asked her to give me a heads-up when Caroline was on her way home. Luckily, by then I'd finished with the doc and successfully sold eight horses to the buyers who had come down. Drew waved me off when I asked if he needed help, but the crooked grin on his face told me he was doing it more because he knew what I had planned and not because he didn't actually need help.

The rest I'm hoping like hell Maverick took care of. Otherwise I'm going to be winging it and not giving Caroline a fraction of the romance she deserves. I can't remember a time I've ever cared about that, but I want to give her memories that have her feeling our love for the rest of our lives.

Moving my hips, I lean back slightly. Dell instantly slows his trot. I wait, giving Onyx time to follow my lead, pleased as hell when he does so without hesitation. I hear Caroline gasp, but keep my eyes on Onyx while he follows Dell to the tie-off post. Dismounting, I loop Dell's reins around the post before taking Onyx's from Caroline and doing the same. Both horses stretch their necks to drink from the large watering basin as I move to her side and, with my hands on her hips, help her to her feet. Only when she's grounded do I look over her head.

This spot has always been my favorite within all our acres: the peak where our land is the highest and the trees are few and far between. From here, you can see part of Maverick's land to the west, where he has a few housing structures for the riders enrolled in his rodeo school. The other side is all Davis land. Nothing but green earth and blue skies. Untouched by any man and unblemished by any structure aside from the fence that used to keep cattle locked in.

"I used to come out here when I needed to get away. When my pops was drunk out of his mind and fightin' with anyone who would look at him. When Quinn's cryin' got too much to bear, knowin' I couldn't fix what hurt her or bring the only person she wanted back. And when Maverick left town, I found myself out here more and more. Wouldn't do anything more than just look out across our land, focusin' on nothin' and wishin' more than anything I could've protected them more. This was the only place on this ranch that felt like home to me, even after my pops passed away. Here the only thing I had to worry about was myself. Still, after he passed, and this place became all mine, I never felt like it was home unless I was out here." I pause, walking over to the table that Maverick set up for me, grabbing the bottle of red wine sitting atop it and filling the two glasses placed next to it. "I felt like that my whole life, Linney. Never findin' peace in my own house, on my own land, long enough to let me find *my* home—my sanctuary. It wasn't until a beautiful good girl, lookin' to be bad, sat down next to me in a dirty bar. There you were, surrounded by drunks and bikers, lookin' like you stepped out of the pages of a magazine—you were pure temptation. That moment, before we even left Hazel's, I felt like somethin' had snapped in place deep inside my chest. I found my sanctuary—my *home*—that night in your arms. I found it and almost lost it forever after just one night. You'll never know how thankful I am that I got my second chance. Knowin' that we might never have found this if I woulda let my stubborn pride keep me from findin' you—that kills me."

Her wide brown eyes stay locked on mine when I stop talking and hand her a glass of wine, then take a sip from my own glass.

"One day, we're gonna bring our children here, Linney, and you're goin' to sit on a blanket between my legs while they run all over this damn hill. Laughter will echo across our land while we bask in what our love created. There'll never be a day that I don't love you. Not one. I wasn't plannin' on you, baby, and I know you weren't plannin' on me, but sometimes what we need to finally feel whole is what we least expect. You are that for me."

"Clayton," she whispers, tears filling her eyes.

"Just a second, darlin'," I interrupt, bending to kiss her nose before taking our glasses and placing them on the table next to the picnic basket.

"Clayton," she repeats softly; this time I hear her tears in her voice.

"Sweetness, one second." When I turn, seeing the worry in her eyes, I take her face between my hands gently. "What is it, Linney?"

She swallows, her whole head moving in my grasp as she does. Her mouth moves, opening and closing, but no words come. I relax my grip and bend to press our lips together. It doesn't take long before our kiss turns hungry and I regretfully pull my mouth from hers.

"You good?" I ask with a smile that grows when her eyes don't open for a few more pounding beats of my heart. Finally her lashes flutter, and she looks at me in a daze.

"I just . . . I don't want you to think that I expect you to . . . I don't know! I mean, I was jokin', wantin' to let that nasty woman know she was wrong about you, but the second the words left my mouth I . . . I'm freakin' out here, Clayton!"

There really is no way to describe what it feels like when all the pieces of you that had been out of sorts your whole damn life start to click together. When all those years of twisting them up because you couldn't figure out what you were missing are unraveled in an instant when you find what your purpose in life truly is. For me, I knew my place was here on the ranch and that my protection and love went to my siblings and only them. Because of my parents, I knew allowing myself to find what Maverick and Quinn had would be something too risky. I had resigned myself to that life, only recently feeling like I was spiraling, with my siblings no longer needing me. But then I met this woman and those pieces started shifting until I knew without a doubt that my crazy, shy, wild-when-she-wants woman was my purpose. My reason for waking and my reason for breathing. The woman who made the risk of loving her unquestionably worth it, because with her love, that risk is really just a reward. I would have done this weeks ago, but it wasn't until today that I knew it was time. I take her hands in mine and wink when her eyes grow a little wider. Not looking away from her, I drop to my knee. Her hands jerk in my grasp as she watches me. I inhale deeply and start putting mental pictures of this moment away so I'll never forget what it looks like to ask for forever with the person who holds your purpose.

"Caroline Lynn Michaels," I start, having to pause when a lump of emotion crawls up my throat before continuing. "There will never be a time in my life, yours, and whatever waits for us beyond that when my heart won't beat a little quicker because of what my love for you does to me. You came into my life and showed me how wrong I'd been about so many things without even tryin'. I never wanted more for myself than what I had runnin' the ranch and seein' my family thrive, but then your love made me need things I hadn't ever allowed myself to think of before. Without you, there isn't anything here on this earth worth findin'. Not a goal I can set for my life that would mean anything to achieve. My purpose. Everything I could possibly achieve. It's all you now. You've turned my house into our home, put me back together when I hadn't even realized I'd been broken, and given me so much more in four months than some people will ever get in a whole lifetime. We burned our way through our own paths in order to find this road we're travelin' on now together. I only hope I'm able to give you back a fraction of what you give me. I was made to love you, Caroline, and there isn't anything that would make me happier than you becomin' my wife. Marry me, Linney. Marry me today, tomorrow, or the next day, and let me spend the rest of our lives provin' that I deserve the honor of you."

"Oh, God," she cries, her whole body shaking with her soft sobbing. The tiniest sounds come from her while she struggles to compose herself.

I release her right hand, keeping hold of her other, and reach into my pocket to pull out the ring I bought almost four months ago. Right after our second dinner at the ranch. I knew then, just like I knew when I stupidly denied it to myself the night I met her, that she's my forever.

When the sun catches the diamonds, Caroline stops trying to control herself and cries harder. I place the ring against the tip of her ring finger and wait, looking at the diamonds as they reflect thousands of colorful prisms in the sun, feeling my own eyes burn, knowing that this moment will forever be one of the greatest triumphs in my life. Her body shudders as she sucks in a choppy gasp, and I glance up just in time to see her looking down at our hands with her chin quivering and more wetness starting to pool in her eyes. This time, there are no sounds, just her tears running silently down her cheeks while she watches me intently. A lesser man would feel some dread over the prolonged silence from the woman he just asked to be his wife, but not me. I know what she'll say. I've known for months now that her answer would be yes, no matter when I asked. It's what drove me to the jeweler to begin with, needing this ring to be ready when the moment came. Confident as I was, I knew she'd be like this. She wouldn't be the woman I love if she didn't need to work through the overpowering emotions slamming into her. If I need to kneel here until the sun dips below the trees, I'll do it. I'll give her all the time in the world to give me—us—the beginning of everything.

By the time we leave here tonight, I'll have my ring on her finger; our bellies will be full with the food waiting for us; and there'll be grass stains on our clothes from when I love my future wife slow and soft under the blue skies, endless green pastures, in the spot that was my only salvation for thirty-five years. Used to be—not now. Not with the love of a damn good woman showing me my way.

Her hand pushes forward in my hold with a sharp jerk, the movement causing the ring to slide down to the middle of her finger, stopping at her knuckle. I'm unable to look away from the big round stone surrounded by tons of smaller diamonds, what it symbolizes hitting me with a maelstrom of emotions. None of them bad, either. No panic, like I had felt when this was almost forced on me by my ex. No fear when I think about my parents' marriage. Nothing but excitement for what my future with Caroline holds. I swallow thickly before glancing back up at her. Her silent tears are still cascading down her tanned cheeks, but she's giving me a huge, blindingly happy, toothy smile. Even though I knew it in my gut, seeing how happy she is and knowing those tears are because she's *that* happy, I feel my own expression break as my joy is given free rein.

"Yes," she finally answers in a small whisper so soft that if there had been some wind, it would have carried her word away with it before it reached my ears. Awe present in her hushed tone, her stare is locked on our hands as I slide the ring the rest of the way down her slim finger. She continues to look down, only giving me her eyes when I lift her hand and press a kiss against the ring. I hold my lips there, watching her chest shake as she pulls in rapid breaths. It's the pure, unmasked joy lighting every inch of her that has me silently vowing I'll do everything in my power to make sure she never loses that happiness while we love each other for the rest of our lives.

I climb to my feet, bending down to dust the dirt off my knee, before stretching to my full height. Caroline looks so tiny standing before me, holding her hand out in front of her face as she admires the ring.

"You look good wearin' my diamonds, Linney, love." My voice must have broken the spell she had been hooked in, because her head snaps up and she jumps. When our gazes collide, I see she hadn't really stopped the crying like I thought. "You're killin' me with the tears, darlin'."

"I'm *so* happy, Clayton Davis." Her whole body

shakes as she gets choked up. I can't help it when my chest puffs slightly. I feel damn good about being the reason she's feeling this way—even if it's coming with some tears.

"How about you get in my arms with your mouth on mine and show me just how happy you are?"

She doesn't hesitate. She jumps, and her arms go around my neck at the same time her legs circle my hips. My hands instantly go to her sweet ass, pulling her closer and keeping her right where I want her. The heat of her pussy is unmistakable against my hard cock, even with the layers keeping us apart completely. She peppers my face with kisses, her soft lips moving frantically as she covers me from forehead to jaw. When she lifts her head, after pressing one last kiss to the side of my jaw, I expect her to finally give me her mouth. Instead, she tips her head back, and shouts up to the sun and the bright blue sky, her back arched, with her tits right in front of my face, while holding on with her hands hooked together behind my neck. Her body bounces, excitement flowing, and I groan when I feel that movement milk some pre-come from my needy cock.

"My dark cowboy is goin' to be my husband!" Caroline shouts. Her whole body quivers with excitement as she looks back at me. "You're goin' to be my husband, Clayton," she tells me, her lips curled in a beautiful, happy smile.

"You're gonna be my wife."

"Oh my God!" she starts bouncing and I almost fall to my knees as pleasure zaps up my spine.

My fingers clench, grabbing her ass cheeks and pushing her roughly against my cock, stilling her movements instantly and groaning loudly. I hiss when she manages to wiggle just a fraction against me.

"Keep that up, sweetness, and I'm gonna strip us down and forget about our dinner so I can fuck my love into you with the sun shining down on us."

She moans, her cheeks turning a light shade of pink.

"You want that, baby?"

Her thighs clamp tighter around my hips and her fingers dig into my shoulders. The bite of pain just makes me crave her more.

"Linney, love. You want me to feed you or eat you?"

"Oh, God," she whimpers.

"Give me the words, darlin'. Tell me what you want. I'll give you the world, but you gotta use the words to ask for it."

"You," she breathes heavily. "I just want you."

My chest vibrates with the hungry sound of approval that bursts free and I lean my head toward hers as she moves to meet me halfway. Our mouths are already opening before our lips press together. Her tongue glides against mine in a slow caress. Her hands drag up my neck as we both give everything we have. Her moans meet mine as our tongues dance. Our bodies become frantic as she rolls her hips and I flex my ass to push my length harder against her, needing, craving more.

I have to rip my mouth from hers, unable to wait any longer to feel her heat hugging me tightly. Caroline starts to kiss and lick down my neck and that sound fills my chest again—a mix between a groan and a growl that her intoxicating body brings out in me. I see the thick flannel blanket Maverick placed under the small two-person wooden table. The huge swath of red-and-black material gives me all the space I need.

"As much as I hate to say it, you're gonna have to get down."

"No, honey," she hums, licking me from my collarbone to my ear before taking a tiny bite with her teeth, nipping me and making me falter as the shock of it creates waves of pleasure through my body.

"Linney," I grunt when she sucks the flesh she just nipped into her mouth. "Get down and get naked, *now*," I hoarsely command, quickly losing the battle with my control. I can already feel my balls pulling tight, ready to explode and not giving one shit that the only place I want to pour myself into is the woman drunk with arousal and high off happiness.

I don't waste a second seeing if she's heeding my demand. My fingers curl in my shirt and I give it a tug. Buttons scatter all around as I pull it and my undershirt off and reach for my belt. When I see Caroline moving just as frantically as I am, not even hesitating to strip out here in the open, I clench my jaw and pray for control. Her small, perfect-handful tits are free and jiggling slightly against her chest as she wiggles her jeans down, kicking them in the direction of her boots and hooking her thumbs into her white lace thong. Her hands freeze, though, and I lick my lips before looking up at her.

"You're too dressed," she pants, rubbing her thighs together.

Knowing she's desperate for me to ease her ache between her legs sends an animalistic need bursting through me. I tear my clothes off wildly and so fast that when I'm taking the few steps separating us, she's still standing there with her thumbs hooked in her underwear. Her breath rushes from her lungs when my body collides with hers and I take her mouth again. My hands turn her head as I deepen our kiss and moan in her mouth when her soft belly presses against my cock.

It doesn't take much before I know I'm seconds from coming, and I'm not going to do that shit on her stomach. Shifting our bodies, I grab her hips and lift her. Her legs hook behind my ass and she slams her center against my cock. Her wet heat slides against my shaft as she rocks her hips and mewls a knee-weakening moan. Our bodies move without prompting until I'm on my back, her knees at my hips, and her hand circling as much of my cock as she can while lining the tip up with her entrance. She pauses, and my eyes practically cross when her heat kisses the tip of my cock. When she doesn't move past that, I look up at her face.

"Fuck me," I breathe. The sun, high in the sky, casts a

glow around her naked body. The brilliance of the bright light hitting her back makes it seem like little beams are shooting around her. She looks like a fucking angel. I have no idea what I did to earn the love of this woman, but I'll never take it for granted. "Get on my cock, Linney, and ride me. Show me how much you love me and take what you need."

"Oh, Clayton," she gasps, her chest heaving with her rapid breaths.

My hands move until my thumb is pressing and rolling against her clit as the other goes to her tit. She inhales with a hiss, her eyes slits as pleasure takes hold of her. I pinch her again, a little harder, before soothing the tight bud with my thumb.

"Take me. Give me you while I give you me. Show me what having my ring on your hand makes you feel."

She drops down, impaling herself on every inch of me. Her eyes squeeze shut and her mouth drops open. She's only taken all of me at one go once, and that was after I had fucked her with my mouth until she came over and over. Even as wet as she had been after that, she still couldn't take all of me. But with the lips of her sex pressed against my pelvis, she greedily takes every inch, her hands curling against my abs as she begins to fuck my cock. Pulling herself up and dropping back down, she rakes her nails over my skin in a burning path. I keep thumbing her clit, her walls fluttering against my cock, milking me.

"I'm not gonna last, baby," I groan when I feel her wet-

ness on my balls and her pussy start to tighten to the point
of pain before sending me rolling into blinding pleasure.
"Fuckin' hell," I moan, taking her hips and thrusting up
as she starts to scream out my name, clamping down on
me with her wet heat. I pull her hips down and flex my
ass to feed her all of me while I start coming with a shout.
I hold her firmly against me, not willing to lose any part
of our connection, and lift off my back to take her mouth
while she milks her release.

She falls against my chest and I grunt when the movement slides my cock a little deeper, closing my eyes when
I feel another burst shoot deep inside of her. The tension
from my release finally drains out of my muscles a minute
later, but I keep my hold on her hips so I don't lose her
heat. We lie there in comfortable silence, the only sounds
our ragged breathing as we both come down. Every few
minutes my cock, still more hard than soft, twitches inside her, making her moan. Caroline shifts in my grip,
bringing her hands to my chest as she pushes against me
to lift up. As soon as there's some space between our bodies, she looks from my face to my chest. She starts moving
her hand in small degrees, staring at her ring, and I can
only guess that the sun hitting her ring is the reason she's
doing so. I watch her beautiful face as she smiles, still
looking at her hand.

Then her hand drops, but her smile grows.

"Oh my God," she gasps, giggling a beat later, the ring
forgotten as she points to where the horses are grazing,

patiently waiting for us. "Dell . . . he's all white, Clayton!" My fingers tighten when I feel her laughter in the walls of her pussy, still surrounding my cock. "You," she snorts, unaware of what she's doing to me. "How did I not see it before! You rode in on your white horse, knocked me on my butt, but saved me in the end. My knight in pressed flannel and Wranglers."

"You're a nut, darlin'."

Her giggles multiply and I can't help but join in. "I'm goin' to make a whole section on hot, flannel-wearin', white-knight cowboys when I get The Sequel back open. Just you wait."

Her body rocks against mine as she continues to laugh softly, looking at our horses again with a tiny shake of her head. Unable to stand it anymore, I thrust my hips. Her giggle quickly turns into a whimper.

"I love you, Linney," I tell her, giving her a few more thrusts.

Her soft brown eyes darken and her lips take on a smile that will forever be branded in my mind. The sun is still swirling around every inch of her as I look up from my spot on the ground. She's never looked more beautiful than she does in this moment, joined with me as we start our forever.

"Never gonna stop lovin' you, Caroline."

Her breath hitches. "And I love you, Clayton. Always."

22

CAROLINE

"Forever and Ever, Amen" by Randy Travis

- ★ -

"**I** don't want to wait," I tell him, helping him pack up the rest of our lunch. He stops folding the blanket we finally climbed off of to actually eat the lunch I was cleaning up, but seeing the material in his arms against his naked chest makes me want him all over.

"Wait for what, darlin'?"

I place the last empty storage container into the basket before looking back at him. The rush of him loving me is still surging through my body and mingling with the euphoric high I've had since he knelt in front of me, making me feel as if I could take on the world and win it. And right now, becoming his wife is just as grand in my mind as owning the world would be.

"To become your wife," I answer confidently. No

more, not with him, will the shy Caroline Michaels hold back because of her insecurities.

His shoulders move in silent laughter. "What makes you think *I'd* want to wait?"

"That's usually what happens, honey. Man asks woman, woman spends every waking moment planning her dream wedding until months of stress and preparation form the most perfect day that you'll ever experience."

His lips twitch before he smiles his heart-stopping grin. His green eyes squint as his smile grows. "Darlin', you planning on takin' that long?"

I shake my head. "Well, no."

"How long you need?"

I tilt my head, thinking about it, but don't get far before he starts laughing deeply. He tosses the blanket on top of the picnic basket a second before his arms are around me. The light peppering of hair against his rock-hard chest tickles my palms and I regret getting dressed before we ate when my nipples harden. I love the feel of his chest hair against my skin as he takes me.

"Linney?"

"Hmm?" I answer, rubbing my hands over him.

"How long do you need?"

"For what?" I lick my lips when I feel him grow harder, the length of him no match for the denim covering it.

"Baby." He laughs.

I blink, looking from his chest to his face. "Don't laugh at me, mister."

"You loved me hard, Linney, then you still let me take you slow. My cock shouldn't have anything left, but with you lookin' at me like that it damn sure does. How about you answer me and I can get you home, in our bed, with my cock buried deep."

I feel his words dance through my body, lighting a fire of need in their path, wetness dampening my panties.

"I forgot the question," I tell him honestly, breathless for him.

"How much time," he starts, pressing his mouth to mine quickly, lifting his head to smile down at me, "do you need to plan our weddin'?"

"None," I hum, pressing myself closer and shifting my hands to glide over his skin until I've got a palm against each side of his neck and my face tipped up to look into his. "I don't need any time, Clayton. I just need you."

"Baby," he responds thickly.

"I don't want anything big, Clayton," I say. "Your family, Lucy and Luke. That's it, honey. I don't want to wait weeks, months, years. We've both wasted too much time in our lives while we dealt with our ugly in order to find our beauty. I don't need to continue to waste time now that it's even more precious. I just want you. You and me and whatever blessings we find together."

"You sure you don't want somethin' big?"

"Why, Clayton? You have your brother and sister, their families, and I have Lucy and Luke. There aren't grandparents; my parents and yours didn't have siblings. I don't want the town turnin' our weddin' into somethin' crazy because they're just nosy. All we need is a small ceremony, our family together, and us."

He drops his forehead to mine, smiling. "I like that, Linney."

"I don't want to wait," I reiterate.

"Then don't. I wouldn't have asked you to be my wife if I wasn't ready to make that happen. You aren't the only one not wantin' to wait, darlin'. I don't want you lookin' back and wishin' you had some big weddin' though either."

"I would never."

"Then, Caroline, don't wait."

"The whole town's goin' to think you knocked me up. They went crazy when news got out about us livin' together, I can only imagine what they'll think when they hear about us bein' engaged."

His eyes flash, something I don't quite understand flickering there for only a second before vanishing. I feel his heart thundering against my chest as the silence continues. His throat bobbles when he swallows.

"Clayton?"

He clears his throat.

"I don't want to rush you," I finally say when it becomes clear he isn't going to stop staring at me mutely. My words get his attention, but I keep going. "I'd marry you tomorrow, but I don't want to rush you."

"Tomorrow will still be longer than I care to wait."

"What?"

"Caroline," he breathes, "I've had that ring for damn near the whole time we've been together. I had you one night and it took everything inside of me to walk away. I might be a foolish man, but when I saw you at the girls' baby shower, I knew I wasn't strong enough to walk away a second time. Every single day since, I've been ready, and every day from this moment will feel like it's not soon enough. Trust me when I say there isn't a damn way to rush somethin' that every second you don't get it feels like a lifetime."

"Oh," I say lamely.

"Take the time you need to plan the weddin' you want. Small, big, or in between. Just don't take *that* much time, darlin'."

"I won't," I mutter.

"That's good, Linney. That's damn good."

He lets me go with a short kiss. Silently, we finish cleaning up and stacking the things he'll pick up later on top of the table. I take one last look at the land around us and feel lighter than I've ever felt in my life. His words from earlier return and I can almost see our future kids running around the green grass. One day, one day that's going to be ours, and I can't hardly wait for it.

The ride back to the ranch is a lot easier—Onyx proved himself to be trustworthy already. I imagine it will take some time for me to get over my fears, but I no longer look at Onyx as part of that. He's been patient with me and I know, deep down, that Clayton was right when he said there's a bond between the dark beauty and me. During the time I'll have to wait to reopen The Sequel, I hope to learn more from Clayton when it comes to riding. A horse as perfect as Onyx deserves that.

We pass a few ranch hands working with a couple of Clayton's newer horses in the riding course that's set up between the Davis personal horse barn and the huge one that houses their stock, for lack of a better word, on the way back. Ignoring them, Clayton continues until we both have our feet on the ground and I've finished the last task that he's coached me through in getting Onyx ready to go back in his stall.

I caress the horse's neck, not really ready to leave. "I'm goin' to be back in the mornin', handsome."

Clayton laughs. "Handsome?"

I look over my shoulder at him. "Uh, yeah. Look at him."

"Such a nut," he mutters, walking Dell down to his own stall.

"Clay," I hear someone call from outside the barn right before one of the younger cowboys comes in. His eyes go straight to me but shift back to Clayton when Clay makes a disapproving sound deep in his throat. "Sorry, Mr. Davis. Drew had to run to town and you didn't bring your phone or the radio, but your brother's been callin'."

"For how long?" Clayton questions, walking to me and taking my hand before heading toward the younger man. He pauses to grab his hat, placing it back on his head while waiting for a reply.

"Reckon 'bout a half hour ago, maybe close to an hour now."

"Thanks, Tim," Clayton says, walking right out of the barn and toward the house.

"Is everything okay?" I quicken my pace to keep up with his long legs but feel like I'm more jogging than walking.

"He knew what was goin' on, darlin'. Only reason he'd be callin' is if it's important. Seein' that Leighton is so close to havin' the baby, I'm guessin' that's why."

"You'll get to your phone quicker if you go ahead, honey," I rush out, pulling my hand from his hold. "Meet you in the house. I'm goin' to run to my car and grab my phone so I can call Quinn."

He nods sharply, turning to continue up to the main house. I quickly snatch up my phone before sprinting back toward the house. I pull Quinn's name up and press the phone to my ear before I even reach the porch steps.

"Are y'all on the way?" she questions when the call connects.

"About to be. Is everything okay?"

"I think so. I haven't talked to Maverick since he called to say it was time. We had to wait for Jana to get to the house so she could watch Grayson. Tate's tryin' to get some information with his doctor magic."

Clayton comes barreling down the hallway, phone to his ear. "That Quinn?"

I nod. "Here's your brother, Quinn."

His breathing is harsh when he takes the phone and places it to his ear. "Quinnie?" Whatever she says to him must ease some of the worry, because his shoulders loosen up and he closes his eyes before exhaling slowly. "We're on the way."

He hands me back my phone and visibly struggles with his emotions. "I'll never be able to hold my shit together when it's you about to have a baby. I feel like I'm too big for my skin right now. I've watched those two fight for this moment for damn near our whole lives. Knowin', like us, they could have never found it because of that shit they had to deal with in order to do so. This baby of theirs is somethin' we've all of us been waitin' for so long to meet. I can't imagine, feelin' this much over their child, what you givin' me one of our own will do to me. Never, not until you, did I ever want this for myself. To my knees, Linney, thinkin' about somethin' as perfect as our future children brings me to my knees."

"Oh, Clayton." I wrap my arms around him and hug him tight.

"I don't want to wait either, darlin'," he says against my temple, his head bent and his arms around me. "There's nothin' better than travelin' with you and doin' it in a way that we don't waste a second of our time hesitatin' in takin' what we want. You've got two weeks. Two weeks, and I'm not goin' to wait any longer than that."

"Two weeks," I echo breathlessly.

"Not a day more."

By the time we make it to the hospital, Tate was able to find out that Leigh was being prepped for a cesarean section. Her baby is just too big and the natural birth she's been hoping for is out of the question. Tate assured both Quinn and Clayton that they had nothing to worry about, but even with him explaining how common this is, it's still major surgery. That was almost three hours ago, and even Tate has some worry in his eyes now.

The tension in our area of the waiting room is thick, but when the doorway opens to reveal a crying, smiling Maverick, that tension vanishes instantly. I look over at Tate and smile, both of us letting the two waiting Davis siblings go to their brother first.

"Congratulations," Tate says after Clayton and Quinn reach Maverick's side.

"Huh?" I respond in confusion, not taking my eyes off Clayton. When he grabs his brother by the shoulders and pulls him into his arms, I feel the burn of tears start. When both of them drop their foreheads to the other's shoulder, Clayton's hat falling carelessly at his feet, and both their arms tighten as they embrace, I know I'm not going to be able to keep my tears in as I witness such strong men be overcome by their emotions. Then, as if they practiced the move their whole lives—each man lifts the arm closest to where Quinn is standing out. She moves instantly, all but diving into their embrace with her arms going around each brother.

"They've been through a lot of shit in their lives," Tate whispers, moving to the seat next to me. "Thick and thin, those three have been each other's rocks through the worst of it, only sharing that responsibility recently. Maverick findin' Leighton. Quinn and me. Now you and Clay. Lot of time has passed since they were young kids livin' a shit life without the love of anyone other than each other, but when you get right down to it, they're always goin' to need each other's support."

I blink furiously, trying to get my stupid tears to back off, but when Maverick lifts his head and looks at me with his piercing emerald eyes swollen and wet, I feel them start to fall. His don't stop, but he smiles at me with a small nod before bending his head back to his brother's shoulder.

"Felt that when Gray was born. There's no way to explain what you feel when your child is born. Not sayin' that my son's birth wasn't as important, but for them, this is so much more. Me and you, we weren't around for all of it, but you know as well as I do that they had a dark childhood. Leighton was there. She loves my wife as a sister. Your man as a brother. And her husband owns the rest of her heart. Those three, they finally have it all, and more importantly, they know it. Makes moments like this hit a little harder because there was a time they all thought this would never happen."

"Their gifts," I whisper.

"Pardon?" Tate asks.

I look away from the huddle across the room and smile at Quinn's husband. "It's their gift for all that ugly they survived."

I don't think I really believed Clayton when he told me that months ago, but there are no doubts now. I've seen it in Clayton during the course of our relationship, but never as clearly as I do today. I spin the ring on my hand, loving the weight of it, and grin when I realize just how much of a gift *my* Davis has received today.

"Yeah, you get it."

"I do, Tate. I totally do."

"Like I said, congratulations." He taps my hand, stilling my fingers.

"Thanks," I breathe, opening my mouth to say more but snapping it shut when I see the siblings release each other and turn to us.

"That's our cue."

We both stand and walk over to them.

"I knew it!" Quinn exclaims with a shake to her voice when her husband reaches her side. "Since I was six years old, Tate. I've always known it."

I glance at Maverick, seeing him look down at his boots, but not hiding the smile on his face. Clayton pulls me to his side and I wrap one arm around his back, place my other hand against his hard stomach, and tip my head up to look at him. His eyes are wet and red, but his smile is huge.

"I've got a niece," he tells me in a soft voice full of happiness.

"I knew it!" Quinn cries out again. "What's her name?"

Maverick looks up, his lips tipping even further.

"Promised Leighton I'd let her tell y'all."

"Well, bucko, what are we waitin' for? Take me to my niece!"

Maverick smiles at his sister and we all follow the new daddy down the hallway. Clayton's been quiet since his brother came into the waiting room, but every time I glance at him he just smiles, so I leave him to his thoughts, knowing he's anxious to meet the newest member of his family.

We stop behind Maverick when he reaches a closed door. James, their last name since he took Leighton's when they married, is written under the room number.

"She's still tired but didn't want to wait," he rumbles low, looking down at his hand on the doorknob. "I'd keep y'all here with us all night, but I'm askin' because I need this time with my wife and daughter. Please, keep it short tonight."

"I swear, if you don't get your tail outta my way, I'll take you out."

"Quinn, I mean it."

I look at her as she rolls her eyes. "I know you do, big brother, and I think you understand that I get you. Now get out of my way so I can see my sister and hold the niece you denied me for years, and *then* I'll leave."

Maverick nods at his sister as Tate and I laugh lightly when she starts pushing into the room before the door's even open all the way. Clayton hangs back while Tate enters, causing Maverick to glance his way.

"I spent ten years worried you'd never come home," Clayton tells Maverick, his words low. "Ten years I felt nothin' but fear that I'd lost my brother because I couldn't protect him enough to keep him here. I'm so happy for you right now. Seein' you overcome all that pushed you away and kept you gone to find what you were always meant to have . . ." He pauses as his arm tightens around my shoulders. "You made it possible with all that for me to be able to see what I was meant to have. I'm so fuckin' proud to call you my brother, Mav."

"I'm just goin' to . . ." I point toward the open door and try to step out from under Clayton's arm.

His head tips down to look at me. "Don't you dare move."

"We're all gettin' what we were meant to have, brother," Maverick says, breaking the staring contest I had apparently entered with Clayton as we both look to him. "You'll be in my shoes sooner rather than later, I reckon." He steps closer to his big brother and lowers his voice. "Don't let me hear you say you didn't protect me again, Clay. You've always done that. You did it when I was a kid, when I left, and you continued doin' it when you look care of Leigh when I didn't. I overcame all that because I had the love of a good woman and the support of you and Quinn. Don't forget it was *you* who helped me see my way to her. Means the world to hear you're proud of me, seein' that you were the man who taught me how to be one myself."

I don't hesitate to step away from Clayton when Maverick finishes, walking into the hospital room and leaving them to have the rest of that moment privately.

An hour later, much to Quinn's irritation, the four of us walk out of the hospital, leaving Leighton and baby Laelynn Quinn James resting peacefully in Maverick's strong arms.

23

CAROLINE

"All My Ex's Live In Texas" by George Strait

I wave at Marybeth Perkins and back out of the grocery store as quickly as I can without making it look
obvious that I'm trying to get away from the sweet, but
extremely nosy, older woman. I could tell she was itching for some gossip with the way she kept looking at my
stomach. I knew this would happen the second our en-
gagement news started circulating. What should've only
taken me fifteen minutes, tops, took close to an hour.
Everyone, and I do mean everyone, I encountered asked
me a million questions.

It's been almost two weeks since Clayton asked me to
be his wife. I've spent every second of that time planning
our wedding and going between our home, Maverick
and Leighton's, and Quinn and Tate's. Since both couples

have such tiny newborns, I didn't want them coming out to our place. It was just easier to go to them. Plus, this way I get tons of time cuddling babies without having to fight off someone else in order to do so.

Lucy's been out a few times, Luke as well, but we've had little time to get together like we normally do. They understand, and I know both are happy for me.

"Caroline."

I freeze, my body locking tight.

"Please," the voice continues. Instead of making me feel uneasy, though, the broken tone in his pleading gives me what I need. *He* doesn't get to feel broken here. *He* doesn't have that right, seeing as he's the person who did everything in his power to ensure *I* was the broken one.

I suck in a cleansing breath before turning. "What do you want, John?"

He looks terrible. The once handsome man I knew is long gone. His hair is a little too long. His eyes are bloodshot and sunken, with shadowy bags under them. And he's lost weight. Not too much, but enough that I know he's not taking care of himself.

"I'm so sorry," he rushes out, looking around frantically. "So, so sorry."

"I moved past needin' to hear that a long time ago, John."

"It wasn't supposed to be like that," he continues like I didn't even speak.

I cross my arms and arch a brow, not willing to turn my back and continue loading the car, but I realize my mistake when John's panicked eyes drop. I glance down and see that my left hand and big diamond ring stick out like a billboard announcing my relationship status.

"Is that . . . Are you . . . to Clay Davis?"

"Why does it even matter to you?" I sigh, shaking my head. "You have no say in my life, John. You haven't for years. Why now, after all this time, is tellin' me you're sorry so dadgum important?"

He keeps shaking his head, not looking away from my ring. He mumbles something I can't hear under his breath before looking up at me with worried eyes. "I loved you, you know," he finally says. "I don't know what to do now."

Clayton's words about John being on drugs filter through my thoughts when I realize how odd he's acting. Knowing what I do about his past here in Pine Oak and having firsthand knowledge about just how violent he can be, I should be blind with fear. Heck, months ago I would have been. But I've come too far to let him push me right back into that person who was afraid of living.

"I want you to leave me alone. I want you to leave Clayton alone. And if you're goin' to be livin' in Pine Oak too, then I want you to avoid us at all costs. I survived what you did to me, John. I made it through that, and even though it took me a while to find my reward, I have it, and I'm not goin' to let you try and dirty that up with everything that is *you*."

He opens his mouth to say something, but I release my arms and hold one up to stop him silently.

"I don't want to hear your apologies, because they mean nothin' to me. Just like you. Do you understand that, John?"

He shakes his head sadly, looking down. "I loved you."

"No! No, you didn't. You loved owning someone who feared you. You loved the power of breakin' me. You loved *you*!"

"You're wrong, Caroline. I've done everything for you."

I snort. "You must be delusional."

"Don't marry him. I won't be able to save you."

This time I laugh in his face. "You? Save me? You're a riot."

"I tried," he says, but stops and shakes his head.

"You inflicted pain. Don't get that mixed up. It's been years, John. I've finally moved on and I'm so happy, it's ridiculous. You're sorry? Great. If it's my forgiveness you want or need, then you'll be waiting for a while. You can't give forgiveness to someone you've forgotten. And you, John, are just a forgotten memory."

I turn my back and load the last four bags into my trunk before shutting it and walking the buggy back to the return. When I start walking back to my car, I don't see him anywhere.

The first thing I do when I climb into my car is grab my phone and call Clayton.

"You on your way, darlin'?"

"I just ran into John."

Silence.

"Clayton?"

"I heard you," he answers with venom in his tone. "He touch you?"

"What? No, Clayton."

"What did he want?"

I sigh, then tell him what happened, trying to remember what John had said, but knowing I probably got some of it wrong. Still, even though it was pretty harmless, I can tell Clayton is about to lose his mind.

"He wanted to apologize. It doesn't make any sense to me, why he'd feel that's somethin' to be done so many years later, but nevertheless, he did. He startled me only because I wasn't expectin' him, but Clayton, I didn't feel anything but done. I don't fear him or what he did to me anymore."

"He could've hurt you," Clayton finally says, letting me know what's really upsetting him.

"He didn't. And I'm not the weak little girl who won't fight back. I've got all the reasons in the world to fight, and if he had been stupid enough to try and touch me in the middle of Main Street, I guarantee I wouldn't have been fightin' by myself for long."

He grumbles under his breath.

"We're gettin' married tonight, Clayton Davis. Don't you dare let this put a cloud over our weddin' night. It happened, it's done, and you know about it because I didn't want you hearin' it from someone else. I'm fine, and in just a couple of hours, we're goin' to be husband and wife. No one can stand in the way of that kinda happiness."

"Get home, Linney. Get home and no more of that shit about me not seein' you before tonight. I need to see with my own eyes that you're fine."

I smile, leaning my head back against the headrest. "I'll see you in our spot tonight, and not a second earlier."

I laugh outright when I hear him bellow out his complaints before I can disconnect the call. Not wanting to make him suffer too much, I quickly take a picture of myself and text it to him, happiness and love written all over my face, my smile big and my eyes dancing. I place my phone on the passenger's seat and back out of the lot to head over to Leighton's place, ignoring the chimes announcing texts that don't stop coming in the whole way to her house.

Not wanting to be distracted, I leave the phone on the seat and walk to the trunk to grab the bags.

"I've got it," Maverick says, making me scream.

"You need a bell," I gasp, holding my hand to my chest, my heart pounding from being snuck up on.

"Leigh's waitin' on you," he tells me, bending over to

scoop up all of the bags and trudging into his house, leaving the front door open for me.

"Well, then."

Earl is the first to greet me when I step into their home. He's sitting on his large rump in front of the baby swing. The huge, kind of scary cat gives me a look that, were he human, would express disapproval, his brow arched and a frown beneath his whiskers.

"Hey, Earl," I greet, stepping up to the swing to look at little Laelynn as she sleeps peacefully. I reach out, wanting to move her blanket down a little so I can see her adorable dimpled chin, but jerk it back when Earl hisses and swats at my ankle. "What the heck," I whisper, frowning at the cat.

"He's a little protective of Laelynn." Leigh giggles, scooping up her huge cat as he hisses and wiggles to get free. "Stop it, you big baby."

"So . . . I'm just goin' to go get changed, then," I tell her. "No offense, I'm sure he means well, but I'm pretty sure your cat could kill me, and as much as I love your daughter, I don't want to die."

Leigh laughs, dropping her cat to his feet. He pads back to his spot and settles in to sit guard in front of the swing.

"Quinn's feeding Gray and Lucy is gettin' dressed. Luke and Tate went up to get everything finished. I think Maverick is on the way back up there. He just happened to be checkin' in on things when you drove up."

"I feel like there's somethin' I should be doin' other than gettin' dressed."

"There is *nothin'* you need to be frettin' about, sister."

My heart warms and I smile at my old friend, soon to be my sister-in-law. "It's really happenin'?"

"You betcha ass it is! Come on. We've got a weddin' to get to and a bride who isn't ready yet."

All thoughts of John and our bizarre run-in are forgotten while my three closest friends help me get ready to marry the man of my dreams. By the time Luke comes back to let us know everything's ready and that the groom is waiting very impatiently, I've been buffed, fluffed, painted, and sprayed. He takes one look at me in my simple, floor-length lace dress and turns to walk back out the door.

I look over at Lucy, seeing her watery smile, and blink furiously to keep my tears from ruining my makeup. I glance at Leighton and Quinn, seeing them wearing the same simple coral sundresses that we all agreed on as their bridesmaids' outfits. All three are wearing brown cowboy boots, and their hair is braided simply to rest over one shoulder. Quinn's holding Grayson, dressed in a miniature version of what the guys are wearing— a black button-down and dark washed jeans. With Laelynn being only two weeks old, there wasn't anything close to the girls' outfits that fit her, but I bet Leighton tried anyway.

"Okay," Luke says, walking back in.

"You okay?" I whisper, walking to his side and hugging him.

"Yeah." He swallows thickly. "I'm just real damn happy for you, Carrie."

"Caroline," I correct with a laugh, not the least bit serious.

"I'm honored that you asked me to give you away, sweetheart."

"Don't make me cry," I warn.

Luke laughs but lowers his head so the girls can't hear him. "I knew five months ago when you sat next to Davis at Hazel's that this would happen. You both looked like you'd been zapped. I'm always here if you need me, but I couldn't be more pleased with the man you've chosen to be your husband."

"Luke," I murmur, my vision getting wonky with the tears filling my eyes.

"Enough of that," he exclaims, clapping his hands and rocking on his booted feet. "You ladies ready? Because there's a man up at the top of that hill who's about out of patience to get his bride in his arms."

Quinn gives me a quick hug before walking out and climbing into the front of the golf cart, next to Tate in the driver's seat. Lucy follows, thankfully having said much of the same that her brother did the night before and sparing me the tears. She winks before settling in.

Leigh is last out the door, holding the pink bundle of her daughter in her arms. "You ready?"

"God, yes," I answer emphatically.

Her grin is as huge as mine, I'm sure, as she walks to the cart and climbs up to sit with Lucy. Tate gives a wave before driving off slowly, careful of the precious cargo, in the direction of the Davis property. I look up at Luke and, with just him there, finally let loose some of the pent-up excitement. My hands go up in the air with the bundle of wildflowers held tight in my hand, and I shake my hips as I dance in a circle on Leighton's front porch.

"I'm gettin' married!"

"Not if you don't stop dancin' around, you aren't. Come on, crazy girl, your man is waitin'."

I drop my arms and turn to him, my cheeks burning from the enormous grin on my face. "This is it, Luke. This is my forever."

His eyes get soft and he grabs the hand not holding my bouquet. "No one deserves it more."

"Thank you, Lucas," I tell him after he helps me into the golf cart. "Thank you for bein' there for me all these years. You didn't have to be, but you were. I just want you to know how much your friendship means to me."

He taps my nose with his finger and grins. "You're family, darlin'. I didn't have to, but I wanted to. That's what family does. That will always hold true. Even with you gainin' a husband I know will protect you completely, I'm always gonna be here if you need me."

I reach out and grab his hand, not trusting myself to answer him without breaking down like a baby, and squeeze. Luke gives me a nod, then presses his foot down and takes off on the trail that will bring me to my forever.

24

CLAYTON

"It Took A Woman" by Craig Morgan

⭐

"**J**esus," I hiss, feeling my heart try to burst out of my damn chest when I see Caroline step down from the golf cart and smile at Luke as he walks around to hold his elbow out for her.

She looks like one hell of a vision. Her dress makes her tanned skin glow, the bright white lace hugging her small frame like it was made just for her. The low-cut neckline highlights her small breasts—and the fact that there is no way she's got a bra on. Her long, dark hair is pulled up into some messy curly bunch at the base of her neck, exposing each delicate inch.

It's her face, though, that holds me captive, openly projecting her happiness to everyone who is with us up on the hill that I used to run to when I needed to feel grounded. The same hill that I made love to her on two weeks ago when I asked her to be my wife. If you'd told me years ago that I'd be marrying the love of my life right here in this spot, I would've laughed you right out of Pine Oak.

She and Luke start to walk down the flower-petal-covered path that'll bring her to the gazebo I built in our spot. I did as much of the work as I could myself, but with limited time to give her something perfect, I had to get help. Drew and I pulled a few of the boys off their normal duties and with the help of my brothers as well, we created something I have no doubt will be standing for many years to come. The large, square base covers the expanse of where I got on my knee, the roof keeps us covered, and the low walls around the opening she's walking up ensure I can keep loving her out in the open while giving us some privacy.

With each step she takes toward me, I have to fight the need to rush to her. Feeling a nudge against my arm, I reluctantly look away from Caroline. The handkerchief in Maverick's hand silently gets passed to mine and I wipe the tears I hadn't realized I was crying. Caroline takes the last step into the gazebo and pulls the material from my grasp, wiping my eyes for me with the most serene expression on her beautiful face. When she's done, I take it from her and return the favor when one tear of her own slips down her cheek.

"Oh, God," one of the girls sobs.

I hear some more sniffles, but I can't look away from Caroline to see who is crying. My eyes don't leave hers once while Judge Allan—the only person available to marry us on a Wednesday night—speaks out for the small group to hear clearly. The whole ceremony is a fog for me, my focus only on Caroline as my heart pounds happily. I slip my band on her finger without breaking our gaze, and she does the same. The second the solid weight of my wedding band registers, I feel my control slipping and my eyes watering. She doesn't miss it either, but I reckon she's too busy holding her own emotions in check to do much about it. It isn't until Judge Allan tells me I can kiss my bride that I move.

My hands frame her face and my feet take a step closer until I bend and take my wife's mouth in a slow, deep kiss. I have to force myself to pull away, but when I look down at Caroline—*my wife*—and see the dazed stare in her dark eyes I smile and drop my forehead to hers.

"I love you. I loved you before you were my wife and I'll love you long after my last breath. Thank you, Linney, for blessin' my life."

She hiccups out a soft sob, closing her eyes and tightening her arms around me. "Heavens above, Clayton Davis. You're an incredible man. You own my heart, honey. Now and forever."

I move my mouth to her ear, making sure no one can hear me, and grin when she sucks in a breath. "I'm gonna be bad with my wife tonight."

Her hand that's resting on my chest trembles slightly before her fingers grip the fabric. Leaning back, I wink down at her and place a quick kiss against her forehead.

Judge Allan signs the papers to make us legal before waving us off and taking one of the golf carts back toward the ranch where he left his truck. He knew we wanted this moment to be as private as can be, shared between family only, and I'm thankful he doesn't stick around, giving us this moment before our marriage news spreads through town.

And spread it will.

I have a feeling that by the time I wake up in the morning with my wife in my arms, the whole town is going to know Clayton Davis finally settled down.

"What's up, sista!" Quinn hoots, her voice carrying in the vast open space around us. I frown at her when she pulls Caroline from my arms and wraps her in her own. The brat just sticks her tongue out at me when I reach for Caroline again. "Someone is goin' to need to learn to share. She's not just yours, big brother."

"Like hell," I grunt.

"Oh, be a good boy, Clay. Sharin' is carin', you know."

I narrow my eyes at Quinn. Before I can say anything, Caroline smiles at me over her shoulder, her eyes dancing with mischief.

"Yeah, honey . . . be a *good boy*."

I arch my brow, place my hands on my hips, and smile

at her. Her eyes widen the second she realizes that, by trying to play me, she's about to get it right back.

"Darlin', need I remind you how much you love it when I'm bad?"

"Clayton!" She hisses, her cheeks turning pink.

"Oh, really?" Quinn gasps with mock shock. "Someone's been holdin' out on us, Leigh!"

"I'm goin' to get you for that," Caroline whispers, closing her eyes and shaking her head when Quinn and Leigh continue teasing. "I'm goin' to tell them you've got a butt fetish."

Tossing my head back, I laugh loudly and pull her into my arms. "Linney, that's not exactly a threat, considerin' I most definitely love your ass."

"That's not what I meant!"

"I might need to show you just how much I love it later," I continue, ignoring her. Her eyes darken and I pull her tighter against me. "Knew you loved me bein' bad for you."

I expected her to ignore me, but instead she holds my gaze—pink cheeks and all—and shrugs. "I don't think there's a single thing in this world that I don't love when it comes to you, Clayton."

"Feelin's mutual, Linney, love."

"We're goin' to head back to the house and start gettin' the food out," Maverick says, stepping closer with his daughter asleep against his chest. "Give y'all some time alone."

I nod. "Thanks, Mav."

He lifts his chin, looks down at his daughter, and kisses her on the top of her blond head. I glance at my niece and feel the tug in my chest. Until Caroline, I never wanted that—what my brother has right there in his arms. I shoot my eyes over to where Quinn is fussing over her son while he grunts in his father's arms. One more glance at Laelynn, and I feel a burst of determination rush over me. I want that. I want children with the woman who owns my happiness, love, and life. I need it. More than that, I want to prove that I can be what my parents couldn't be.

Maverick clears his throat, pulling my eyes from his daughter. My normally stoic and closed-off brother gives me a whole hell of a lot without words when I lock eyes with him. He gets it. The need that's coursing through my veins right now. One corner of his mouth tips up. He adjusts his daughter so he can pull one hand away, placing his large hand on my shoulder. Caroline steps to the side; then my brother has one arm around my back and his head next to mine, voice low. "Real happy for you, Clay. You deserve everything you've gotten and will get with Caroline. You know what kinda peace lovin' her gives you, but just you wait until your woman blesses you with your firstborn. No fuckin' feelin' can compare to the love that grows from that for your child, and for the woman you never imagined possible to love more. Just you wait."

Fuck me.

I clench my jaw, press my lips to my niece's temple, and lift my head to nod at Mav. He doesn't need me to acknowledge his words, not when we both know he isn't wrong.

True to his word, Maverick corrals the small group into carts to head off to his house. The sound of their chatter lingers behind them long after they disappear around the trees that keep Mav and Leigh's property mostly hidden. Caroline steps into me, her front against mine, and wraps her arms around my waist. Resting my chin against the top of her head, I close my arms around her.

"I can't wait to get you back home," I confess softly, my hands caressing the bare skin completely exposed from just below her shoulders to the top of her ass, showing the dimples at the base of her spine. "Is this clasp the only thing holding your dress together?" I continue, flicking the tiny stretch of fabric that goes across her shoulder blades.

"Pretty much." She giggles, pressing herself even tighter against me. "I think it's more for extra support in keeping the front from showing too much."

I pull back a little and look down at the front of her dress. My fingers trail from the strap in question over her lace-covered shoulders, and down her front. The deep V of her neckline stops below her chest, mid-stomach. Sticking my pointer fingers into the lace at the bottom of the V, I glide them up toward her breasts. The bottom swell of her tits is silky smooth as I slide over the flesh. Her teeth bite her lower lip when my fingers finally move to her nipples, and she moans low. I roll each tight bud before pulling both fingers out of the fabric. Her chest moves rapidly.

"Tonight, tonight I'm goin' to love my wife bad and not take this dress off until I'm done." I bend, my tongue coming out to lick her from the bottom of that V and up the middle of her chest until my mouth is at her ear. "I can't wait to feel all this lace against me while your silky heat sucks me dry."

"Oh, God," she breathes.

"One day, when our family isn't waitin' for us, I'm goin' to bring you back up here and we're goin' to break this gazebo in."

Caroline places her hands against my chest and lifts up on her toes. "I like the sound of that, honey."

With a groan that seems to come from deep in my body, I take her mouth in a deep kiss. Her lips open instantly, ready for me, and our tongues slide against each other. With her body pressed tight and her hands at the back of my head, keeping me close, I feel surrounded by her love. She whines when I shift us and my erection pushes into her belly. My hands move and I bend, taking her ass in my palms and lifting her as I stretch back up. Her dress keeps her from wrapping her legs around me, but her arms adjust to wrap around my neck, deepening our connection.

I've never felt more whole than I do right now. High above my land in a place that's always meant something to me, with the rest of my life in my arms.

I've got it all. I truly have it all.

25

CLAYTON

"Ain't Nothing 'Bout You" by Brooks & Dunn

"**M**ore."

I breathe in, the scene and taste only becoming more addicting when I do. How she can taste like the sweetest apple pie ever baked, I'll never know, but fuck if I'm not going to enjoy the dessert of her.

"Please, Clayton," she gasps, the breathy sound turning into a scream when I bite her swollen clit between my teeth before hollowing my cheeks and sucking hard.

Her hands fist in my hair, pulling me closer as she grinds against my face. I look up her body, seeing her lost in pleasure as she writhes against our bed. The stark white of her wedding dress against our dark gray sheets reminds me that only hours ago this woman became mine for life. I growl against her, causing her to yelp, and press my left hand against her pelvis to keep her hips on the mattress.

In the dim glow from the lamp on my nightstand, the black metal on my ring finger can't be missed. Seeing that symbol of our union only drives the need I'm feeling to take her grow to insurmountable levels. It's undeniable, primal, the forceful urge to consummate our union in the most carnal of ways taking on a life of its own.

Dragging my hands up her torso, I take her breasts. The fabric of her dress catches on my callused hands, but it doesn't stop me from flexing my fingers against the small weight of her tits. She moans low and deep as I continue to play with her, her wetness covering my chin. Flattening my tongue, I lift my head and then lick her from opening to clit, dragging my tongue around the bud, then moving back down. Her flavor bursts on my tongue, making me hungry for more. The heady scent of her swirls around me as my balls tighten. Running the tip of my nose over her sex, I inhale and feel my chest vibrate as the satisfying aroma of her arousal fills my head.

"Look at me," I demand, stilling my hands. She rolls her head from side to side but doesn't give me those brown eyes. "Look at me, Linney. Watch me love the fuck outta my good girl. See what it does to me to drink from your pussy. To know that I'm the one your body comes to life for."

"Oh, God," she gasps.

"Look at me *now*," I growl.

Her head lifts slowly as she obeys. Her hair, no longer contained, tumbles around her face and over her chest. The ends tickle my hands against her breasts. Her eyes, so dark they almost look black, plead with me through hooded lids, and incoherent mumbles leave her mouth. Her kiss-swollen lips part as she starts panting, needing this as much as I do.

Opening my mouth wide, I close my lips around her pussy and stick my tongue into her entrance. Thrusting as deep as I can before lifting my head back slightly to lick her again, I hold her gaze and suck, flick, and lick her pussy until her eyes flutter closed and she screams out my name as her orgasm slams through her.

Releasing her breasts, I drag my hands down her body, and with one more closed-mouth kiss to her pussy, I turn my head and wipe my mouth against her thigh. Her legs fall open as I lift my shoulders from between her legs and climb up her body, thankful I stripped down before following her into bed. I glance at the clock on the nightstand and smirk.

"You look smug," she pants drunkenly, out of breath and making my cock jerk, knowing I'm the reason she's trying to catch her breath.

"I just made you come three times and even though I had your pussy wettin' my lips for over an hour, I want more."

"My heart is always goin' to be racin' around you, isn't it!"

I smile at my wife as my hips start moving, gliding

my thickness through her slickness, not entering her. She hisses each time the tip of my cock bumps her sensitive clit. "I hope so, darlin'." Keeping my pace, I watch her dress move against her chest while I rock her body with my teasing. Her small tits jiggle slightly each time I thrust against her. The delicate fabric that goes around her shoulders to meet the strap across her back strains with each heavy breath. I wonder how hard I'd have to take her for those tits to break free of the fabric.

I come up on my knees and drink her in as I stroke my cock. The long skirt on her dress is bunched at her hips, her sex glistening in the low light, and those brown eyes I love are watching my fist as I work my length. When she moves quickly, it takes me a second to realize her mouth is suddenly around my cock and her tongue is swirling against the tip. Her hand wraps around mine, squeezing my stalled grip, and when I don't move, she hums against my flesh. I grunt, clench my cheeks, and with my free hand brush her hair out of her face. Her hand squeezes me again and her eyes meet mine.

"Fuck me." I hiss, seeing clear as day in those dark depths the pleasure she's getting from sucking my cock.

My hand moves, letting her hold guide the movements as we start stroking the hard, needy flesh. Her mouth takes as much of my length as she can, which isn't much, before swirling her tongue around me to repeat the process. It takes every ounce of my control to not come, but when I feel her teeth scrape against the underside of my cock, I see stars. With a bellow, I release my hand from her hold and hook her under her arms and toss her back against the bed. My body covers hers instantly and my mouth drops to hers. The sounds coming from the two of us are hungry as our tongues dance together.

Lifting my hips, I feel her arm move between us, and without any encouragement, she feeds my cock into her body. She screams out with the first hard stroke, but because of how long I primed her with my mouth, she has no trouble taking me completely. The shock of her pussy strangling me from tip to base is almost enough to have my come shooting deep into her, but I hold on and rumble a warning when she wiggles her hips.

"Please," she begs.

"Don't move," I demand through thin lips, feeling a tiny burst of pre-come leave my cock. "Fuck." I drop my forehead to her neck and try to measure my breathing and get ahold of my body.

"Clayton Davis, if you don't start movin' now, I'm goin' to knock you on your ass and move for you."

"Caroline Davis, if you don't stop movin' and let me have a minute, I'm gonna spank your ass and then move for you."

"Yes." She exhales, her eyes widening and her pussy clenching greedily and flexing against my cock.

"Goddamn," I blow the word out with a hiss.

Pushing the thoughts of her liking the sound of me spanking her from my mind, I start to move, slowly gliding through her, in deep thrusts. Her nails scrape against my back, her mewls echoing and mingling with my low grunts, but it's her slick heat rippling against my cock that almost does me in. I drop my mouth to her neck and start to kiss up the slim column until my lips are moving along her jaw. The whole time, my hips start to pick up speed. By the time I've covered her mouth with mine, she's frantic, her hips surging off the bed to meet mine, our damp bodies slapping together, and her voice becoming hoarse as she screams out her release. Between the incredible feeling of her pussy clamping down on my cock and the expression on her face when she does, I can't hold myself back any longer.

Planting my hips against hers, the tip of me as deep as I can get, I feel my stomach clench and my balls draw up. My mouth opens over her shoulder and I bite her against the tender flesh while emptying my release deep into her body. I lift my mouth when the last tremor shakes up my body and lick where there are indentions of my teeth.

"I love it when you're bad with me." She sighs.

"Did I hurt you?" I ask, panting and staring at the mark I've left on her flesh—a mark that only makes me want to put more all over her. Logically, I know it's going to disappear before we wake up in the morning, but I can't deny loving the fuck out of seeing it—wishing it was to stay.

"Hurt me? God, *no*." She moans the last word when I

start to slip free from her heat, that sound turning into a low whine when I pull the rest of the way from her body.

I glance down at my cock, the wetness of our combined releases covering every inch. She whimpers, the pitiful sound making me smile. She isn't the only one who wishes we could keep our bodies connected. When I look back up at her, all flushed skin and bright eyes, I feel like the luckiest bastard in the world.

"Thank you."

She frowns and searches my face. "For what, honey?"

I inhale and shake my head, feeling my lips move as I grin down at her. "For lovin' me. For givin' me you. For wantin' me. Never thought I would have this, Linney, but now that I do, I know I'll never be able to live without it. So"—I kiss her slack lips—"thank you, baby."

Her chin wobbles and she blinks rapidly. "Clayton," she hiccups. "Honey," she sniffles. "Never, *ever* do you need to thank me for doin' what I was made to do. You have no idea what you've done for me, do you?"

When I don't speak, she gives one more sniff before giving up and letting the tears fall, smiling through them up at me.

"You, honey, you saved me. You healed me. You gave me purpose in a life that I had given up on. You've given me strength, confidence, and a fearlessness that only grows with your love. Don't thank me for doin' what comes as natural as breathin' does, honey."

"Linney," I rumble thickly.

"You brought me back to life," she continues.

"Stop, darlin'."

"Showed me just how beautiful my days could be."

"Caroline."

"Offered your silent protection, my white knight, while I faced my demons."

"Baby," I try again, her words making my throat get thicker and my eyes burn.

"Loved me bad and gave me forever."

"Fuck," I grunt, my mouth covering hers so she'll stop talking. I don't even attempt to hold back the wetness falling from my eyes in tune with my pounding heart. Getting emotional because your other half loves you isn't something I'll ever be ashamed of. Not when I never thought I would have this.

I keep my mouth fused to hers while I strip her carefully of her dress and, with her silky-smooth skin pressed tightly to mine, love my wife slow. Our moans and pleading gasps are swallowed as we kiss. The slick silk of her chest rubs against mine as I continue the slow tempo of my hips.

With her words still echoing through my mind, the last thought I have before the sensation of loving her becomes too much is that she's wrong. It was she who brought me back to life.

- ★ -

My ringing phone pulls me from a deep and sated sleep. Caroline curls into my side as the ringing continues and I pull her closer while burying my head in the crook of her neck, content to ignore whoever is calling. I groan when the ringing picks up not even a second after it stopped, but it isn't until I hear Caroline's phone join in that I move.

"Clayton?" she asks, confused.

I roll and grab my phone off the nightstand, jabbing the accept button. "Yeah?"

"Clay."

"What, Mav?"

"The gazebo," he starts, releasing an aggravated breath. "It's gone, Clay."

"What the hell do you mean, it's gone?" Sleep instantly vanishes as my brother's words wake me up as effectively as an ice-cold bucket of water tossed over my head.

"Trey was out on a late ride tonight. He does that shit after a long day—don't ask me why he goes this damn late. He said when he went west, all was quiet. About an hour later, before he could even see where it was comin' from, he noticed the glow of somethin' burnin'. He tried, Clay. Rushed back to grab the extinguisher here, but by the time he got back up the hill, there wasn't anything left."

I swing my legs over the side of the bed with a heavy exhale. I click on the light and brace my elbows on my knees, looking down at the floor. I feel Caroline press against my back, her hands rubbing my arms in silent support. Fuck, I don't want to tell her. I'll rebuild it, no doubt about that, but it won't be the same. I know that, even without telling her and confirming it.

"He see anyone else out there?"

Maverick's silence tells me all I need to know.

"Who?"

"Calm down, brother. You gettin' pissed isn't gonna help shit."

"I'll be there in five." Knowing in my gut that he didn't tell me who it was for a reason, that reason pressing herself against my back, I shake my head and look down at my feet.

"What is it, honey?" Caroline's question breaks the silence, worry in her tone.

"Fuck." I hiss, knowing this is going to put a dark cloud over our wedding day. "I need you to trust me, darlin'. I don't know much, but there was a fire and I need to go meet Mav and find out the rest. I'll tell you everything when I get back, but stay put while I go get answers."

"You're scaring me," she whispers, her voice shaking. "Was anyone hurt?"

I turn and reach for her, pulling her into my lap. "No, Linney, I don't think so. Trey, Mav's uncle, found it and did his best to put it out. I don't want to scare you, darlin', but I need you to stay here and let me handle this. Until I know more, I don't want you leavin' the house."

She nods, but I can tell she isn't happy about me leaving her with no answers.

"I'll be quick and I'll keep my phone on me."

"Is . . . is there more? Is everything okay?"

"Everything *will* be okay."

Her eyes search mine for a beat before she nods and pulls a choppy breath in. "Be careful," she whispers.

"Always."

I climb from the bed and start getting dressed. The whole time her eyes follow me. I see her wrap the comforter tighter around her body and I hate knowing she's worried. She isn't stupid, my girl. She's likely connecting the dots, just like I did when Maverick mentioned a fire. We haven't had a single break in finding the person who set her bookstore on fire twice, but judging by what Mav didn't say, I have a feeling that's about to change.

The question is, will finding those answers do more than give Caroline the closure of knowing the truth? I know she's no longer the scared and shy woman I first fell in love with, but this situation is worthy of a little fear. I just pray that fear guides her to rise through the aches.

"I'll be back," I promise.

She nods. "I'll be ready."

She'll be ready. Fuck me, this girl. She means it, too. I can see her building herself up, steeling herself for whatever news comes back with me, ready to take it on. She isn't building walls, not like she used to do. She's building her emotional army. Even with the shit I'm about to go handle, I can't help but feel pride witnessing just how far my shy and timid Caroline has come. I honestly believe she could take on the world. My Linney, she's always been so much stronger than she gave herself credit for, but just as our love saved me, it helped her see that. I have no doubt about it.

"Yeah. Yeah, you will be."

"I love you, honey."

I bend over the bed and kiss her soft and quick. "I love you too."

26

CAROLINE

"The House That Built Me" by Miranda Lambert

A fire.

Clayton said *was*. Past tense. There had been a fire, not that there still was one. That's something I've been holding on to since he left ten minutes ago. I locked the front door behind him and watched through the living room window as he rushed across the grass and into the detached garage that holds the golf carts and quad bikes. A few minutes later, he's tearing through the night on the back of one of the quads. I expected to see some sign of the fire close, but seeing the direction he's headed makes no sense. The land between our house and Maverick and Leighton's holds nothing. Unless the fire was at his brother's. God, I hate not knowing, being afraid for the family that already owns my heart.

There's no way I'll be able to go back to sleep.

It was just a little past midnight, I think, by the time we finally fell asleep earlier. I lost track of how long we spent loving each other, but the last time I saw the time, it was close enough to midnight that I'm fairly sure that's when we passed out. Glancing at the clock above the oven, I wince. Fifteen minutes till two. No wonder it feels like I just fell asleep—I literally did.

Needing to keep my mind occupied, I start the coffee maker and then go to the fridge to pull some breakfast food out. We haven't eaten since the dinner at Maverick and Leighton's after the ceremony, but even then, we didn't eat much. Even if we hadn't been anxious to be alone, we couldn't keep our hands—and mouths—off each other long enough to eat anyway. I don't even think either of us finished half of our food before we were making our excuses and rushing home.

Not knowing how long he's going to be, I decide to start putting together a quiche. Nothing crazy, but at least it'll keep me busy. If it weren't the middle of the night, I would call one of the girls to talk me through my worry. I take my time cutting the onions and bell peppers, the mindless task not taking my mind off my worries at all.

"This isn't workin'," I mumble, dumping the diced bits into the bowl.

I grab the piecrust I had already prepped and start to add all the ingredients, my eyes moving to the clock every five minutes or so. I blow out a breath, pick up a handful of peppers and onions, and scatter them on the bottom of the pie tin, covering the crust completely. As satisfied as I can be with my mind in such a jumbled state, I pick up the egg, cheese, and spice mixture and pour that into the crust.

Picking up the quiche, I turn from the island and start to walk to the double ovens. Two steps in and the deafening sound of glass shattering breaks the silence. I scream, my whole body jolting in fear. The pie tin hits the floor, the sticky yellow contents splattering my bare legs and the area all around me. I glance down, confused, seeing the mess before another sound by the back door reminds me what startled me enough to drop the quiche in the first place.

"Hello, Caroline."

The heinous heat in those two words slams into me, and without looking, I know this is going to be bad. I just hope and pray that whatever happens here, Clayton won't be harmed.

"Look at me, you stupid bitch!"

I fill my lungs with a deep breath and say a silent prayer. Then I look up from my egg-soaked mess and into the evil glare of Clayton's ex, Jess. Jess, who is pointing a gun in my direction with wild hair and even wilder eyes.

This is it, Caroline. Time to fight for the beauty you've found. No more letting fear win. Not now. Not when it isn't just your life that's in jeopardy here.

"Clayton's going to be back soon," I tell her, proud of the calm I don't actually feel in my voice.

She tosses her head back and laughs sinisterly. The gun jerks in her hold while she takes obvious enjoyment out of her crazy thoughts. "Oh, no, he won't. I made sure he'd be busy for a while."

"What did you do, Jess?"

My worry for Clayton barrels into me, but I push it aside . . . for now. I focus on where I am in the kitchen and weigh my options while hoping to keep her distracted with questions. If I can just move a little to the left, I can reach the knife block.

"What did *I* do? You've got to be kidding me."

"No." I shake my head. "I'm not kidding you."

"You've got some nerve, whore. You show up, move in on my man, and even though I was nice enough to give you a few warnings, you still didn't listen! Not even when I finished what I didn't accomplish the first time."

"*You* set those fires?" I take a step back slowly when she looks away briefly.

"God, you're dense. Of course I did. I would've taken care of you with the first one, but he assured me you weren't worth it. He said you wouldn't stick around. HE SAID I WOULDN'T HAVE TO WORRY ABOUT YOU AND MY MAN!" She wipes her mouth as spit falls down her chin. "He said all you'd need was a little warning and you'd be too scared to leave the house. WHY DIDN'T YOU LISTEN!"

Good heavens, she's insane.

"Who, Jess? Who said that to you?" I take another step back, my heart thundering in my chest when I almost slip on the sticky mess at my feet.

She moves away from the broken back door, kicking the rock she must've thrown through the window out of her way. As the barrel of her handgun gets closer, I feel panic rising in my throat.

"John, you dumbass. He seemed to think you wouldn't be a threat. One fire, he said, would be enough to make the timid little turtle go back into her shell. I thought he was right. You didn't come sniffin' back around *my* man for a while. But, then you had to go and fuck it all up, didn't you? Shoulda trusted my gut the first time I saw you with Clay at that piece-of-shit bar. Shoulda slit your throat when you left that motel, like I wanted to."

I shake my head, blown away by what she's saying. "The motel?"

"The first time I saw you with my man. I left it be because you stayed away and I gave you some time to make sure you wouldn't go sniffing back around what is mine. I knew Clay would get bored of your used goods. I knew he'd come back to me. But then you had to go and move your trash into *my* house with *my MAN*! That's when I knew you needed more of a reason to run far away from Pine Oak—and Clay. John didn't want to help me again, but he did when I reminded him who was in charge. No matter what we did, you didn't take a hint. You were supposed to leave!"

"You and . . . John? Y'all were the ones messin' up things with the rebuild of my store?" It takes everything in me to keep my voice calm as the panic starts to flow quicker. I just need to keep her talking. Keep her mind distracted. One more step. My hand slowly moves behind my back and I wait until I have an opening, finally being close enough to grab a knife, but not wanting to get shot when she realizes what I'm up to.

There's no way I'm going to give up without fighting to keep the beautiful life I have—I've got too much to live for.

"He didn't want me to, but I had to finish what I started. Saw right through his stalling and realized he wasn't really on my team. Stupid motherfucker. You know, I'd hoped it wouldn't come to this. Now I'm goin' to be cleanin' up your blood in my kitchen. You dirty everything up. I should just light this place up so Clay and I can move on without your filth." Her chest heaves and her eyes narrow as her face gets bright red. "You just couldn't leave though, could you! Even with your stupid fuckin' store gone, you still didn't go. NO ONE WANTS YOU! You're nothin' but a paid whore now, moochin' off my man and livin' off his dime. There isn't anything for you here!"

"You're wrong," I whisper, wincing when the unhinged madness in her eyes amps up. In my inability to keep from defending what Clayton and I have, I might as well be throwing out a challenge to this madwoman.

"I'm wrong?! I'm WRONG?! You did NOT just say that. There isn't shit for you here! All you are and all you'll ever be is a warm hole."

"How did you get Clayton out of the house?" I hedge, knowing I need to steer her into something a little safer than my relationship with Clayton so I can get out of this kitchen alive.

She grins, evil and wicked, clearly proud of herself. "That dumbass ex of yours." She laughs, the sound nothing short of vile. "You know, all he wanted to do was apologize. Stupid bastard. I finally realized what he was doin' when he tried to stop me tonight. The whole time he's been tryin' to stop me—I just didn't realize it until today. Slipped up, he did. Told me you had a diamond on your finger—*my* diamond—and that he was fuckin' happy for you. Fool. Found out not long after that Clay married your dumb ass tonight. John couldn't hide it any longer. He was just blowin' smoke up my ass, protectin' you the whole fuckin' time by keepin' me from doin' what I wanted to do all along. Always had a reason why we shouldn't hurt you. Well, joke's on him since he damn sure can't protect you with a bullet through his brain."

"My God," I gasp, not dwelling on the thought of John being dead, but recognizing just how far past sane this woman is. There will be time later, when I make it through this, to reflect on everything she's said tonight—and I *will* make it through this.

"I made sure to leave Clay that stupid fuck as a present. Left him right next to the ashes of that ugly gazebo I hear you married my man under."

My heart clenches. Clayton worked so hard building that in our spot. "He's not goin' to forgive you for this, Jess. You might think hurtin' me is the answer, but he'll hate you more than he already does if you go through with this."

"HE LOVES ME!" The gun jumps as she waves it in my direction, spit flying from her mouth as she growls. "You don't know anything!"

"I know everything!"

"Clay loves me. He always has. He was comin' back to me!"

"He hates you! The second you killed his baby, you made it so he wouldn't ever feel anything more than hate when he thought about you. When he finds out what you've done, he'll do one more than just hate you. He'll forget about you. Because that's what MY husband does when someone wrongs him and doesn't deserve his forgiveness."

"Shut up!" she screams, shaking her head and banging her free hand against the side of it.

Taking advantage of the insanity inside her bubbling over, distracting her enough that she lowers the gun just enough so it isn't pointed at my head anymore and her eyes are no longer wildly hunting me as though I were prey, I lift my hand and grab the first knife handle I reach, pulling it from the block behind my back.

"All he had to do was give me *that* diamond and I wouldn't have had to take care of the problem."

"The problem?" I gasp.

"He didn't even want a fuckin' little snot-nosed brat. He said he never wanted them, but I knew he'd marry me if I was carryin' his child—then I could take care of it and we'd still have each other."

My hand tightens on the knife, my anger for the wrongs she's done to Clayton taking on a whole new life. "You *bitch*! He would have loved that baby. Even with you bein' stuck in his life because of the child y'all shared, he would have loved it. You're right, he definitely didn't want to have a baby with you, but he would've been the best damn father. Who knows, maybe he would've come around, but you'll never know, because you killed his child."

I see it in her eyes the second she decides to pull the trigger, that insane glint that's been dancing there since she broke in turning into something feral. I move on autopilot, jumping to the side and diving behind the island. Before I fall to the floor, though, my arm flies out and over my head as I release the knife. I don't even know if I threw it toward her, but it was the only thing I could think of. Fighting a gun with a knife leaves little room for options.

My thigh burns and I cry out when I land hard. My ears ring, the blast from her gun so loud that I feel its power in my bones. My body slides and slips against the eggy mess on the floor as I back toward the hallway. I had expected her to be on me the second I moved, but when I hit the hallway and press my back against the wall, all I hear is silence. Well, muffled silence. Between the gun going off and my thundering heartbeat, I can't hear much over the bounding tempo of my racing heart and my gasping breaths.

Think, Caroline. You can't just sit here and wait for her to come back for you. Fight.

The gun safe.

Clayton showed it to me a few weeks ago. Gave me the code, but I didn't think anything of it. I listen for movement, but still don't hear much of anything. However, when I go to stand, I realize why my leg is burning, and it has nothing to do with landing on it wrong. There's a small puddle of redness forming under my leg. Now that I've noticed, the bullet wound's pain becomes all but unbearable.

Linney, fight. FIGHT, baby!

Gritting my teeth, I do the only thing I can and rally. I wipe my hands on my shirt before placing them behind me and turning from the wall. Unable to put weight on my leg, I start scooting back with my good leg, pushing my body down the hall toward Clayton's office. The red trail against the hardwood floors is unpreventable, even if it's basically an arrow telling Jess how to find me.

Once I reach the office, it takes me a little while to remember the code, but finally the metal door pops and swings open. I take in the different guns inside, but, not knowing anything about them, I just grab one and pray it's loaded. I start moving back toward the door but pause to look down at the gun I'm holding, remembering the safety that Clayton had mentioned. He hadn't been teaching me how to use the gun, merely mentioning how, if I needed it, I would have to click the safety off.

"Where the fuck are you, bitch!"

"Oh, God," I pant, blinding white fear slamming into me. "Where the heck is it?" I turn the gun around in my hand, finally seeing the small button. After making sure it's off, I try to move behind his desk, but the fire in my leg makes it hard to breathe without it throbbing.

"I'm goin' to find you and gut you from your nasty, used cunt all the way to your chest so I can rip out your heart and stuff it down your throat."

I raise the gun, leaning my back on Clayton's desk and try to calm my racing heart. I hear her moving, swearing as she does.

I look down at my still bleeding leg. *Shit.* Using the desk, I pull myself up from the floor and hobble as best I can to the attached bath, cracking the door and placing the tip of the gun between the gap in the direction of the office doorway. I hear her as she moves down the hall, her words incoherent as she rants and slurs. My vision is getting gray around the edges, and I know time is not on my side.

"Gotcha, bitch," Jess yells, jumping into the office doorway and searching the room wildly. "The fuck did you go?"

My hands don't even tremble as I adjust my hold on the gun and wait. She takes three steps into the room, stopping right next to where I'm hiding, and with one last slow exhale, my vision now a dull black, I pull the trigger.

27

CLAYTON

"Sometimes I Cry" by Chris Stapleton

— ★ —

Pulling up to the still-smoking remains of the gazebo, I park next to Mav's four-wheeler and cut the engine on mine. I expected Sheriff Holden to be here, but not the three other patrol trucks pointing their headlights toward the ash- and ember-filled space that I'd married Caroline in hours before.

What I also hadn't expected, was the body of John Lewis to be here.

"What the fuck?"

"Shit, Clay," Mav answers, blowing out his breath. "I know you thought it might have been him, but fuckin' hell."

I don't look away, my eyes struggling to make sense of what's before me. John Lewis, the man who deserves whatever hell is waiting on him, lying half burned on my property. "What did he do? Start the damn fire and fall in?" I ask no one in particular.

"Not sure, son," Holden says, coming to stand next to me. "Your brother tells me that there's a connection here?"

I nod, looking away and at the older man. "He's my wife's ex. There's not one good thing about what he shared with her either. Not to mention his history of erratic behavior from a few years ago."

He clicks his teeth, looking back down at the body. "That's right. I remember that. Such a shame, those horses of yours."

"I hadn't seen him after that until a month or two ago when I was pickin' up Caroline in Wire Creek. Didn't say a word to us, but saw him there watchin' and not hidin' it one bit."

"Has he contacted your wife?"

"Shit," I hiss, looking away from the dead man. "Earlier today. I don't know everything that was said, but she mentioned him approaching her briefly. Shit just got busy with the weddin' and I haven't talked to her about it since."

"Tucker says he saw them outside the grocery earlier yesterday."

I glance in the direction he's pointing to see the younger police officer. He dips his chin but doesn't say anything.

"With all due respect, Sheriff, I hope you can understand how it slipped my mind, seein' that aside from us sayin' I do, there wasn't much time to talk about our day."

"I didn't mean anything by it, Clay. Just pointin' out that this clearly wasn't a spur-of-the-moment thing if not even twenty-four hours after approaching your wife, he's here."

"What the hell was burnin' somethin' down in the middle of my property goin' to prove anyway? It doesn't make a lick of sense."

"I understand your wife's store in Wire Creek had some fire issues as well recently?"

I scoff. "You could say that. Someone tried to burn her inside of there the first time. Shit got tampered with while she was in the rebuildin' stage, and the second she put the place on the market, they came back and sparked it up real good. That wasn't long before when she officially moved in to the ranch."

Holden bobs his head, listening to me while one of the younger cops writes some notes down.

"Coroner's here," someone mumbles.

I glance up at Spencer Russell, the town's coroner, as he climbs down from his truck. The man's old as dirt but wise as hell. He walks toward our huddle and shakes hands with Holden and Mav before getting to me.

"Nice night for a barbecue?" he cryptically jokes, grunting out a belly laugh while walking toward John's body.

Mav snickers under his breath and I see the sheriff shake his head, a small grin on his lips. I keep my silence. It's not like John being behind all this isn't believable. But Caroline's words about how he wouldn't have hidden behind the fires echo through my mind. That's why I'm having a hard time believing this is clear-cut. Someone like John Lewis would have made his point in an irrefutable kind of way. He would have been in your face and proud, hungry to see the fear he had produced. What he wouldn't have done was spent months hiding behind fires and petty construction-site mischief.

"Well, well," Spencer mutters, using his gloved hands to turn John's head. "Y'all see a gun anywhere round here?"

Ice-cold dread fills my veins.

"No, sir. We checked the area real good when we got here, too."

"Linney," I wheeze, already turning and running back to the four-wheeler. I toss my leg over the seat and reach for the key. Before I can fire it up, the unmistakable sound of a gunshot echoes through the night. "Caroline!"

"Clay!" I hear bellowed at the same time my engine kicks over. Before I can get the four-wheeler into gear, my brother is jumping on the back rack with his legs hanging over one side. I don't spare him a glance, flipping my wrist and gunning it back to the ranch knowing he'll hold on but not giving a shit if he falls off. I need to get back to my wife.

"Kill it back behind the barn," Mav yells into my ear.

I nod, changing gears and picking up speed. When we come into the clearing that the house is in, I flip the lights off and drive to the back of the barn and turn off the four-wheeler, running toward the house not even a second later. I don't look to see if my brother is following; the only thing I care about is making sure Caroline's okay. My feet have just cleared the top step of the porch when I hear the second gunshot and all rational thoughts vanish. I lift my boot and kick the front door, the wood splintering as the lock gives. Shouldering the broken door out of the way, I stand in the doorway, my eyes searching and my heart praying.

"Clay," Mav whispers, pointing to the red smear that looks like someone dragged a body down the hall.

"Caroline!" I scream, rushing forward and following the trail, Mav hot on my heels. I hear more footsteps rushing up the porch and I have no doubt that Sheriff Holden didn't waste a second following me.

"No," I pant, coming into my office and seeing a nightmare coming to life. My world stops spinning a second later when I see through the cracked door of the office bathroom the delicate hand lying limp—the hand adorned with the rings I had put there.

"Holy hell," someone says behind me.

I jump over the very dead woman on the floor in the middle of my office, noticing that not only is her head missing, she's got a knife sticking out of her chest, directly under her collarbone.

My girl fought.

"Linney, love?" I sob, pushing the door open enough to get into the bathroom. "God, darlin'." My knees slam into the floor and I reach out to check her pulse, feeling instant relief blast through the dark pit of dread that had settled over me when I find one, though it's weak. "Get an ambulance here, now!" I bellow out. "Stay with me, baby. You stay with me, Linney."

I rock her in my arms and pray, plead, and beg. My throat burns and my eyes sting. I bury my face in her neck, breathe her in. Her limp body is heavy in my arms, her face drained of color.

"Ambulance is five out," Mav says, his own voice betraying his calm outer appearance. He grabs a towel off the rack and presses it against her leg. "She's gonna be okay, Clay. Believe it. Ain't room for any other outcome."

I shake my head, my tears falling faster. I don't say a word. Not while my brother helps to stop the blood flowing from her leg, pulling my shirt she's wearing down to cover her underwear. When the paramedics burst through the door and take her from my arms, though, I break. Break into so many pieces that I know if something happens to her, I'll never put them back together again.

The stretcher makes her look even tinier than normal. The men work on her for only a second before rushing down the hall. I jump from the floor and sprint after them.

Mav grabs my arm, stopping me from getting to the ambulance. I turn and punch him in the face when the ambulance door shuts, one of the men yelling out that they're on the way to the hospital in Law Bone and taking off without me—taking my *everything* away from me.

"Get in the fuckin' truck," Mav demands, spitting and wiping his split lip with the back of his hand.

He stomps toward my truck, not looking to see if I'm following. We both climb in, and he punches the gas while I hunch forward to push my hands through my hair. Silence and the sound of my engine speeding through the night ring in my ears, the vision of Caroline lying in a pool of blood, lifeless, etched in my brain.

"She's gonna be okay, Clay."

"I'm nothin' without her," I mumble, feeling the pain of my words like a knife to the heart.

"Stay strong. She needs you fightin' too."

"If she doesn't—"

Mav slams his palm against the wheel and bellows a string of curses. "Shut the fuck up. You've got another ten minutes before we get to the hospital, and I fuckin' swear, you better fix your shit by then. You're doin' her no good already placin' her in the ground when she fought to make sure you never gotta know what it's like to not have her. You fight, knowin' she's doin' the same."

I blow my air out and lean against the seat, closing my

eyes and doing my best to bat the fear back. The vision of Caroline as I saw her last makes it hard, but finally we pull up to the emergency room entrance, and I'm out and rushing into the brightly lit waiting room.

"Caroline Davis. My wife. She was brought in by ambulance."

The young nurse nods before typing something into the computer in front of her. "She's here, but I don't have any news right now. If you have a seat, someone will be out as soon as they can tell you more."

"I need to be with her," I tell her frantically.

She gives me a sad smile and shakes her head. "I'm sorry, sir. It's hospital policy."

"Come on," Mav says, taking my shoulder and turning me to walk over to one of the empty seats.

And we wait.

We wait and I pretend my world isn't ending.

28

CAROLINE

"Wake up Loving You" by Old Dominion

The heavy weight against my hand is the first thing I notice.

The warmth from that weight, the second.

With the cobwebs in my mind, though, it's hard to register much of anything else.

Slowly, the rest of my body starts to connect back with my groggy mind, the weight on my hand forgotten when the burning sensation in my leg comes into focus. I groan and try to open my eyes.

"Linney," I hear whispered, but the only thing I can focus on is the pain in my leg, which is getting more and more intense with each passing second. "Darlin', please calm down."

"Hurts," I moan, my voice gravelly and thick, like I just woke up.

"God, baby."

"Carrie, stop fightin'. You're safe. Calm down before you hurt yourself more."

At Luke's words, my body stops moving. I hadn't even realized I had been thrashing against the bed. My eyes are still not opening, but more around me registers now. I hear sniffles, some farther from me than others and some right next to me. I hear the beeping of machines and soft, pleading whispers at my side.

Clayton.

Knowing he needs me just as much as I need to see him is what helps me to push the cobwebs away and take control of my mind and body. It takes a couple minutes, but I finally pry my eyes open. I blink frantically as my pupils adjust to the dim light. Luke is standing at the end of my bed, his sister in his arms while she cries against his chest. I turn my head when I see movement to see Maverick in much the same position with Leighton, standing under the TV mounted in the corner. Next to them, Tate is standing behind Quinn, his arms around her shoulders as she wipes her eyes.

Then, when I look away from them, my handsome husband fills my vision.

His hair is wild, like he's done nothing but run his hands through it. The stubble that had been on his jaw when we went to bed is even darker now. And his red, swollen eyes look like they're glowing as he openly and silently cries. Tears spill over his lashes and fall down his face before landing against our joined hands resting next to my side. He doesn't look away, doesn't dry his tears. He just stares at me, breathing heavily, like he can't believe I'm right in front of him.

"Hey," I whisper.

His eyes shudder closed and he sucks in a jerky breath before dropping his forehead against my belly. He shakes his head as his strong shoulders hitch as he loses whatever control he'd been holding tightly to.

"Clayton," I plead, my heart breaking over seeing my strong husband falling to bits in front of me. "Please, honey."

He mumbles something against me, the words muffled. I look around the room, frantic to get help in easing his pain, but I see not one dry eye as they witness the strongest man we all know unable to keep himself together any longer.

"Cl-Clayton," I wobble out, my chin quivering and my eyes filling with tears. "You're breaking my heart." My chest literally feels like someone is pulling my heart from my body with each second that passes.

His body shudders and I hear him suck in a breath. "I thought I lost you," he admits, lifting his head and looking down at our hands. "I saw you there, blood everywhere, and knew if I lost you I'd be losin' myself too."

"I'm okay," I gasp, needing him to stop. "I'm here."

"There's nothin' for me on this earth without you by my side," he continues. "She almost took you from me."

I choke on a loud cry as it bursts from my throat. I gasp for air, but I can't stop wailing. Through my tears, I see Clayton jump to his feet, and then his hands push under my shoulders as he pulls my upper body off the hospital bed and into his arms. I wrap my arms around him the best I can with the IV and cling to him, soaking his shirt while he drenches my gown, the early-morning events coming to a head as we hold each other.

"I'm so sorry," he mumbles against my neck after we both calm.

"For what?" I question, opening my eyes. The first person I focus on is Maverick. His jaw clenches and his eyes are just as wet as I imagine mine are.

"I should have done better at protecting you."

I gasp, pull back, and stare up into his tortured eyes. "This is *not* your fault. No one, not even you, could have seen this comin'. You *did* protect me, honey. All I heard in my mind was your voice remindin' me to fight. Your strength filled me up without you even bein' there. I remembered you tellin' me where you keep your firearms, and that gave me a chance. You might not have been there, but it was you nonetheless who protected and saved me."

"It's because of me you were in this situation to begin with, Caroline."

I frown. "No, it was because of your crazy ex. Don't you dare take this on, Clayton Davis."

"Linney," he breathes.

"Don't you Linney me. We're both victims here. And she does *not* get to win. Not now. Not ever."

I see my words take root, the despair in his eyes lifting. His forehead comes to mine and he rocks against me, shaking his head. "I'm never gonna let you out of my sight."

"I'm thinkin' that's not goin' to be a hardship, honey."

"I've never been more scared in my life. If she wasn't already dead, I'd fuckin' kill her myself."

Knowing I'm the reason Jess is dead doesn't even faze me. It was either her or me, and I'm not about to feel guilty that I battled for the beautiful life I've earned. Maybe one day I'll feel differently, but I doubt it.

"Why am I here?"

He exhales, his eyes looking pained again. I hate that, but I know it's unavoidable if I want to know what happened.

"When she . . ." He sucks in a deep breath. "When she shot you, the bullet lodged deep enough in your thigh that you lost a good bit of blood. They stitched you up, and the doctor assures me that, aside from the scar, you'll have no lastin' issues. But the bump on your head is what's got you here for the night. When you passed out, you hit the edge of the toilet on your way down."

"And the rest?"

"That's it, darlin'. Stitches, fluids in your IV, and monitorin' you overnight, and they assure me you'll make a full recovery."

I search his eyes, feeling my brows pull in. "What aren't you tellin' me?"

He searches my eyes before dropping his head and shaking it slowly. "John was part of this."

My shoulders droop and the tension I felt in them drains away. "I know."

"What do you mean you know?"

"Jess admitted it." I look down at my lap. "I know he's dead. And I know she did it too. I'm not upset he's gone, but knowin' that, in his way, he tried to stop her doesn't exactly make me feel good that he died doin' so."

"And him? What did he say to you?"

Pulling my head back, I look into his face, confused by his question. "Pardon?"

"I forgot about it until I stood over his body and told Sheriff Holden that John approached you yesterday afternoon."

"Oh, that," I whisper, nodding. "I wasn't keepin' it from you, Clayton. Things were just, well . . . He was the last thing on my mind when I was gettin' ready to marry you. I only had room for happiness and it slipped my mind."

"I'm not mad, darlin'. I just want to know what he had to say. Piece this shit together the best I can."

I search my mind, replaying everything I can remember. After what Jess said, some of John's confusing words make more sense.

"He tried to stop her," I finally say after the silence stretches on. "It didn't make any sense when he came up to me in town, but after what she said about him, I get what he'd been tryin' warn me about."

"Explain that to me."

I sigh and recount everything from when I was starting to cook, to when Jess broke the door, and every word she had to say before what happened in the office. I know it costs him to sit here and not react. The tic in his jaw muscle and the twitching of his left eye betray the calm he's trying to project. Once I tell him everything, I take a gulp of air and lean back, instantly exhausted.

"I don't give a shit that he thought he was protectin' you. He should've gone straight to the fuckin' cops when he realized what Jess was up to instead of helpin' her with some misguided belief that he was doin' it to keep you safe. There's no fuckin' gray line, Linney. You could have died tonight, regardless of what he tried to do leadin' up to it. You could have been lost to me forever, and I'll take your life over theirs any day."

"I wasn't justifyin' his actions. I agree with you, but even though he failed, he tried."

"And failed. All that matters is that he failed."

I nod. "Our ugly isn't goin' to touch us anymore."

He closes his eyes and his nostrils flare while he composes himself. "Nothin' but good's gonna touch us, darlin'."

I nod, resting my head against the pillow with a yawn. Clayton leans over me and presses his mouth to my forehead. I blink up at him and smile. "A honeymoon might be a good idea now," I slur, exhaustion pulling me under.

"Seein' that we're gonna be mighty busy in the next handful of months, I think you're right."

I hear some feminine giggles but give in to the tiredness and fall asleep, knowing that I'm safe, Clayton's safe, and there isn't anyone else out there who can hurt us.

29

CAROLINE

"My Best Friend" by Tim McGraw

- ★ -

"**W**hat?!" I screech, looking at the doctor like he's lost his mind.

I woke up ten minutes ago when the doctor and the evil nurse who'd been torturing me all night clattered into the room pulling some equipment. Okay, so she hadn't been torturing me, but each time she came in to wake me up, it sure did feel that way. Logically, I know head injuries aren't anything to take lightly, but I'm exhausted and sleep is the only thing I want.

"Pardon?" the doctor questions, looking up from the chart in his hand.

"I get that I bumped my head and all, Doc, and I'm not tryin' to tell you how to do your job, but maybe we should be checkin' my noggin . . . or better yet, yours, because nothin' you just said makes sense."

Clayton's manly chuckles tickle my fingers and I glance away from the doctor to see my husband hiding his smile behind the hand he's been holding all night.

"Mrs. Davis," the doctor says, and I look over from Clayton to narrow my eyes at him. "Tracey's monitored you all night and we have no reason to believe that further testing is needed regarding your injuries. I've given your husband your care instructions and he knows what to look for in the event that more medical treatment is needed—which I'm confident won't be the case."

"So you're just goin' to let me leave without makin' sure the head you've kept me here all night for is fine?"

Closing the chart, the doctor crosses his arms over his chest and smirks. I'm not sure what he thinks is so dadgum funny. At this point, I wouldn't mind knocking him over the head. When his grin grows and two dimples appear, I make a mental note to find out if he's single. He's young, clearly successful, and handsome—though not as handsome as Clayton. Perfect for Lucy, even if I want to shake some sense into the crazy-talking man.

"We wouldn't let you leave if there was even a slight concern, Mrs. Davis."

"Well, clearly there's somethin' wrong with my head, Doc. I'm hallucinating, hearin' things or somethin'! Either that or I'm dreamin', because there isn't any other reason you'd be standin' there with Nurse Pokes-for-fun, tellin' me I'm pregnant." I take a deep breath, my eyes widening. "Oh, my God! I'm losin' my mind, aren't I? The fall knocked somethin' loose and you're about to ship me off to a home!" I turn my head to look at Clayton. "I don't want to go to a home!"

His shoulders shake as he laughs at me. "Linney, love, no one is puttin' you in a home."

I narrow my eyes at him. "Well, maybe we need to put him in one, then," I snap, pointing at the doctor.

"Maybe it'll be easier if we show you, hmm?" the evil, poking-me-all-night nurse says in a sugary sweet voice.

"Show me what?"

"Your baby." She smiles and I stare, my mouth hanging wide-open.

I stop arguing and, with a huff, lie back on the bed. There's no way I'm pregnant. I haven't missed my period. Aside from the whole being-shot-and-passing-out thing, I feel fine. I haven't been sick, tired, or sore.

Clayton sits up straighter when the nurse holds up some long, ET-looking finger and starts covering it with a condom. I frown when the doctor starts moving the sheets from my legs, taking the condom finger from the nurse. My hand is squeezed at the same time the doctor starts explaining to me that he's about to insert the finger into my vagina.

"Whoa!" I swat at his hands when he moves my gown. "You can keep your kinky alien probe away from me, mister."

"Mrs. Davis." He sighs, his lips twitching as he obviously tries to keep from laughing at me. I'd like to see him be all calm and doctorly when someone wants to stick a long, skinny, condom-covered piece of plastic inside of him! "This is the most accurate way to determine how far along you are. Your numbers are high, but that could mean one of quite a few things. My guess is you're somewhere between six to nine weeks along, which means this is the only form of ultrasound we can actually see the baby with."

"This is such a waste of time. I haven't even missed a period!" I pull the hem of my gown down, covering my naked sex. If I could reach the blanket, I'd put that back over me as well.

"Some women, though few, experience their cycle throughout their pregnancies. I know this might be a surprise, but I assure you there's no way we aren't going to see a baby."

"Linney," Clayton huskily whispers.

I stop glaring at the doctor and look at my husband. His stubble has grown out even more, the black shadow highlighting his strong jaw. The lips that can drive me wild curve, a small and happy smile across his mouth. His dark-as-night hair is still a mess, but instead of seeing the raw pain that had been in his green eyes last night, all I see is a whole lot of love and even more . . . hopefulness.

"Had a little more time for this to sink in, darlin',

and I get you not believin' the good doctor, but please, baby . . . let them show us what our love created."

The wind in my sails evaporates instantly and I study my husband, the emotions written all over him infectious as a flicker of hope starts to ignite inside of me.

With a nod to the doctor, I follow his instructions as he embarrassingly bares me, then inserts his ET finger into my sex. It's uncomfortable as hell, but I keep my eyes on Clayton and hold my breath. I watch his face as his eyes go wide and stay trained on the monitor. Tiny wrinkles form between his eyebrows as he concentrates.

Then his hand convulses in mine and his whole face goes soft. I've seen what my husband looks like with love shining bright, but this . . . this is something I've never seen on his face. It's as if his heart jumped from his chest to beat right behind his blazing bright eyes. Wonder, love, and pure elation beam out at me. My own heart starts to pick up speed when I realize there's only one thing that could make him look as if the world is being handed to him.

"Amazin'," he says softly.

I feel lightheaded as my head rolls against the pillow to look in the direction of Clayton's stare. I see the doctor's face first. He arches a brow and smiles smugly. The nurse is beaming, but I let my attention pass over her and fall on the monitor.

"Oh my God," I gasp, my eyes burning as a beautiful kind of bliss slams into me.

The doctor reaches out and presses some buttons, then the quiet room fills with what can only be described as the sound of muffled hooves racing.

"What is that?" I whisper, not looking away from the monitor, my grip on Clayton's hand tightening.

"That, Mrs. Davis, is your baby's heartbeat."

"Oh," I breathe.

"Strong and healthy. You're measuring right at eight weeks, and everything with the baby looks just fine."

"But . . . are you sure? Nothin' is wrong after last night?"

The doctor shakes his head. "Not a thing. The baby is nice and protected in there, Mrs. Davis."

"A baby." I shake my head, smiling so big my cheeks hurt, and blink rapidly to clear the tears even though I know it's fruitless to try. "Honey, a baby!"

"Heard the doc," Clayton says, his voice thick and even deeper than normal.

I look at him, seeing the same things I'm feeling in his eyes. "Can you believe it?"

"It's our beauty, darlin'. 'Course I believe it."

"We're havin' a baby," I cry, the image of him swimming now that my eyes are full of happy tears.

"I'll print some images for y'all and get out of your hair," the doctor mumbles.

I don't pay him any attention, not when my husband is looking at me like I've just given him the greatest gift. We continue to stare at each other, ignoring the other two in the room. I don't even flinch when the doctor pulls the probe free from my body and drapes the sheets back over my legs. I hear one of them mention that the pictures are on the table next to my bed and that they'll be back shortly with my discharge papers, but I don't look away from the blazing green orbs that have me transfixed.

When the door clicks signaling their departure, Clayton pounces. My hand falls from his grip and lands on the mattress with a soft bounce the same second his lips land on my mouth. If I thought our kisses before were magical, I was wrong. He devours me and fills me with so much love that I'm drunk on it. This is the kind of kiss you only experience with the person who holds the other part of your soul. With every swipe of his tongue, I feel like my heart is swelling, every swirl and sweep feeding my very being. His panting breaths against my face fill me with the all-consuming power of his love.

And I give him just as much as he's giving me.

The knowledge that our child, one who is wanted and loved already, is growing healthy and strong inside of me is nothing short of incredible. Our love, while it flickered to life with a brilliant boom, grew into what we're sharing right here—perfection.

"You're goin' to have my baby," he finally says in awe after pulling his lips from mine.

"I'm goin' to have your baby."

"Everything, Linney, love . . . your love gives me *everything*."

I hiccup a sob, smiling at the man who owns my love. "You're wrong, honey. *Our* love gives *us* everything."

"This is it, darlin'. This is our forever startin', with nothin' and no one standin' in the way of what kinda beautiful we create. Told you before and I meant it then just like I do now, the ugly we had to face to get here only made us unbreakable. Havin' you and our child as my reward for makin' it through mine only makes it all the sweeter. From this moment on, we're not lookin' back and I'm gonna love you so bad you won't ever have a day without knowin' your husband is everything because of you."

"Oh, Clayton."

"Thank you, darlin', for takin' that seat next to me, makin' that crowded bar feel empty with your shy smiles, takin' a chance on us, and, in the end, givin' me life."

I'm openly crying now. I couldn't have held it back if I wanted to. Not with him giving me so much.

"I love you, darlin'," he rasps, his lips pressing against my forehead.

"I love you, too, honey. So much."

Epilogue

CAROLINE

"Holdin' Her" by Chris Janson

I lower the camera and smile. It's moments like these that make me want to pinch myself. Moments that fill my every day, giving me a life that's so unbelievably beautiful it doesn't ever seem real.

"Pretty sure you've got a million pictures just like that one, Linney love."

I scrunch my nose at my husband, turning the camera in my hands and bringing up the image I just took on the screen. "I could have a million more, Clayton, and it still wouldn't be enough."

He grunts out a few low chuckles. "You're a nut."

"Whatever, honey."

He stands and I lean my shoulder against the door-frame to watch him. His head dips once he's on his feet, pressing a light kiss atop our daughter's head. Her tiny little rosebud mouth purses, but she doesn't wake up. His eyes close, lips still pressed against her head while he takes a moment, like he always does. Never fails, he works hard all day and the first thing he does when he comes home is strip his shirt off, wash his hands, and hold our daughter to his chest until she's asleep; then he kisses her sweetly and breathes her in.

Since before Harlow was even born, Clayton would end his day much like this, only with his mouth against my belly and our daughter kicking against his touches.

My pregnancy was the kind that women dream of. I was happy, full of energy, hungry for my husband's touch, and hardly gained any weight. Of course, when you have a man like Clayton Davis showering you with his love, there isn't a snowball's chance in hell you'll feel anything other than pure bliss.

Not everything has been sunshine and rainbows. In the year since the fateful night that almost stole this from us, we've continued to move forward—but it was the early days when we both were frantic to erase the memories of that night that put a dark cloud over the beginning of my pregnancy.

The first thing he did was buy an RV—not just any RV either. This was the luxury of luxe, grander than some homes. And after he pulled it down the drive and parked it in the grass away from the house, he told me we were moving in—temporarily—to his deluxe home on wheels.

I didn't argue with him because I could see it in his eyes, the wild hunt for control driving him.

So we moved into the RV.

And we lived in it for almost four months while Clayton put all his responsibilities on hold so he could oversee the complete renovation of our home. I didn't need to ask to understand why. I knew why he needed that. Even if it was to erase what Jess had done, I have a feeling he was also banishing the ghosts of his childhood as well.

The first time I saw all the hard work he poured into our home, I cried for an hour. Not only had he gutted and updated everything, he'd turned the spare bedroom closest to ours into the most heavenly nursery I've ever seen outside of a showroom.

The nursery had me crying for another hour.

While our house was being renovated, he also hired someone to rebuild our gazebo. This time he created a wraparound porch outside the structure with a freestanding hammock and an outdoor table. We've had a few dates in our spot and not once has our time out there been anything short of perfect. All the painful memories from that night are completely eradicated.

What we didn't do though was worry about The Sequel. Not until six months ago, when I was entering my last month of pregnancy. I hadn't been sure that I wanted to reopen my store, but in the end, Clayton helped me see past the sadness I've been associating with rebuilding. I think a little part of me hasn't been sure I could reopen without continuously looking over my shoulder. I knew Jess and John were gone, but with so much of their evil being connected with the store, I had a hard time seeing past it.

Until Clayton.

Until my husband reminded me that we've got nothing but beautiful now.

It didn't hurt that he reminded me while filling me with his cock and loving me slow.

"She's out," Clayton says softly, standing in front of me and startling me out of my thoughts.

I lean to the side and look around his delicious naked torso to see the blanket-covered bundle in the middle of the dark gray crib. When I straighten and blink up at Clayton, nervous flutters start to fill my belly when his smile grows.

"You got somethin' for me?" he questions, smiling.

"Maybe," I hedge, a nervous giggle breaking free.

He tilts his head and studies me.

"Come on, honey," I request, placing the camera on top of Harlow's dresser and taking his hand in mine. He follows as I pull him from our daughter's doorway and into our room. I drop his hand when we reach the middle of our room and turn to him. My eyes roam from his chiseled chest, over his defined abs, and down his denim-covered legs to his bare feet. I take a deep breath and smile at the floor before looking up at my husband.

"Strip, handsome."

His eyebrows shoot up, but he brings his hands to his buckle without questioning me, making quick work of shucking his pants and briefs, standing to his full height in all his naked glory.

With a wink, I reach down and pull my sundress up and over my head. My breasts bounce free, reminding me that they've taken on a life of their own since having Harlow. Clayton's eyes burn as he looks down at them. He's made it no secret that he loves the changes our daughter brought to my body—especially my breasts. Anytime they're out, he's licking his lips and staring, and with a breastfeeding four-month-old, they're out often.

"On the bed."

Silently, he walks around me, not without reaching out and grazing my thigh with his fingertips. He climbs into our bed, right in the middle, and lies down with his arms up and hands behind his head.

I climb up on the bed and shuffle my knees forward until they're pressed against his hip. He watches me intently with his emerald gaze, his erection bobbing when my eyes look down at it. When I lick my lips, he groans.

As much as I'd love to sit here and drink him in, I need to feel him. Shifting, I climb over him, spreading my legs and sitting back on his knees. His eyes look down his body and straight between my legs, his nostrils flaring wildly. My hands go to his thighs and I start moving them, caressing him slowly while leaning forward until his cock is right at my mouth. My tongue comes out and licks him. He hisses but doesn't move. God, I love the taste of him. Opening my mouth wide, I take him as deep as I can and lift one hand up to work his shaft while flicking the head of his dick with my tongue. I hum when I taste his salty essence, moving my other hand down and between my legs. I don't take my eyes off his, wanting him to see the pleasure I get from using my mouth on him. I also know what he looks like when he's about to come, and right now, as much as I love it, I want him inside me when he does.

Removing my mouth with a loud pop, I start to crawl up his body.

"I've been waitin' all day to give you my bad, Clayton Davis." I place my hands next to his head and lean down, placing my mouth close enough to his to feel his hot breath as he pants. My pussy glides against his erection, making me moan. "You're goin' to sit there and let me give that to you. You're goin' to keep your back on the bed and let me take everything. I want to feel you, so deep, Clayton."

"Fuck yes," he hisses.

"You gonna sit there and let me give you my bad while I love my husband?"

"Baby," he breathes.

I lift my hips, moving one hand to his abs, the other wrapping around his thickness, moving my body until he's kissing my entrance. I swirl the blunt tip around my wetness, moaning when he hits my clit. My head rolls while my body burns with need. Then I stop my hand and drop my hips, impaling myself on him. He shouts a deep grunt that turns into a low moan when I roll my hips again. We don't look away from each other as I begin to move, both our mouths open. Our heavy breathing fills the room. He lets me drive as I take his body, using my legs to pull my hips up and drop down. Each time he hits that sweet spot deep inside of me, I feel myself growing wetter and wetter. I won't last much longer.

Feeling it build, my body trembles. "Help me," I beg, moaning when he takes my hips in his strong hands and starts lifting me, pulling me down, and thrusting up from the bottom. My cries turn wild when he quickens the pace. "I'm goin' to come, honey," I breathe, my vision getting hazy as fireworks start to explode behind my eyes. I clamp down on him and cry his name out, his own groan of completion echoing around us.

I fall to his chest, sucking in air as my body comes back to earth. His heart thumps wildly against my cheek and I smile.

"I would've put money on us makin' another baby just now, but . . . seein' that you took care of that weeks ago, I'll just enjoy the practice."

He jolts under me, the hands that had been roaming my back stopping, and I lift up to look at him. His eyes are wide, happy, and wet.

"You tellin' me my baby is growin' in there?"

"Yeah honey," I sigh, tears slowly cascading down my face and landing on his chest.

"You tellin' me I'm goin' to get more beauty from you?"

I sniffle and nod.

"Linney, love," he breathes, kissing me deep and quick.

"Are you happy?" I ask, knowing he is, but still worried about my handsome husband.

"God, yes."

"Good, honey. I am too. So happy. Tate did a scan and said everything looks perfect."

He frowns slightly. "Tate? Darlin', how long have you known you were carryin' my baby?"

I shift, making both of us groan from the connection we haven't broken. "A few weeks. I didn't . . . I, well, I wasn't sure if it was a good time to tell you before now."

His face gets soft and I know I don't need to clarify. Three weeks ago, the day I found out I was pregnant again, Clayton took a call from his brother, and after he said hello, he didn't speak again. Not during that call, or for hours and hours after. He ended his call, placed his phone on the counter, and walked out the back door. It wasn't until four in the morning that he came back. I listened from our bed while he moved through the house, seeing his shadow enter Harlow's room before coming into ours with her in his arms. He got into bed, made sure our girl was situated, and reached over to pull me into his chest.

With my daughter's face close to mine, the heart of the most important man in both of our lives beating under us, he told me that his mother had passed away. I kept my mouth shut but tightened my arm over his body. He didn't say anything else about it, just kissed my head, then Harlow's, before all three of us went to sleep.

And until today, I hadn't been sure how to tell him that I was pregnant because I wasn't sure if he was handling his feelings over his mama.

"I understand why you didn't tell me, but darlin', you don't need to worry. I didn't have her in my life for a long time. I don't miss her, haven't in a long time."

"You haven't talked about it though, Clayton. I've been so worried about where your head's been that I wasn't sure if it was a good time to tell you about the baby."

He tightens his hold on me, and his lips form a tiny smile. "I let her go that night. I left because I didn't want her—even the thought of her—in our home with our daughter. The only thing I could think of, even now, is how anyone could walk away from their children. When I think of Harlow, there isn't anything I wouldn't do for her. I'd die for her—you—and any children we have. When I think of my mama now, the only thing that goes through my mind is how thankful I am that, because of her inability to love her children, I know I'll never be what she was. She didn't have what it took to cowboy up and live each day for someone else. But I do."

"I've been so worried."

"I know, darlin', but I wasn't keepin' it from you. I meant what I said: she doesn't have a place under this roof."

I nod, understanding what he's saying. "Okay."

"Okay." His smile grows, teeth flashing, and the corners of his eyes crinkle. "You, Caroline Davis, are the best thing that happened to me."

I rock my hips, my happiness mirroring his. "Ditto, honey, ditto."

His hands move from my hips to my lower belly. "Just when I think I couldn't love you more, you go and give me more beauty. Give me your mouth, baby, and let me love you slow this time so I can show you how much you givin' me another baby means to me."

I squeal as he flips us and moan when he starts slowly gliding his hard length in and out of my body. He takes his sweet time, not breaking the steady rhythm he's built. His eyes hold mine and his lips part only a breath above mine. I'm surrounded by and filled with the man that owns me—heart and soul—as he loves me slow and steady. My heart pounds against my chest, calling out to his, and with his name leaving my lips on a whisper, I tumble over the edge. Clayton follows me not even a minute later, turning our bodies, keeping us connected, and wrapping his strong arms around me.

"Never dreamed that this existed. You fill me with so much, darlin', that a lifetime will never be enough for me to repay that."

"Far as I can tell, honey, it's me who gets filled to the brim. I reckon if we both keep tryin' to repay the other, there won't be a day that passes where we aren't ridin' high."

"I'll love you forever and always, Linney."

"And I'll be lovin' you right back forever and always, Clayton."

- ★ -

Fifteen years later

High on the hill located on the back end of Clayton and Caroline Davis's property, there isn't a face without a smile on it. The painful memories that used to haunt the three Davis children are a distant memory. Each in the arms of his or her spouse looks down from the gazebo that's stood through six tornados over the years and only grown since the eldest Davis realized just how important this spot had become not just to his wife, but to his family, as their children run, laugh, and love. There hasn't been a day that happiness didn't sound from the Davis property for the past fifteen years.

Clayton Davis looks from his two daughters over to his son, wrapping his arms a little tighter around his wife, knowing that without her, he wouldn't have this wonderful life. Glancing over his wife's head, Clayton takes a second to appreciate the same contentment-induced happiness on his brother's face.

Maverick, not having missed the attention of his brother, turns to meet his gaze. Gone are the hard lines and stoic disposition. His wife made it impossible for him to keep his old flinty edge throughout the years. But it was with the birth of each of his children that whatever pain he had left inside of him vanished. With a year separating each of his four daughters, something inside of him changed forever, but it was when his son was placed in his arms that Maverick Davis finally found out what it was like to have the world. There are days when he wakes, the house still silent, and he's slammed with just how lucky he truly is. His heart swelling, his wife pressed tight to his side, and his house full of the children his wife blessed him with. Seeing what he feels on those days in his older brother's gaze, he smiles even wider.

Both the Davis boys look to their left and down at their baby sister tucked tight to her husband's side. Her youngest son leans into his mother with his hand wrapped around her belt loop and her hand rubbing his raven-black hair. It was a long road for Quinn Montgomery and her husband to have the last of their four boys. She struggled through two miscarriages but never gave up, knowing that they weren't whole. It was during those days that Quinn got quiet and her smiles came less and less. When her husband delivered their last baby almost six years ago, she changed. Holding their miracle in her arms, Quinn had laughed so loud that her family heard her outside of her birthing room, her laughter sparking something in each of them that well and truly made them realize how far they had all come.

And that's how Clayton and Caroline, Maverick and Leighton, and Quinn and Tate . . . came home.

Acknowledgments

— ★ —

As always, to my family. Your support, love, and understanding is the reason I'm able to continue living my dream. Without the four of you, I would be lost and my words would have no meaning. Knowing my three daughters are never allowed to read Mommy's books, I doubt you'll ever see this: but every time you ask about what I'm writing, I hope your dreams are weaving knowing that the sky is the limit.

To my team at Pocket Books, especially my fabulous editor, Marla. Thank you for giving me this chance. Thank you for believing in me. Thank you from the bottom of my heart for showing me that anything is possible. Even seeing your books at the grocery store next to someone's forgotten bag of pasta!

To Danielle Sanchez, the best publicist a girl could have. Honest to God, I would be lost without you. Thank you for always being there, even when I'm in another country and confused about life.

To the two girls that were with me every step of the way during each book in this series. You both know how much I love you, Felicia and Lara. Felicia, don't expect more . . . I've dedicated a book to you already and feed you from my minifridge. Lara, what can I say, other than Clay's yours.

To Marisa Corvisiero, thank you for everything! And I do mean everything. I can't believe that this series is over, and I can't wait to see what other trouble we can get into together.

And lastly, to my amazing readers. Every word I write is for you. Each dream I pen. Each love I create. I love you all.

Lost Rider

Maverick Austin Davis has been a rodeo star for ten
years. But when family duty calls him home, Mav
is forced to admit to his siblings that one too many
head injuries has put paid to his career – and the only
dream he ever had for himself is over. When sparks
fly between Mav and his sister's best friend Leighton,
could it be time for a new dream?

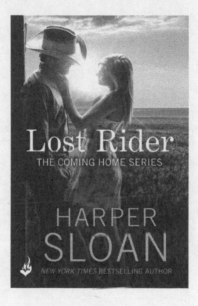

Available now from

HEADLINE
ETERNAL

Kiss My Boots

Quinn Davis is the stereotypical tomboy who prefers to live her life quietly. Of course, it doesn't help that her heart has been hardened when it comes to devilishly handsome cowboys with silver tongues. That is, until Tate Montgomery rides back into town . . .

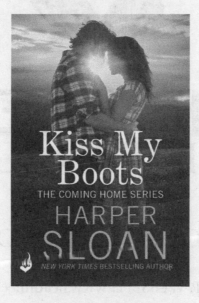

Available now from

HEADLINE
ETERNAL